W9-AYX-723

Gods and Angels

BY THE SAME AUTHOR

Oranges from Spain

The Healing

The Rye Man

Stone Kingdoms

The Big Snow

Swallowing the Sun

The Truth Commissioner

The Light of Amsterdam

The Poets' Wives

Gods and Angels

DAVID PARK

BLOOMSBURY

LONDON · OXFORD · NEW YORK · NEW DELHI · SYDNEY

Bloomsbury Publishing
An imprint of Bloomsbury Publishing Plc

50 Bedford Square   1385 Broadway
London   New York
WC1B 3DP   NY 10018
UK   USA

www.bloomsbury.com

BLOOMSBURY and the Diana logo are trademarks of Bloomsbury Publishing Plc

First published in Great Britain 2016

British Library Cataloguing-in-Publication Data
A catalogue record for this book is available from the British Library.

Library of Congress Cataloguing-in-Publication data has been applied for.

ISBN: HB: 978-1-4088-6607-8
        TPB: 978-1-4088-6608-5
        ePub: 978-1-4088-6610-8

2 4 6 8 10 9 7 5 3 1

Typeset by Integra Software Services Pvt. Ltd.
Printed and bound in Great Britain by CPI Group (UK) Ltd, Croydon CR0 4YY

To find out more about our authors and books visit www.bloomsbury.com.
Here you will find extracts, author interviews, details of forthcoming
events and the option to sign up for our newsletters.

For Alberta

And the Lord God formed man of the dust of the ground, and breathed into his nostrils the breath of life; and man became a living soul.

Genesis, 2:7

What a piece of work is a man! How noble in reason! how infinite in faculty! in form, in moving, how express and admirable! in action how like an angel! In apprehension how like a god! the beauty of the world! The paragon of animals! And yet, to me, what is this quintessence of dust?

Hamlet, Act 2, Scene 2

Contents

Learning to Swim   1

Boxing Day   23

The Kiss   44

Keeping Watch   60

The Strong Silent Type   73

The Painted Cave   87

The Bloggers   107

Skype   129

Heatwave   155

Man Overboard   178

Gecko   199

Old Fool   227

Crossing the River   271

Learning to Swim

Then, since fortunes favours fade,
You, that in her armes doe sleep,
Learne to swim, and not to wade;
For, the Hearts of Kings are deepe.

IT'S FROM A POEM by Henry Wotton that I came across when completing my doctorate on John Donne. The lines caught my eye because I've never succeeded in taking his advice. It was an attempt to address this gap in my otherwise unblemished CV that found me early one Sunday being taught by Maurice in a hotel swimming pool in suburban Belfast. Maurice who worked in the leisure complex prided himself on his track record with reluctant swimmers, frequently informing me of his stats, the way driving instructors like to do with new customers. So before the pool opened to hotel guests or the leisure-complex members, I was in the shallow end wearing armbands like a child on the first day of his holiday.

'Trust the water, Henry,' he repeated, but his mantra failed to persuade me to take my standing foot off the bottom and put my faith in anything that seemed so yielding. After this first lesson I stayed in the water, thankfully no longer adorned with armbands but bearing a float in each hand. When I got out I used the gym, exercising only long enough to justify the membership fees to myself, and it was when I went to get changed that I saw them for the first time. They stopped talking for a second as I sat down to catch my breath. One nodded, one stared silently a little too intently to be polite and the third said, 'All right? Is that you then?'

'Fine, thanks,' I replied, as always in those first few months immediately conscious of how my English accent conflicted with the brick-hard consonants of the Belfast vernacular. Getting dressed I was able to observe them and tried to work out why their presence seemed to weight the room, right from that very first encounter making me feel slighter, less substantial, in some way I didn't fully understand.

It wasn't just that they were older – I guessed in their late fifties – with their bodies over-ripened and fleshy, and it wasn't the gold jewellery or the old men's faded blue tattoos decorating their forearms – bluebirds, Indian chiefs in feathered headdresses, serpents coiled round daggers – but something to do with how they held themselves slightly apart from the shape time had imposed on them, and the weariness that permeated all their movements, as if they had travelled a great distance.

When I was leaving the leisure complex I paused and glanced back through the glass to where they were sitting in the Jacuzzi, their arms draped along the top of the tiles, and just for a moment it looked as if they formed a chain.

I probably would never have considered a post in Belfast in normal circumstances. Despite the Peace I still thought of it as a frontier town, but the scarcity of post-doctorate university jobs meant beggars couldn't be choosers, so when a last-minute temporary cover for a staff illness came up, I applied and got lucky. The university turned out to be a leafy, elegant oasis of calm and I managed to get a bedsit fifteen minutes' walk away. But I didn't know anyone in the city and I suppose joining the leisure complex a few weeks later was a way of helping me feel I belonged to something.

About a month later, after Maurice had written me off as one of life's self-induced failures, I found myself sharing the Jacuzzi with two of the men I had encountered in the changing room. By then I had registered their first names. Only the one called Sam used the pool. When he swam, despite my expectations, he moved gracefully in the water, his blue-scribbled arms rising and falling languidly in a rhythmic backstroke that made me envious.

George liked to wear expensive suits but his face bore the hints of a heavy drinker and once I saw his hand shake in anticipation of the glass the hotel bartender was slipping to him across the polished wood. And it was already obvious that they looked up to Eddie who sat opposite me in the Jacuzzi, his face slightly bloated and puffed, as if water had seeped behind the surface of his skin.

'How's it going?' he asked.

'Not so bad,' I answered and, wondering if I had assumed the right tone, added, 'Can't complain.'

'That's good, son,' he said, turning his head briefly to catch Sam gliding by and then stretching his hand across the water until our crimped skin touched, 'too many complainers in this world. My name's Eddie and this is George.'

I went through the same ritual with George and as I told them I was called Henry I had the same thought I had every time I introduced myself to someone in that city, that as soon as they heard my voice they silently prefaced my name with 'Hooray', or secretly considered me personally responsible for countless centuries of colonial oppression. Their faces gave nothing away.

'So where are you from?' George asked.

'North London.'

'Arsenal or Spurs?' he enquired as the cauldron bubbled up around his gold bracelet and made it look as if it was being formed by some ancient alchemy.

'Arsenal,' I said, knowing little about football but just enough to be able to add, 'but we'll never win anything if Wenger keeps selling our best players.'

'True enough,' Eddie said. 'We're all United men but I miss the way those games with the Arsenal used to be – Keane and Vieira getting ripped into each other in the tunnel. Some of the passion's gone out of it.'

'The passion's in the money now,' I said as I played my last card about football, worrying that even the simplest of questions would expose my ignorance. But thankfully they both nodded in agreement and then turned to watch Sam drift by once more.

'He does twenty lengths each time,' Eddie said, 'and then we retire to the bar and he puts it on again. We don't even bother trying.'

'Are you here on holiday?' George asked.

'No, I'm working here – I teach at the university,' I told them a little too quickly and a little too obviously pleased with myself, the way young doctors wear their stethoscopes in breast pockets like silken handkerchiefs.

'What do you teach?' Eddie asked, his face flared by the heat of the water.

'Literature,' I said, having stopped myself adding 'seventeenth-century'.

'You must be a smart guy, Henry. We're University of Life men and even then some of us got expelled,' George said.

As he smiled at the joke Eddie's eyes fixed on me, the rush and bubble of the water subsided, and impulsively, not wanting in that moment to be separated by education, class or anything else, I offered them, 'I'm not so smart. I can't swim.'

A couple of weeks later when I was leaving the hotel I passed Eddie standing in the foyer and we both nodded. Then as the automatic doors opened a woman probably in her mid-thirties entered. I'm not much good at describing women so the most I'm going to say is I found her very beautiful. Instinctively I glanced back and saw her greet Eddie, her arm extended towards his neck. I assumed she was his daughter until through the slowly closing doors I saw her kiss him full on the lips and knew I was hopelessly mistaken.

5

My path mostly crossed with that of my new acquaintances on Sunday mornings, but one late Friday afternoon after spending an hour in the pool pretending to myself that I was finally about to take my foot off the bottom, and then not wanting to try and conjure a miracle from the barren waste of my fridge, I decided to eat in the hotel bar. I saw them as soon as I went in, grouped round a table in one of the window alcoves. The bar was full with the lingering remains of a funeral party, their dark suits and white shirts lending the room a formal feel. Changing my mind I decided to pick up a takeaway when I heard my name called and saw Eddie's hand raised in the air as if he was summoning a taxi. I wasn't sure at first if he was signalling to me but he called my name again and feeling it impossible to ignore I went over.

'You getting something to eat, Henry?' Eddie asked and when I nodded he pointed to a spare seat. 'We're about to order, sit down and join us.'

There wasn't any way out of it and so, setting my bag on one of the broad window ledges, I sat down. Eddie raised his hand once more and after we had ordered asked what I wanted to drink.

'A Diet Coke please.'

Sam sniggered until Eddie shot him a glance and by way of apology for my apparent lack of manliness I added, 'I'm on my bike.'

'Sam'll put it in the back of his van, drop you home. Have a drink with us.'

I ordered a beer and was almost pleased when George, who permanently wore the smell of alcohol like a favourite cologne, slapped me slightly on the shoulder and said, 'Good man.'

When we were finishing, the woman I had seen meeting Eddie arrived. My back was to the door so I didn't register her approach but caught the way the smile breaking across Eddie's face made him almost handsome. I stood up and offered her a chair. Her hands were full of shopping bags and as I helped her find somewhere to put them she thanked me and asked Eddie who this 'gentleman' was.

'This is Henry,' Eddie said, 'a friend of ours. He works at the university. Henry, this is Alana.'

'The university? What do you do there, Henry?' she asked.

'I teach literature,' I told her, trying not to stare.

'You teach?' The surprise in her voice suggested she had assumed I worked there in some other capacity. 'You must be a bit of a brainbox,' she said, holding out her hand. But while she was saying this there were other words unravelling across my consciousness and as my eyes caught the diamond ring on her finger I thought only of 'My myne of precious stones ...' and, feeling the soft warmth of her fingers slip away too quickly, 'Then where my hand is set my seal shall be.' And for the first time I realised that all those thousands of theoretical words I had written didn't mean anything compared to this, when the pure physical reality of a woman brought Donne's lines spinning off the page in a way I had never experienced.

Whether it was that powerful realisation or simply because of what she had said – I hadn't been called a brainbox since first year in secondary school – I felt myself blush like a teenager but even when I glanced away my senses were still steeped in her brown eyes, the layered fall of her black hair and her skin's patina, all pulsing to the involuntary rush of words shaken free from the dusty page.

'Yes, Henry's a brainbox. But he can't swim,' Eddie said while George and Sam smiled into their drinks.

'Everybody can swim, Henry – it's not that hard,' she said as she picked a leftover chip from Eddie's plate then when he asked her if she wanted something to eat said no before adding, 'Have to keep myself good. Important to look my best.'

'You always look your best,' Eddie insisted with no trace of embarrassment.

'Bless you,' she said playfully and then in what seemed like an afterthought, 'I tried not to spend too much money.'

'Doesn't look as if you tried very hard,' George said, pointing at the clatter of bags all embossed with designer brands.

'Nothing that wasn't needed.'

I began to feel uncomfortable, momentarily brushed against strangers' lives, so I started to make my excuses but when I tried to attract the waitress for my bill Eddie said, 'Don't worry about it, it's George's shout.' I muttered some objection but stopped when George raised his hand and peeled some notes off a rolled wad, then tipped the waitress a tenner.

'Thanks,' I said, 'that's very kind of you.'

'Don't worry, Henry, George'll be printing some more over the weekend,' Eddie said.

'And for fuck's sake don't forget the Queen's head this time,' Sam said and they all laughed.

After a while Eddie asked Sam to drop me home and I took my leave, wondering what they would say about me when I had gone. As I followed Sam out of the bar a group of increasingly jolly mourners, their ties now recklessly askew, were cheering the rugby on the television and singing 'Stand Up for the Ulstermen'.

Sam's large van was empty apart from a mattress still in its protective plastic. He held the doors open while I slid my bike in, then as we left the car park asked me if I minded if we did a quick stop-off.

'No problem,' I told him before trying to edge towards what I had been wanting to ask, but because there wasn't any subtle way, I came right out with, 'What do you guys do?'

'We're in partnership,' he said, 'the three of us.'

There was silence for a few seconds, long enough for me to wonder if that was to be the extent of his explanation.

'We're in a lot of stuff – property, buy to lets, a couple of clubs and franchises, some retail units – that sort of thing.'

'Right,' I said, 'and you guys go back a long way?'

'A long way,' he repeated and I sensed as he stared out of the side window that the conversation was concluded. The only other sound was the smoker's cough that rattled somewhere deep in his lungs, which suggested it wasn't just his fingers holding the wheel that were heavily dusted with nicotine.

We stopped in a side street off the Lisburn Road and I watched him knock on a door. When it opened I caught a brief glimpse of a woman's face – she might have been Chinese – and then without asking for my help he humped the mattress out of the back of the van and slalomed it into the hall before the door closed again. After five minutes he returned and we didn't speak during the rest of the journey.

A week later I got a note from the English Department secretary asking me to return a call. On the way to the library I used my mobile and found myself talking to Eddie.

'Listen, Henry, son, you're a sporting man,' Eddie said as I stood balancing my armful of books, 'so why don't you come out with us next week? A friend of mine is organising a boxing gala for charity in the Ulster Hall and I've bought a table. What do you say?' I hesitated for a second trying to think of excuses but he insisted, 'Give it a go, it'll be a good night out. It's for a good cause and there's a meal.'

'How much does it cost?'

'It's all taken care of. But you need to get yourself a bib and tucker – it's a black-tie job.'

'I need to pay my way,' I said.

'You can donate something to the charity if you want. But don't worry about money, everything's sorted.'

On the night, I waited outside my flat in the dark trousers I had brought with me and a dinner jacket and black tie I had bought for £10 in a charity shop. I was looking for Sam's van but what stopped was a very large BMW with Sam sitting stiffly in the back like a black and white Buddha. Soon we were in the Ulster Hall at a ringside table. George was already there and when Eddie arrived with Alana who was wearing a black sequined cocktail dress I tried not to stare. There was a short speech given from the centre of the ring by the organiser and his wife who had lost their youngest son to leukaemia, followed by a raffle of various items supplied by local businesses.

After the meal, during which I had consumed too many of the drinks being pressed on me and the MC had outlined the night's programme, a very long-legged young woman in a swimsuit and high heels strutted round the ring to announce the first fight and the actual boxing got under way. Nothing in my experience had prepared me for it, not even that bitter little ten-second flurry of stick arms and legs I once had in primary school with a boy called Toby over conkers. So the ferocious, visceral exchanges between two skinny greyhounds of flyweights took my breath away as they sought to inflict instant physical damage, accompanied by the dull slap of their gloves on flesh, the constant squeak of boots on the canvas and the raw roar of the crowd.

Red-petalled bruises bloomed on tattooed upper arms and any punches connecting to the head were greeted with furious encouragement until gradually all boxing technique seemed to have been replaced by windmilling limbs and head-to-head slugging. Not long after it had started it was all over, a judge's decision had declared a winner and the crowd slumped back, as if exhausted, to concentrate once more on their drinks.

I blinked and tried to clear my head then George passed me a brandy and perhaps it was the alcohol but I suddenly had the sensation that I was living in my body. I glanced at Alana again, trying discreetly to harvest as much as possible, and then as another swimsuited young woman squeezed her way through the ropes with her placard I looked at my soft hands, splayed the fingers before clenching them into tight fists. It was as if all those hours in university libraries and days spent with books had withered into dry husks and as I reached the bottom of the brandy too quickly I felt that, if I had to, I would swim the Hellespont and if my name were called I'd strap on the gloves and give it my best shot.

I had a second brandy as we progressed through the fights until the lumbering heavyweights, whose bodies falling against the ropes sagged them towards us and whose gloved hands looked like the heads of sledgehammers, knocked steady hell out of each other and everyone was standing and taking and giving every blow, sometimes forgetting they were holding glasses until drink slopped over wrists. One of the fighters got cut above the eye and the trainer was called. We fell back into our seats glad to draw breath. I put my hand over my glass when someone attempted to fill it again and watched the trainer smear what looked like grease over the cut, smoothing and pressing it like putty into a window frame, and then the fight recommenced.

As gobs of blood started to splat round the ring I felt something lurch in my stomach. Both men locked into a shuffle that looked like some drunken smooch of a dance under artificial starlight. They pushed against the ropes above us and a swinging blow glanced across the open cut, making a sleet of blood stipple our suits and shirts. I felt sick. Despite the crowd's cries of disappointment the fight was stopped and we used our napkins to dab at our lapels and shirt collars. The night was over.

In the toilets I emptied my stomach. Eddie was there when I came out of the cubicle.

'Must have been something I ate,' I said when he asked if I was all right. I splashed my face, checking it in the mirror for any remnants of puke or blood. 'And I think I've drunk too much.'

'We can all do that,' he said as he patted my back.

He sounded subdued and in the glass he appeared older, more tired than I had previously seen him. His face was puffed, malleable-looking, as if the lightest of touches might have moulded it into a new expression. He handed me paper towels.

'There's something I need to talk to you about, Henry – maybe in a few days when you're feeling better.'

I tasted the sick in my mouth and spat out again then nodded, no longer really taking in what he was saying, and as I caught one last glimpse of myself in the mirror I felt foolish and the euphoric sense of living in the body, instead of the head, seemed nothing more than an embarrassing drink-fuelled fantasy.

When we started down the corridor I thought of what excuse I could make for my departure. And then it happened. I don't know who he was – he may have been one of the catering staff or part of some other service provider – but he stepped sharply across our path and spat fully at Eddie, hitting him on the shoulder and the side of his cheek, then shouted stuff that in my befuddled state I didn't quite grasp, but there was no missing his use of the word 'bastard' and then something about his father. Suddenly Sam was there and he slammed the man against the wall, one hand clamping the base of the assailant's neck and one hand twisting his arm up his back so he was pinned motionless. But he was still shouting, the words as violent and vicious as any blow we had seen in the ring, until Sam tightened his grip and they vanished into an exclamation of pain.

'Enough, Sam,' Eddie said as he dabbed at his jacket with the handkerchief I had handed him. Soon other men in suits were arriving and still with his arm pressed up his back the attacker was shuffled along the corridor and out of sight.

'I'm sorry you had to see that,' Eddie said, smoothing his palm across his cheek. The shoulder of his jacket still glistened.

'What was it all about?'

'Some people have moved on, some find it harder to forget. That's all.'

There were so many questions but something – perhaps it was fear – stopped me from asking and it felt as if I had stumbled by chance into a world far beyond mine whose existence was governed by rules and principles of which I had only the most tenuous grasp.

'Put it out of your mind, Henry,' he said in the very second that I realised it was probably one of those events whose physical reality presses itself indelibly into the memory and which is liable to reassert itself at any given time. 'And, Henry,' he said, 'I do need to talk to you but not now and not here. How are you fixed tomorrow?'

'It's pretty hectic tomorrow, lots of meetings.'

'Day after?'

There was no way out of it so I told him I could see him at noon in two days' time.

'Thanks, son, and thanks for coming. Don't let that little tiff spoil your night. Just another bit of Belfast confetti.'

When two days later I met Eddie, who was wearing a black overcoat as a defence against the cool autumnal air, I took him through to the university quadrangle and we sat on a bench, the youthfulness of the students ambling by accentuating his age. He was uncharacteristically nervous, his eyes flitting to everyone who passed, and taking a little pleasure at his discomfort I set my briefcase and a pile of books between us.

'Thanks for agreeing to meet me like this, Henry. I know you're a busy man so I'll not be keeping you more than I need to.' But he paused and we watched two young women kicking up leaves for a second before he said, 'It's like this, Henry. You see, I think I'm dying.' The girls rucked up new flurries against each other in a pretence of aggression. 'I've prostate cancer. They say I might survive it but the odds are slipping out of my favour.'

I didn't know what to say other than I was sorry but he simply raised his hand as if there was no need for me to offer sympathy.

'Life's a bitch, Henry, but you know that already. I'm getting chemo and, who knows, I might dodge the bullet.' He paused again as a student went by. 'But I have to get things shipshape, everything organised, and because of that I'm getting married to Alana. Second time around but I want to make sure everything goes to her and no one else gets my share of what I've worked hard for. There's too many grabbing hands lurking in the background. It has to be watertight. You understand?'

I said I did, and I thought he had misunderstood my subject and intended asking me for legal advice, but he continued, 'Alana's been good for me – she deserves everything that's going. And part of that is the wedding.' He hesitated and pursed a little stream of breath through his lips. 'And this is where you come in, Henry. As part of the ceremony, when we do the vows, Alana wants us to have a poem to say to each other. She wants me to find one and for it to be a surprise until the actual day. And, Henry, I'm not talking about roses are red, violets are blue sort of crap or Whitney Houston, I'm talking the real McCoy, something old and classy, something out of a book. You know what I mean?'

I nodded as I tried to take in what he was saying and probably conveyed more conviction than I was feeling so as a way of buying time repeated, 'Something classy.'

'That's it, Henry. Something that will please her and do the business. So what do you think?'

'It's a big responsibility.'

'You're the man, Henry, you're the expert,' he said as he touched the pile of books that separated us. Then he talked about some of the arrangements for the wedding and how naturally I was invited and before I had fully assessed my newfound commission and devised an exit strategy he was patting me on the shoulder and taking his leave with, 'And, Henry, something preferably that doesn't make me look a complete tit.'

So there it was, the weeks of cultivation all came down to this – I was charged with finding a poem, an old and classy poem out of a book, for Eddie to deliver as part of his marriage ceremony. Even though I was shocked by what he had told me about the cancer I couldn't help but feel a sense of repugnance at this sick man being married to Alana. When I shivered I tried to tell myself it was because of the cold breeze blowing through the quadrangle.

That night I started writing a paper on Donne called 'The Ecstasy of the Spirit and the Flesh' but I couldn't help getting distracted by the task that had been foisted on me and no matter where I looked I encountered lines that I couldn't imagine Eddie ever speaking. I tried Shakespeare's sonnets, *Romeo and Juliet*, Auden, a host of others, but found myself returning to Donne. In the end I settled for 'The Good-Morrow' – I had to rejig it, leaving out the parts about sucking on country pleasures and snorting in the seven sleepers' den as potential snigger inducers, modernising some spelling so that the first stanza simply read:

I wonder by my troth, what thou and I
Did, till we loved? If ever any beauty I did see,
Which I desired, and got, 'twas but a dream of thee.

I typed it up, conscious of the poignancy of the final

If our two loves be one, or, thou and I
Love so alike, that none doe slacken, none can die

then wondered whether it would please him or if he would reject it out of hand.

A week later we met in the Victorian Palm House in the Botanic Gardens and as I read it to him I wasn't sure whether it was the humid heat or my nervousness that made my voice quiver a little. He stared at his copy, his face expressionless, while I explained everything in it as simply as I could.

'It's beautiful,' he said. 'The business.' Then, shaking my hand, he added, I suppose as one sporting man to another, 'Back of the net.'

'If you're not comfortable with it I can look for something else.'

'No, Henry, this is the one. But you've got to help me say it right. I'm going to learn it so I don't need the page.'

'OK, let's give it a go.'

'Here?'

'Why not, there's no one about.'

We leant arm to arm on the railing above the tropical ravine and he started to read. He wasn't bad and I let him finish without interrupting and then showed him where to pause and where the lines ran on. We went through it a couple more times, adding a little more subtlety of emphasis or pacing in the delivery. Then he shook my hand again and I watched him walk away, his feet shuffling through leaves and the spiked shells of plundered horse chestnuts.

Before the wedding he had two more practices and by the final one he was word perfect. I made him occupy the middle of the bandstand and address the poem to his single-person audience. He spoke the lines in a way that showed an understanding of the words and I found it strangely moving as he stood there in his black coat, hands dug deeply into his pockets as if for ballast, while on the other side of the grass young mothers played with their children. Then as he finished I saw him shade his eyes as if suddenly blinded by the sun and realised he was crying.

I waited stock still, unsure whether to go to him or pretend I hadn't seen, but he made the decision for me by holding his palm up before shaking his head several times like a dog throws off water. He wiped his face with the back of his hand then scrunched his shoulders and asked, 'So how did it sound?' his voice as he intended, inflated with renewed, if simulated, buoyancy.

I wanted to tell him using my own words but after a second's searching I simply said, 'Dead on,' then repeated it again and he nodded with what looked like relief and not a little gratitude.

At the wedding in Belfast Castle he did the lines faultlessly, and when I glanced round no one was rolling their eyes or looking at each other blankly. By then of course I had completed my Internet searches and knew what had been done. And yet despite this knowledge I found it difficult to associate him with what I had read, almost as if it existed in some other life that had rusted away and been buried deep in the discarded debris of the past. It may well have been a dangerous and hopelessly naive sentimentality but I thought of the opening line of Donne's 'The Calme' – 'Our storme is past, and that storms tyrannous rage' – and repeated it silently to myself because in those moments I wanted to believe it was true.

At the reception I danced with Alana. They were going to Paris for their honeymoon and with every step I imagined waking beside her in 'loves hallow'd temple, this soft bed' and, as embarrassing as it now seems, the predictable image unfurling in my mind was of the early morning Parisian sun slipping through curtained windows and as she lay in my arms I was of course chiding the 'busie old foole' for daring to disturb us.

That's almost all there is to tell. With the cheering, confetti-throwing crowd I watched them drive off in a vintage car that looked like it might have been borrowed from Jay Gatsby. Then in the coldness of the next day's light that belonged to winter I finished my paper on Donne and started to trawl for a post closer to somewhere I could think of as home.

I only saw Eddie, Sam and George one last time – two weeks after the wedding and just before I cancelled my membership of the leisure complex and bought a new phone. They were in the Jacuzzi but I stayed in the pool clutching my two floats. I knew that Eddie was due to have his last bout of chemo but wasn't sure whether this was a good or a bad thing. Then he was calling me over to face the ritual question of how was it going, to which I simply said, 'Can't complain,' before out of politeness I asked about Paris.

'Very good, Henry, very good. Alana really liked it, so good choice all round.'

There was a moment's silence until Sam asked, 'You still can't swim, Henry?'

'No, not yet.'

'I'll teach you.'

When I hesitated George said, 'He's a good teacher, Henry – he's taught lots of kids, lots of older ones. Isn't that right, Eddie?'

'Trust him,' Eddie said, nodding up at me. 'Never known him to fail.'

I started to make excuses but all three stepped out of the Jacuzzi and the weight of their collective encouragement made me follow Sam along the side of the pool. We got to the deep end, and then he turned, smiled and offered his hand in a friendly gesture before the start of the lesson, but as soon as I took it I was hurtling past his shoulder with so much force that I hit the middle of the pool with a stiff splayed-arm splash and then a bursting panic as every limb frantically kicked and threshed. And as I looked up Sam was leaning over the edge making slow-motion swimming movements that I tried to copy while the others urged me on, shouting as if they were cheering a racehorse home. Spluttering, water in my mouth and eyes, beating a desperate, fear-fuelled path towards the edge, I glanced up only long enough to hear someone say, 'You're doing it, kid, you're doing it,' but then just before my flailing hand found safety my face went under again. And this is how I have come to remember them and every-thing that happened during those months – finding myself floundering in that strange element of a city, their faces and voices increasingly blurred as if they too were cast adrift in some world that was partly of their own making, but in part of things they didn't fully understand, and, despite what would always separate us, all of us equally uncertain about when fortune's favours might fade and whether our outstretched hands were ever going to reach.

Boxing Day

FOR FOUR YEARS MY father drove me on Boxing Day to spend time with my mother who lived on her own in a small bungalow facing the sea. He took me after lunch and as arranged always collected me at six. Each year I argued that he should collect me earlier, only to be met with the same reply that it wouldn't be right to make my stay any shorter. All his life I believe my father tried to do what was for the best and perhaps he was right about this, but I made my first journey when I was thirteen and when you're that age nothing seems as important as what you want. And I didn't want to visit my mother on Boxing Day. I suppose he didn't either but understood that although he had legal custody of me it would be a kindness if she was able to see me at Christmas and so for four years we took the same half-hour drive to the coast.

I made the last one when I was seventeen. On that final journey we didn't talk much and used the radio to fill the silences but already it sounded as if those tired old festive songs needed to be stored away until next year, and their insistent jolliness seemed as meaningless as the discarded wrapping paper from the day before. I mostly stared out the side window in my best effort to convey my reluctance to converse and, when he tried, didn't say much in reply, or even turn my head in his direction. What I was punishing him for was that each of those four journeys signalled the end of my Christmas and I didn't want it to end so soon because what my father had given me was happiness which is a diffi-cult thing to give up.

The day he told me he was leaving my mother we were sitting in the rickety stand of our local lower-league football team and as usual at half-time sharing a flask of tomato soup and the sandwiches he'd made. I remember clearly that my first impulse was panic so strong that it was a wonder I didn't grab his sleeve and refuse to let go but already he was tell-ing me that I was coming with him. The questions tumbled out. Did Mum know? Where were we going? When was it going to happen? Some of these ques-tions he answered fully, others he seemed less sure about, but the one thing I understood was that the worst was over because he had already told her. As the second half began and he set the flask aside then dabbed my orange moustache with his handkerchief, I tried to work out when he had done so. There was no obvious moment that I could think of, no recent screaming voices or slamming doors, no sense of final crisis.

You see, my mother was ill. 'Your mum's not well, Robbie,' was the earliest explanation I remember my father giving me. When I was older he added medical words and tried to help me understand. And as the wind snaked through the tiered seats he repeated those earlier words before adding, 'and I tried very hard but I couldn't help her to get better'. It was strange to hear him refer to her in the past tense and that afternoon as we sat watching the game, even though the pattern of play seemed increasingly disjointed, devoid of rhythm or purpose, I didn't want it to end, didn't want to go home.

In the car on this last Boxing Day the world skimmed past under my disinterested gaze. There had been much talk of snow but it didn't look as if it would come to anything and as we drove towards the coast, although it was very cold, the sky seemed untroubled and layered only with a thin wash of brightness.

'It'll be fine, Robbie,' my father said.

'It won't be fine. You know it won't be fine,' I answered as I clutched the present Bethany my step-mum had bought on my behalf. I couldn't even remember what it was.

'It's only a few hours and you know it means a lot to her.'

I said nothing but if I had, it would have been to say that I couldn't remember my presence all through childhood, or on any of my visits, ever seeming as if it meant that much to her. One Boxing Day after a makeshift lunch that looked as if it had been squeezed out of pretty ancient leftovers she lay down on the settee, curled herself into its narrow softness and fell asleep for a couple of hours. She didn't have a television and the house was filled with an eerie silence that I didn't want to disturb by switching on the light or even in desperation the radio. When she woke it was as if she looked at me through a swirl of fog and for a moment I wasn't sure if she knew who I was.

'It's Robbie,' I said.

'Robbie, of course you are. Robbie – I know that, silly.'

I remembered it as I drove with my father and as he struggled with the radio to find the football commentary on 5 Live it seemed to me that my mother never fully grasped who I was or how I had come to be part of her life. When I was younger she had a habit, almost as an afterthought, of lightly patting my head when she passed and I began to think of it as the closest she could come to giving me her blessing.

'Find the football for me,' my father said but when I located the station the reception was poor and the voice kept breaking in to booming echoes before fading again. 'Must be the weather,' he said.

We passed through a hamlet where the local pub was decorated in fairy lights and where, despite the cold, smokers hunched over an outside table, their smoke like a wreath of frost above their heads. A little further on we got diverted briefly because the local hunt was out and as we drove we glimpsed red coats and horses coursing across a distant field that sloped up towards the horizon.

'A drag hunt,' my father said. 'At least I hope so.'

It was childish but I felt a momentary annoyance that he should be expressing his concern over some dumb animal when he was about to deliver his son to misery.

'Why do I need to keep doing this?' I asked, turning off the radio to signal my seriousness.

'Because it's the right thing to do and because when all's said and done she's still your mother.'

There were many things I wanted to offer in reply to this but I held back, saying only, 'I'm eighteen next year.'

'When you're eighteen, it's up to you what you do. Fair enough? Let's not fight over it, Robbie.'

I slumped back in the seat and put the Christmas music on again. The DJ must have drawn the short straw to be working on Boxing Day and then I wondered if it was recorded in advance and it was all an elaborate charade of jollity. So this was to be my last year. There was some comfort in that at least. And I wanted to tell my father that one of the reasons I didn't want to come was because I loved my new home and family so much. I had a new mother I called Bethany and Mia, a new older sister. Bethany was funny, good to me and made my father happy. When she hugged me I felt myself trampolining against her ample body and as I'd bounce away I was always conscious of her scent that was a mixture of something sweet and the antiseptic smell of a hospital. Mia had started art college four months earlier and I thought everything about her was cool, from the art she produced to the weird self-made clothes she wore. Dad had met Bethany on an Internet chat site and then discovered they both worked in the same hospital. He was in administration and she was a nurse. I think they were going out for a year before he told me about her. So on the first day of the summer holidays and before I started a new school I left my home and moved in with Bethany and her daughter. We stayed there for about a year then moved to a slightly bigger house within walking distance of my new school. My mum also moved shortly afterwards – 'a necessary downsizing,' she called it and said the sea air would be good for her although my father worried that she didn't know anyone. But I think it didn't really matter where my mum lived because inside her head she was only ever in the one place.

It's not easy to describe this place she lived and I don't know what it was like to be her but when I think about it, it always felt as if there was something separating her from life itself and even perhaps from herself. And it was as if nothing was ever fully in focus for her and she didn't have the inner strength to force the world into clarity. I suppose too because of that I found it difficult to know who she was although I told myself that when she met and married my father she must have been her real self and not this one who had slipped behind a veil. There were periods of sustained lethargy where getting out of bed in the mornings represented a challenge for her and all the small necessities of the day such as getting dressed or making a meal for herself became increasingly difficult. When afflicted like this she stayed in her dressing gown and watched television with the sound down. 'It's too loud, everything's too loud,' she would say and there were times when sounds seemed to hurt her – my dropping of cutlery into a drawer, the judder of the washing machine – and she would go to her room and close the door quietly behind her. Sometimes I didn't see her for days.

I got used to this and preferred it to the other state that she entered from time to time – I now understand that it was probably her medication, or perhaps one of the numerous changes to it, that resulted in a sudden flaring of energised intensity that saw her supposedly about to embark on a range of activities – spring-cleaning the house, wanting to help me build a tree house, planning a camping holiday – all of which were destined to fade into complete failure and then be erased from memory. But there was something else I understood on that journey and it was that although we were separated she was always there, lingering silently on the edge of every new happiness, always only a thought away.

Little half-hearted plashes of sleet began to lace the windscreen. The wipers scudded and squeaked.

'Looks like it might snow,' I said because by then I'd started to feel bad about giving him a hard time.

'No chance – it never snows this close to the coast.'

'Are you coming in when you drop me off?' I asked.

'I'll stay awhile,' he said as he peered up at the sky. 'Everything will be fine, Robbie, and I'll be back for you at six.'

'Don't be late.'

'I won't and Bethany'll have something hot cooked up for us when we get in. And there's a couple of top films on later we can watch.'

He didn't know how good a prospect those simple things seemed and I didn't try to tell him as we started to drop down towards the sea, the road unspooling in narrowing ribbons and falling away until eventually we were able to glimpse it in the far distance.

'Will you and Bethany get married?' I asked, for some stupid reason tormenting myself by imagining that my newfound happiness might prove only temporary and naively believing that the exchange of rings would increase the prospect of permanence.

'I think so, but not for a while yet. Is it important to you?'

'No, not really. But you think you'll stay with her?'

'I hope so – you like her, don't you?'

'Yes.'

'That's good.'

And then to avoid further conversation I tried the football again but the commentary was still broken by static and I switched it back to the music.

'That's doing my head in, Robbie,' my father said and he shuffled through his CDs ignoring the Leonard Cohen, the Van Morrison and Fairport Convention until he found one of the compromise discs we kept in the car and so for the rest of the journey we listened to *The Very Best of The Smiths* but didn't, as we sometimes liked to do, sing along with 'There Is a Light That Never Goes Out'. Then we passed frozen stubbled fields until we were funnelled into even narrower roads where the high hedges had been cropped so they were topped by ragged swathes of pointed spears. And when Morrissey sang about driving in his car and begging not to be dropped home, we both glanced at each other and my father drummed a nervous little tattoo on the steering wheel with his fingers. Then as he smiled he started to sing song titles at me:

'Heaven Knows I'm Miserable Now'.
'The Boy with the Thorn in His Side'.
'Please, Please, Please, Let Me Get What I Want'.

I didn't know the song titles as well as him so I had to lift out the CD cover and scan it before I said, '"Bigmouth Strikes Again",' and he chuckled a little the way he often did and which always made me think he had something soft and warm slipping slowly down his throat.

We were almost there now and we could see the sea but it was a disappointment, seemingly stripped of any drama or colour, a grey stretch of nothing fading into a similarly coloured sky.

'It'll be all right,' he said and this time I didn't argue with him.

Parked outside the house we both paused and with our seatbelts still on glanced up at it and for a second I thought there was just the possibility that he would drive us both home but then I heard the click of his and a few moments later we were standing at the front door. My last time.

It was a while before the door was opened and when it did she was a little flustered, smoothing her hair that looked exactly the way her hair always did but as if somehow she hadn't been expecting us.

'Hello,' she said, smiling, but for a second she didn't move and I wondered if she thought we had come to sing carols.

'Merry Christmas, Jane,' my father said as I felt his hand gently pushing me forward.

'Yes, Merry Christmas. Come in – it's getting really cold,' she said, holding her hand palm upwards across the doorstep as if testing for rain.

Then despite what he had suggested earlier my father said he'd head on and after a few minutes of conversation that I didn't quite catch I heard him drive away. The living room was cold, warmed only by the single bar of an electric fire, and over the back of the settee was a red woollen coat and I could tell from the wisps of the same coloured threads on her jumper that she had been wearing it before our arrival. I felt sorry for her the way I always did in those first moments and so I handed her the present and wished her Happy Christmas. I even came close to using the word 'Mum' but at the last moment decided not to break my stubborn resolve from an earlier age. By then I had remembered what the present was and after she had removed the wrapping paper in such a slow and careful way that suggested she was going to preserve or reuse it, she thanked me and putting the cardigan on wore it for the rest of my visit. In return she handed me a small package telling me it was 'nothing much', just a little thing she had picked up in a local shop. I remembered with apprehension some previous presents that had required an intense effort to simulate gratitude so although it was a long way off the best thing I had received that Christmas, I felt some relief that I was looking at a magnifying glass. It was a nice object with a prism about the size of my palm and a black ebony handle. A little smudge of frosting on the glass and some small scores on the handle suggested it wasn't new but that didn't matter and although I had no idea what I was supposed to do with it I thanked her and she seemed pleased in turn. Then I held it to my eye and looked at her through it as I said, 'Perhaps I should become a detective, use it to look for clues.'

'You could be the next Sherlock Holmes,' she said as she fastened all the buttons on her new cardigan then plopped down on the chair closest to the fire before standing up again and plumping a cushion and smoothing out wrinkles from the chair's arms. 'I read somewhere there's a new one on television and they've messed about with the stories. Updated them or something. Why do they do that, Robbie?'

'I don't know,' I said as I lowered the glass.

'It's beyond me. Things never change for the better.'

And as I thought of the warm house I had just left awash with decorations and fun, part of me wanted to tell her that yes they did but it wouldn't have been a kindness, would it? I looked around the room and saw our old box of Christmas decorations sitting under the sideboard, a string of fairy lights lolling out over the side, saw too that the only thing she had used was the garland of reindeer which looped across the fireplace, each end weighted by ornaments.

'You didn't put up all of the decorations.'

'Seemed a bit silly when it's just me. But I put up the reindeer in honour of you coming. When you were small you always liked them.'

I had no memory of this but then I had no real memory of what anything was like when I was a small child and she was my mother. Perhaps that was a time when she was well so it seemed a bad thing that I couldn't remember. I was curious about this part of our shared past but it wasn't something I knew how to pursue. So I nodded as if I did remember and thought how much better it would be if there was a fire burning in the hearth. I don't think she had much money but knew my father still paid for certain things – it was the only argument that I had heard with Bethany. And I'm not sure but I think she got to keep most of the profit on the sale of the house.

'How's school going?' she asked and I tried hard to think of things that she might find interesting, and knowing how many hours needed filling rambled on about my subjects and teachers, telling her what universities I was considering until eventually I ran out of steam.

'That's good,' she said and she stifled a little yawn with the back of her hand.

'And how are you keeping?' I asked and when I spoke these words I knew it sounded as if I was the parent talking to his child.

'You know how it is, Robbie. Good days and bad days. Trying my best. Got to keep going. Nothing else for it, really.'

'That's good. And your medication is working out all right?'

'Mostly, but it's a bit hit and miss sometimes. And I don't think my doctor here is as good as Dr Hamilton who never made you feel she was in a hurry to see the next patient. And this one is still reading your notes on his computer when you're talking to him.'

We both stared at the bar of the electric fire that had started to burn more brightly as the first strength of light seeped out of the day. Then she stood up suddenly and went to the kitchen, returning with a piece of chocolate cake on a saucer and a glass of cordial. Her own glass was filled with wine. I looked at her as she handed me the cake.

'It's Christmas, Robbie. I don't think the world's going to stop after one glass.'

'Are you sure?'

'You're such an old fusspot,' she said as she took her first sip. 'And tell me, is she looking after you properly? You look a bit thin?'

'Bethany?' It was obvious that she had resolved never to use Bethany's name but after she had nodded I told her everything was fine.

'That's good, Robbie, good that you can play happy families. Very good.'

I said nothing and then I thought for the first time that my mother was probably glad that we had both left because it removed what was an often painful distraction and allowed her to focus exclusively on herself in the full way she needed to. The house would be quieter without any of those sharp-edged noises that tore at her as we moved through it. It was quiet now even though on the other side of the road the sea's low moan was a constant presence.

The cake tasted stale but I finished it and drank the cordial as she sipped again at her wine.

'This is a good place to live, Robbie,' she said.

'Why's that?'

'The sea air is good for me. I try to walk on the beach most days. Some days the wind's so strong it feels like it's blowing all your cobwebs away. Know what I mean?'

I said I did and she talked about how earlier in the year there had been a great storm and lots of strange things got washed up on the beach – a large branch of a tree still with some green leaves on it, bits of wooden crates and battered lobster pots.

35

'Perhaps later we could go for a walk on the beach,' I said.

'Well it's a bit cold today and I'd get the blame if you caught a cold. Sometimes there's a wind would cut you in two.'

I walked to the window. The sea seemed locked into a stupor, slumbering in some forlorn memory of its former motion.

'They say this used to be a smugglers' cove hundreds of years ago,' she told me.

'What would they have smuggled?'

'I'm not really sure. Brandy, silk, goods from France, I suppose. There's a mobile library comes round once a week and I should try and see if they have any local histories.'

We ran out of conversation and after a while I could see that she was tired. She finished her wine but continued to hold the empty glass.

'Shall we listen to the radio?' she asked. 'I think there might be something interesting on.'

And so for the next hour we listened to an abridged version of *A Christmas Carol* and sometimes we smiled at each other at some of the jokes. Sometimes too she closed her eyes but whether it was to take more in or to keep something out, I don't know. And so we sat in the thickening gloom while the Ghost of Christmas Past carried Scrooge over the rooftops towards the person he once was and it made me sad that I would never know my mother as she must once have been, and perhaps it was brought on by the sentimentality of the story but to my shock I felt as if I wanted to cry before that impulse was replaced by a resentment over what had been denied. And

I wanted to go home to the scented warmth of Bethany's embrace and Mia's stupid jokes about my wardrobe and her offer to give me a makeover. I wanted to be sitting in that rickety stand with my father as we played our local rivals.

Then before the programme had finished she set the glass on the hearth and curled her legs under like a young girl and as if her head had assumed a weariness that couldn't be resisted she rested it gently on the side of her chair, moving her neck slowly until she had sought out the most comfortable spot. In a few minutes she was sleeping just as she had done once before, so I was left listening to the radio on my own. Her breathing was steady and she snored occasionally, once so loudly that I thought she was going to waken herself but she simply snuggled into a new position. It was getting colder and I tried to put on a second bar of the fire but nothing happened. Taking the red coat I draped it over her and sat down. My father wouldn't return for several hours. I put on my own coat. There was nothing I could do but wait.

I grew nervous about her sleep. Sometimes in the past it didn't always bring the calm that might have been expected but rather a swing in mood and a greater disturbance that expressed itself in old resentments about people and moments from her past. In this state she might talk more rapidly and her words, edged with bitterness, would focus on some aspect of her earlier life that had supposedly sent it spinning into the wrong direction. And on occasions I had seen my father's efforts to calm her rebuffed and then her invective would turn on him and he'd always take it without defending himself, except for saying quietly, 'If it makes you feel better.' Sometimes when my father took me out of the house and after we'd run out of ways to put in time we'd share a palpable nervousness as we stood at the front door and we'd look at each other and inhale a deep breath before he turned the key in the lock. And she might have merely refuelled in our absence rather than burning out and would criticise us for 'running away', or for 'sneaking back', but if we were lucky she would have gone to bed and then in the kitchen my father would make us toast and when we'd eaten it we'd butter the crunchy crusts and eat them too.

I looked round the room until my eyes fell on the box of Christmas decorations. It was always the true start of Christmas when the box was brought down from the roof space and I was allowed to unpack everything. I'd help my mother decorate the tree and she was good at things like that. She'd gone to art college and knew how to make things look right. Sometimes she told me she should have been an artist and occasionally drew in her sketchbook but always seemed dissatisfied with the results and never liked me looking at what she had done.

I quietly removed the box from under the sideboard and started to examine the contents. As well as the run-of-the-mill plastic decorations that had been bought in the supermarket there were other things to look at and which to my surprise still held an echo of the curiosity and pleasure I had felt in childhood. So there were the handful of much older glass decorations that had survived from my grandmother and which because of their fragility only my mother was allowed to hang.

There were the carved wooden nativity figures we had brought back from a holiday in Austria and all the various bits and pieces I had made from shiny paper and cardboard in primary school. I remembered how my mother would tell me to put the nicest objects at eye level and those that weren't so wonderful on lower branches. And there were the little children's story books about Christmas she liked to use to decorative effect, a collection of birds with brightly coloured tail feathers and the large snow globe containing a winter landscape complete with village encircled by fir trees. Then on impulse I lifted the coloured fairy lights and draped them across the fireplace and plugged them in and taking some of the different decorations arranged them beside the garland of reindeer. I didn't know if she would be pleased or not but the lights softened the room and although it was only in my imagination momentarily made it seem warmer. Finally I placed a framed picture of me sitting on Santa's knee with an unopened present, my mother beside us, her eyes angled away from the camera's stare. She was wearing a kind of woollen beret and a long scarf that almost reached her knees. A thin trim of black velvet edged the collar of her winter coat and I liked to think that when the photograph was taken it was during that part of her life when she was truly herself.

She made a snuffling noise then went on sleeping in her curiously childlike position with her head resting on the pillow of her hands that were clasped as if in prayer. Music came on the radio and I turned it off. I stood perfectly still and stared at her, thinking she seemed older, slowly leaving behind my memory of her physical reality. Then taking the magnifying glass and standing behind my mother's chair I looked at her hair, saw the pale gleam of her scalp at the parting and the way the bristly toughness slipped into a finer greyness at the roots. Saw too the delicate coral neatness of her ears that seemed like a young girl's. But it was after I had moved the glass to her hands and looked at the white-flecked nails that I saw the cross-hatching on her right wrist and stopped looking through the glass. The marks were no longer red as they must once have been and were now scabbed over and dulled but they were there all the same. I went and sat down again. I wanted my father to come, wanted him to take me where the reality of such things didn't exist, and as the shadows in the room thickened I didn't want us to be the people who were to blame.

She shifted in the chair and used her arm to settle the coat on to her shoulder then made the snuffling noise again. I couldn't see her wrist now and I was glad. So far as I knew she had never done that sort of thing before but I didn't know everything and there had been times over the years when she had been hospitalised.

'Well isn't this jolly,' she had said once when I was younger and we were visiting her in a day room, surrounded by people who looked as if they didn't know where or who they were and a woman who had to be helped away by staff when she started to ask the same question over and over again, her voice getting ever louder. But I remember too whenever we were leaving my father asked me to wait for him in the corridor and through the glass panel in the door I saw her clutch at his arm in an attempt to hold him longer as he bent down to kiss her on the cheek. On the drive home he cried – it was the only time I have ever seen him do this and he stopped as soon as he saw me looking at him, then in an attempt at mutual consolation we went to McDonald's and had a Happy Meal.

I looked at the decorations on the fireplace and wondered if I should take them down because now they seemed a foolishness. I wasn't sure about what to do and certain only about one thing. As I fastened my coat I realised again that this was going to be the last time I would visit on Boxing Day and in that moment couldn't convince myself that I might return on any future day. Going to the fireplace I took the framed photograph and nestled it in my coat pocket beside the magnifying glass then closed the door as quietly as I had opened it.

I had over an hour to wait before my father's arrival so I walked along the sea front until I found a seat in a green-painted wooden shelter where graffiti and cigarette butts suggested it was the hangout for local kids. It faced the sea and I sat there knowing I couldn't phone my father to come earlier without inventing a reason that I could carry off convincingly. There was a coldness eddying off a sea that still looked bored by its own motion as it broke lifelessly on the shingle beach. Above it the clouds hung low and heavy and as I tried to shelter from the cold the air was suddenly flecked by a dreamy breath of snow. I had this stupid idea that if I could let a flake land on my skin I could look at it through the magnifying glass and see one of those ice crystals, all of which are supposed to be different to any other, but of course it didn't work and the snow seemed to melt just as quickly as it was swallowed by the sea.

By the time my father appeared it was coming down in a steady fall. I pretended I had walked to the end of the road to meet him and made a show of buttoning my coat.

'OK, Robbie?' he asked as I got in the car. 'Everything go all right?'

'Yes, good.'

'And your mother was OK?'

'She was fine,' I said as I turned up the car's heater.

'And she liked the present?'

'Yes, she liked the present. You told me it never snowed this close to the coast,' I said as fat flakes softly drifted against the windscreen.

'Never seen it before. And by the way we didn't miss anything this afternoon. We lost four–one – stuffed like a Christmas turkey. Now let's get you home. You're shivering,' he said, stretching his arm across to mine.

'The house was a bit cold, that's all. I'll be all right in a minute.'

He blasted the heater on full and I held my hands against the vent. We didn't talk much as ahead of us snow slanted sleepily across the headlights and when we started our climb through the narrow roads I thought of the fairy lights I had left on the fireplace and how behind us the snow was silently disappearing into the sea. And as I felt the objects in my coat and the car carried us ever further away, I knew that we could never travel far enough, no matter how much we tried, and I wanted something to hold happiness bigger and brought up really close, a glass that made misery fade. The jagged hedges channelling the car bristled with white-tipped spears, the road ahead a trembling splay of snow. Morrissey started to sing about the light that never goes out but as my father started to accompany him, and with a glance invited me to join in, I wanted him only to tell me that it wouldn't be our fault, that we weren't the ones to blame.

The Kiss

WHAT IS IT GIVES them their annunciations and beatifications, the gilded transfigurations and their holy miracles, but his flesh? They're incarnated only through the tightening rack of pain in his shoulders, the throat's dry river-bed, his tired eyes that feel as if he's swimming through gravel. He knows that life is only in the flesh and nowhere does he know this more than when he's in some church, the supposed place of the spirit, as he hangs himself high on rickety scaffolding to paint a ceiling, or works on an altar panel, the lingering smell of incense and candle wax mixing with the dampness of stone and the sweat of the supplicant poor. When he stops to scan the work of others it makes him want to echo the vaulting space with the most beautiful obscenity that can caress his lips, at the spit-thin, perfect alabaster skin, the vapid expressions, the weightless bodies – so much ethereal spindrift that looks as if the next breeze might blow it into eternity. How it pleases him to paint the face of the moment's favourite whore and think of her unashamed stare meeting the gaze of the penitents below and it pleases him even more that they will turn their widening eyes to her and seek her forgiveness for their sins.

Christ knew about the flesh. It was what he chose to become. So more than anyone ever born he knew the shock of its pain, its weariness, its constant longing. But that's the trouble – they don't understand and so they splutter and whine, renege on their agreements when he gives them their God made flesh. Strange how it's always different with his women and while the robed cardinals and their lackeys stand at the unveiling with sagging mouths – he's even seen one lick his lips – there isn't one of them who doesn't shuffle a little closer to touch with hungry eyes and store something for the lonely comfort of the night. Only a fool would fail to see that the greatest claim to holiness of the spirit is always manifested in what it offers the flesh. He's lived in their palazzos, drunk their wine, let his eyes feel the richness of their clothes, enjoyed their feather beds. And now they think of him as their pet monkey, turn a blind eye to his fleshly loves in return for the paintings they use to bolster their egos and climb the ladder of their papal careers. But for him there is no spiritual ladder that he can climb and so he knows he must paint himself into heaven.

Today he's almost spent. The narrow street outside is baked hot, speckled with flies and stinking with fish heads, the puddles of horse piss stagnant breeding grounds before the sun burns them dry. So what Christ will he give them in this the moment of his betrayal? A thin shiver of a dog wanders in through the open door of the studio, its ringed ribs ridged against its scabbed and mottled skin. The boy shoos it out again with a broom. A fat-bellied fly that looks as if it's been inked-up in a shimmer of indigo lumbers lazily over the heads of the models.

'How much longer,' Christ asks, 'do I have to be kissed by the scabby lips of this Judas who has the breath of a donkey? What privy did you dig him out of?'

'Just a little longer, Pietro, while the light is good,' he says, squinting as if the same light is in his eyes and trying to get the angle of the heads exactly right. 'Just a little longer and then we can wash it away with as much as you can pour down your throat.'

There are sudden cries from the street – a woman's voice splintering into jagged curses and the counter-point of a man's dismissive laughter – and the dog appears again in the doorway. He aims a kick at the boy and tells him if he wants his supper and a bed that night then he'd better get rid of it once and for all. The dog lifts its leg against the jamb of the door but scuttles away as the boy runs at it shouting. The blue fly settles on the black armour of one of the two soldiers and for a second he stares at it, imagines it's warming itself on the body heat of the soldiers that seems to seep even through the heaviness of the metal. He'd almost feel sorry for them if he wasn't paying for their time and sweat.

He needs to paint Christ's face and as if to see it afresh changes the angle of his vision, then walks closer before pulling back again, pushing a lock of hair from his brow and tinting it white.

'Try to be a good Christ,' he tells his friend. 'There's too much anger in your eyes.'

'As if you wouldn't have taken a dagger to this betrayer's innards,' Pietro sneers. 'And where did you find him anyway?'

'You were right about the privy – he's one of the collectors.'

'Shit,' says Pietro, pulling his head back slightly from the permanently proffered kiss.

'Indeed. But he comes cheaper than most. Now hold your head still just a few moments more. And stop your mouth. Just a few moments more while the light's right and then we'll be out of this Gethsemane for ever. I swear.'

He'll finish the face in the morning when the studio is empty and his head has cleared from what he will drink in the coming hours. Already he has given him downcast eyes – that look of meek acceptance of his fate. He despises it already. His hands are clasped but look powerless in the face of the armour and helmets. Judas's hand on his shoulder is like a claw. Pietro was right about the dagger. Step closer with a smile and then up and in under the ribs. A quick twist for luck and pull it out, as always shocked by the flesh's willingness to shamelessly expose its vulnerability, its willingness to bleed and bruise, its bones to snap and splinter as though everything on the seemingly invincible surface was nothing but a vain boast.

His boy attempts to reinstate some favour by bringing him a drink and a cloth to wipe the sweat from his brow. He grunts at the boy, dabs his forehead with the rag and then knuckles it into his eyes before flinging it back at its giver.

'So now you'll torment me by drinking in front of me.'

He sets his brushes and blade down and walks to his friend, lets him have the first sip, holding the cup to his lips while one hand cradles the back of his head so that he doesn't have to move position. Pietro with the pale blue eyes that are the colour of eggshell and which have looked at him with simple love since childhood: faithful co-conspirator through the wild escapades of youth back in their home town and who has followed him to Rome because he thinks that he too can be a painter. Because it looks easy. A painter of bordello signs or obscene graffiti about the Tomassoni brothers, perhaps, but a painter, no. For everything they had shared – not least the women and the fights, the drunken nights they had slept in the olive groves – he grants him the pretence of a kind of apprenticeship, lets him prepare the paints, work up some unimportant parts of the composition, the sort of menial task that bores him. He rubs his thumb along his friend's lips to dry them and looks again at the pellucid blueness of his eyes. They have their own beauty. Somewhere the fly rattles into momentary flight.

The main composition of the painting exists now despite the details that need to be completed, not least the slash of light he will throw into the pressing darkness of the night. It's his favourite trick – the dramatic signature. A little cheap, perhaps, but effective nevertheless. Here it will run the length of the soldier's black-armoured arm that reaches out to imprison Christ so it stretches like an arrow into his heart. There is only one unresolved part of the painting which he sees now as he stares at the tableau that has started to wilt like flowers in a vase. It's on the extreme right and he needs a figure to fill the space and hold the lantern that will supposedly illuminate the moment of capture. But there will be time for that in the morning.

Now the sitting is finished, ended not by the light but by the stiffness in his shoulders and the dryness of his throat. He signals to the boy who hurries to help the models remove their costumes and props – it wouldn't be the first time someone thought what they were wearing was part of the payment. Judas grovels forward for his coins with bowed head. He looks at the outstretched hand with its ingrained grime, the thick rim of dirt under the nails, and presses the few coins into Judas's palm, for a second feels their skin touch.

'You were underpaid, my friend – you should have asked for thirty pieces of silver,' then as the man turns to go he grabs him by the shoulder, feels the sinewy strength of muscle under the cloth and says, 'To honour your contract you must go now and hang yourself.' Judas looks at him with confusion in his rheumy eyes and smiles uncertainly. But he doesn't smile back and instead says, 'It's what the story demands so it's a question of honour – you understand?'

He hears Pietro sniggering and as the man bows again he looks at his exposed scalp that is the colour and moulded texture of days-old bread. 'Be sure to use a good rope, one that won't let you down. Now go quickly.'

As Judas hurries away the boy brings a basin of water and a cloth which is the same one as offered before so he cuffs him and demands a clean one. The soldiers unbuckle the last of the clunking armour and as compensation to the boy for cuffing him he allows him to pay them, watching the bright wink and clink of the coins while he steeps his hands in the coolness of the water, paint spuming out in globular flurries. Then he splashes his face, still smelling the paint on his hands that makes him think it has wormed under his skin. Pietro is slumped on a chair and furrowing a hand through his hair. Being Christ has worn him out.

'Be grateful, Pietro, that it wasn't a crucifixion they wanted,' he calls, drying his face. 'Now let's burn what's left of this day.'

'I can't be out all night. You know how it is.'

'I know that marriage has made you sound like an old man. Two months married and already under the thumb. Have you no shame?'

His friend stands and smiles his embarrassment. 'There are compensations,' he offers but without conviction when faced with the fixed stare of the painter.

'To drink only from the one cup, to whistle one tune day after day ...' Caravaggio says, raising his palms together again to smell them and holding them there for a second as if he is praying. 'When we go to the Ortaccio what you do is your own business but I intend to have my fill.' Then, for some reason he doesn't understand, he thinks of the night in Lombardy they rustled horses, their sleek hollow flanks sheened with moonlight, the steam from their nostrils smoking the air. The hot fetid smell of their fear, their tossing heads trying to escape the bridles. Then he covers the painting, gives the boy a long list of instructions and they are gone.

At dusk when swallows seamlessly stitch the sky, the food eaten, the drink flowing, Pietro hoists himself carefully to his feet and apologises to his friend for unfaithfulness, his unwillingness to match him drink for drink. Caravaggio's face is fully hidden from him, seemingly inspecting the throat of the serving girl who slops across his lap, her laughter tinkling out as now he examines the skin tones of her breasts.

'So scurry home to Fillide before she bars the door to you, shuts you out all night,' he calls, his hand waving a dismissive farewell, but suddenly the girl is off his lap and sliding to the floor with a squeal. Pietro is staring at him and he signals with his eyes to where one of the Tomassoni brothers has swaggered through the far door. He hasn't seen them despite the way he languidly lets his eyes flit around the room establishing his ownership and yet as if it's all unworthy to merit his gaze.

'I've no stomach for it,' Pietro whispers as he leans across the table. 'Let's just take our drinks and be gone. There are a hundred other places you can take your fill.'

'I like it here,' Caravaggio says as he reaches out his hand and pulls the girl off the floor and back on to his knee. 'What happens happens.'

'Let it go,' his friend says. 'You don't need it. You have a painting to finish and they're already knocking on your door for it.'

'You always give good advice and I always pay it no heed. It's not your fault.' He thinks again of the night when they chased horses through the fields, the way the animals jerked their heads in fear of the bridles, their eyes rolling white in the moonlight.

By now they have been seen and Caravaggio smiles as their eyes lock. He pats the girl on the back to send her on her way and straightens on the wooden bench, pulling his outstretched legs closer to his body. Already the world is tightening as if all the air is slowly draining away.

'No,' Pietro says while he leans even closer as if he's about to whisper some secret. 'Let me speak to him, tell him we want no trouble.'

'Here's your chance,' Caravaggio says as he turns his attention calmly to his wine.

And then what happens breaks in a sudden blur of fragmented movement like the shattered jagged glass of a mirror which later even memory can't piece together. It happens without words but in the dagger's silent glinting smile as it catches Pietro's protective arm which tries to knock it from its intended target and then there is a splay of bodies and fists and kicks, the screams of the serving girls and clatter of over-turned tables.

'No! No!' Pietro shouts as his companion crouches over the fallen Tomassoni, his knee on his chest, his dagger poised in the air like a scalpel about to dissect. He pauses, looks at his friend and smiles, looks too at Pietro's ripped tunic sleeve that is slowly staining red and thinks of the flurries of colour in the water when he steeped his hands. He smiles again and straightens.

'Just a signature,' he says and then, bending, he scores his trademark along the stubbled canvas of the cheek, turning it in that moment into a ripped palimpsest that slowly exposes the world beneath. The sudden vibrancy of the hidden colour makes him blink, deafens him even to the scream, and for a second he stands transfixed, oblivious to the tug of Pietro at his back. Then they are gone into the night where the sky is purpled with cloud and the faces that stare at their fleeing forms are white and pocked like the moon.

Pietro's is a flesh wound and he washes it and dresses it, will get a doctor in the morning. There will be a price to pay for the night's business but Caravaggio never concerns himself with the future. He gives Pietro his bed and clothes him in fresh linen and yes he will go and tell Fillide that he has survived, that he hasn't betrayed her trust, tell her everything that the shuddering brush with death loosens from the tongue of his companion. Before he goes he lays a hand on his friend's forehead to assure himself that there is no fever burning, kisses him on the cheek and then slips into the great echoing hollow of the night.

The children swarm about the gallery, worksheets and pencils clutched in hands, excited at having escaped the predictable patterns of the classroom. They do stage whispers behind the sheets in obedient deference to the rules of behaviour that have obviously been well rehearsed. The young woman she guesses is their teacher blesses a child by placing her open palm on his head then directs him to where he should find the answers to their given questions. Strange how even set free and clearly enjoying their independence they still stay in her orbit, coming close from time to time then spinning off again. The teacher is helped by two other people she guesses must work for the gallery and who are less sure of themselves.

The children remind her of her own two who in a little while will be picked up by their grandmother, bags slapping against their backs as they run in anticipation of the spoiling that awaits them until their mother returns. That she shall return, and will always do so, is because this afternoon and all the other afternoons that have taken place once a week for six months make her certain. She will tell her husband that her art course has finished, that it wasn't for her, that she wants to go back to being at home until the children are grown and because he is kind and loves her he won't talk about wasted time and expense, or criticise her for giving up something that never existed in the first place. She is surprised at how easy lying is and how quickly meaningless it becomes. It's just a form of truth that exists in a different plane, a parallel existence that is neither right nor wrong so long as it never meets the other one that she has always thought of as her real life.

A knot of children tightens in front of the painting. They count the figures, identify Christ and Judas, argue about the numbers and have a collective recount. When she comes to the city she is always too early so she passes the time in the National Gallery. It almost makes her feel as if she really is doing an art course but she waits there because it's quiet and allows her to think and recently to decide that this afternoon will be the last time. She's decided it before but tells herself that she means it this time. So soon she will take the same walk to the same rather expensive hotel in Temple Bar and spend two hours with a man she has failed to persuade herself that she is in love with. She wants to be in love because she tells herself that love exonerates, gives its licence, and without the belief in love there are only uglier words that clamour on the consciousness. One of the children smiles at her and she is brought back to the reality of the moment, slightly startled before she smiles back.

She looks at her watch. It's time to go. She knows exactly how long the journey will take. What seat he will occupy in the bar. How long they will wait before going to the room. Already the rituals have become predictable like marriage – the way he draws the curtains; the way they simultaneously turn off their mobile phones and set them at their respective sides of the bed, decommissioned arbiters of other lives; the way they sit back to back on opposite sides when they undress, as if face to face is an intimacy too far. Even the rules of pillow talk are established so they don't ever trade stories of their separate lives and in that absence there is a vacuum so that it feels inconsequential, unanchored, the words drifting purposelessly. Perhaps it lessens the guilt to have only the other and the moment, to find meaning in what is given and taken in the world that is the room.

So this will be the last time. She doesn't know the words she will use, or what he will say, but tells herself that without either of them admitting it to the other, they know that it's run its course. So the last few weeks she's had to pretend and there's already enough pretence in marriage to fill a life for ever. She wonders if it's been the same for him.

Perhaps he'll be secretly grateful that things will end in a quiet and civilised way, that she's not about to turn into some avenging, stalking harpy threatening to arrive on his doorstop. He is a man who values discretion, who pays for the room in cash, who never personalises the encounter with talk of his children or his wife, who treats her always with respect and whose desire flattered her into believing that a new and better self, however ephemeral, could be found in the silent exchange of the flesh.

As she walks she fingers the gold necklace that has been his only present and which broke some unspoken rule but which pleased her. She looks at the faces of those who hurry past her and wonders what secrets their lives contain. So she supposes it was the excitement that first brought her here, the sense of being led back into the memory of a life that felt as if it had escaped her, of being awakened to an inner world that wasn't bound by chore and the repetitive rhythms of keeping a home, or always defined by the constraints of responsibility to someone else. As she enters the hotel she asks herself if she wants to give it up and into the slipstream of her earlier certainty spins a new sense of doubt, a doubt that's intensified when she sees the pleasure her arrival brings him. But he sits in the same chair with the same drink and the same glass of white wine waiting for her. Today the predictability irks her and she thinks of telling him before they go to the room but knows it would be an unkindness and an insensitive indiscretion in this public place.

Afterwards he lolls across the furthest frontier of the bed as if embarrassed by his deep desire to sleep.

She watches the smooth stretch of his back, the thin swathe of freckles that stipple his shoulders, and feels the urge to touch them, to get back in the bed and snuggling behind him try to blow them gently away like dandelion seeds. His breathing rises and falls as if he's carried into sleep on the soft heft of the sea. Taking off the necklace she leaves it on the pillow beside him and lightly kisses the top of his tousled hair. As she turns she catches her shaded reflection in the mirror and is momentarily startled. She looks like a ghost of herself, drifting between worlds, close to home and far away, unsure of how to get there.

A full moon has again insisted its path through the clouds as he makes his way home keeping a watchful eye out for the papal police, while above his head is a cold scatter of stars like a handful of coins thrown to the poor. It hadn't been a challenge, just a matter of opportunity. But there is no sense of achievement, no lasting satisfaction, no sensation stronger than writing his signature on a man's skin. He paints the story of faces so he knows how to read them. It was in her eyes – right from the start. There was no eyelid or fan could silence what they whispered. He doesn't delude himself that it was his looks or charm. She wanted something more than that – it was to do with power, with money and reputation, with wanting the thing that's better than you think you have, and what surprised him even at the very moment of conquest, even as she arched her back, her words broken breathlessly by pleasure, was that she wanted him to put her in a painting.

And why not? It shall be her reward, her binding to silence, her elevation into sainthood. He will use her in some fresco, halo her head with the holiness of her desires.

He goes to his bedroom where Pietro still sleeps. Blood has seeped from his wound and snakelike slithered across the sheet. He stands a long time in the doorway watching his friend and then approaches him until their faces are as close as they were when he leaned across the tavern table. Everything is drained away in submission. It was the expression he needed earlier. He carries it in his head as he goes quickly to his studio and lights every lantern he can find until their flames quiver and shudder to let him finish Christ's face. He works quickly as if frightened that the image harboured will slip away. And then it's complete and all that remains is the as yet undetermined character who lurks at the edge of the painting holding a lantern and is part of the betrayal. He thinks of Pietro, his arm thrust forward like a shield, the lives they shared in Lombardy. He thinks of Fillide whom he took as if merely drinking from a cup placed before him. The wine tastes bitter in his mouth. He rubs the back of his hand across his lips and is almost sick at the smell of the paint on his skin. He stares at the painting, for a second thinks of ripping it open to see what truth, if any, it hides. Then he walks through the flickering fantails of light and brings the full-length mirror and places it at the side of the painting. And it is his own face he paints now, the painted lantern's light illuminating his features, his eyes searching the blackness of the night for the God made flesh. For the kiss. He works quickly on towards dawn and as the flames begin to splutter their exhaustion, he looks at himself one final time in the glass, sees the tint of white in his hair, then blinks his image away and tries to slash light into the darkness.

Keeping Watch

It's not exciting. It's not sexy television cops and robbers stuff. It sounds like an easy touch but isn't what you want to be doing day after day, each slow hour rubbing hard-edged against the next. And what it usually means is that you're sitting in a car staring at a door in the hope that someone will come out of it, or go through it; or you're watching a container in a windswept storage depot washed in yellow sodium lights that after a while makes you feel you're in some remote landscape existing only inside your head. After about the fourth hour the hallucinations begin and that's when you imagine behind the door exists something other than what you know is probably there, so now instead of this being an entrance to a backstreet terrace where marijuana plants weaned on stolen electricity bloom the rooms green and tropical, it becomes that spick and span guest-house in Margate where every summer for five years your parents took you and your brother for a week's holiday. And then in your delirium you smell the morning fry-ups and hear again the springs of your parents' bed creak and complain, despite their best efforts to stifle all sounds, when you and your brother are supposed to be sleeping head to toe in the little single bed that has been shoehorned into the room. Or it might morph into a particular day and what she said and what you said, playing over and over in a loop in your memory that although you want to never lets you change the words you used. Sometimes it becomes the entrance back into your life, a momentary nostalgic portal to what you imagine things were like before.

Television detective shows always have cops watching someone – I like to time how long the scenes last but have never counted more than twenty seconds. That's just about how long surveillance is interesting, I suppose, and another thing that always cracks me up is when it's a male–female team and inevitably to avoid detection the guy has to snog the face off some invariably gorgeous blonde who only exists in the imagination of scriptwriters. I'm never going to snog George, never going to touch him other than to prod him awake when it's his turn to keep his eyes peeled, or in a pathetic attempt to relieve boredom flick his ear when he's looking out of a side window. Because by and large you never do surveillance alone, just in the unlikely case that the low-lifes you're hoping to apprehend actually turn up and things have the potential to get heavy.

Surveillance is no good when you've a partner. Conversation dries up after the first hour and then you just have the stress of another human being sitting too close and whose every idiosyncrasy soon becomes a nagging irritation. And it doesn't matter how good their personal hygiene is, and let's face it, that's not always a given in this line of work, it never ends up smelling like a bed of roses. It's not just the body's natural reaction to being locked up in a small space while being fed cheap coffee, junk food and lurid-coloured energy drinks, it's as if other toxins seep silently out through the skin – all the years of encounters with piss and blood and puke, all the hours rubbing up against the scum of the world have to find their own release. It's inevitable, I suppose. And the spores that lodge in the brain, those dark spots like malignant growths, sired out of what you've seen, what your hand had to touch – these things don't wash away with the shower you always try to take after work. So there's no soap or gel, however expensive, and I've a work locker full of them, ever cleans that stuff off. There were times when I went home to Gina and shivered at her touch, felt as if I risked contaminating her by breathing the spores in the place I loved the most, and when she'd ask if someone had walked over my grave I'd nod and try to smile. So call me the Filth to my face and I'll have you, but not because it isn't true.

'There's nothing happening here,' George says, 'it's a bum steer. I'm going to call in and say we're jacking it in. And I've a date tonight. Need to have a haircut and shave before they close, get home, freshen up. Look the part.'

'With the woman in the garage?'

'Yes, and she has a mate if you're interested. I've seen her – looks not bad.'

'You're all right,' I say, hoping that someone might exit the door or go through it as a distraction from the predictable course of the conversation and the inevitable repetition of George's favourite mantra. But no one appears.

'Need to get back in the saddle sometime,' he says.

I say nothing. The streetlights haven't come on and in the dropping dusk two kids in white sportsgear cycle down the street, their piston knees almost hitting the handlebars. As they go past one angles himself back and gives us the finger before they fade into the gloom. Rain starts to spot the windscreen. I let it stay there. George often has dates. None of his relationships seem to last long. He pats a tattoo on his thighs – it's his usual way of saying he's had enough. Perhaps they don't last because he's no patience, no staying power, because the cheap aftershave he uses makes him seem a little desperate. But what do I know?

I know that I have lots of patience and I'm not a quitter, that I've staying power. So I've had my own shower, changed my clothes and I've even bought one of those scented trees in the garage and hung it from my rear-view mirror. And I'm back on duty and I'm sitting in the car under the shadowing canopy of trees alongside the park railings and have the house in an angled view. The lights are on downstairs and in the child's bedroom – it's probably his bedtime, although I'm not sure what time exactly he goes to bed now. I like being on my own after spending most of the day with George and that's no offence to him – it would be the same no matter who it was. This surveillance isn't official – I suppose that makes it a kind of homer – but the skills needed are just the same; so patience of course, an experienced eye for detail and the ability to form the bigger picture by piecing together all the tiny parts. I don't play music – it's just a distraction, the words, the tunes making your mind drift to different places. Already leaves have started to surrender to the coming winter, giving themselves to the fall without the need for a struggle. Others cling on ready to endure to the end. I admire that. When all the lights finally go out and it's time to return home there are two leaves on the windscreen. The wipers brush them into the air where they hover for a second before slowly drifting out of view.

'So everything go well last night, George?' I ask out of politeness but immediately regret my attempt at good manners.

'Spot on. Early days, of course, but I have a feeling that this could be the one. It's a bit weird but she likes the idea of me being a cop. Says it makes her feel secure.'

The car is already getting colder after George has turned off the engine and although the early morning tastes like having metal in your mouth we both laugh, a kind of suppressed giggle at first and then more openly. There is a half-hearted mist lolling lazily about but not enough to obscure our view of the door, and whatever a woman should feel about her partner being a copper, secure isn't one of them. We both know that. There are career criminals who offer their wives more security. On every level.

The car has already started to smell. Maybe George's late-night meal – a curry, probably, accompanied by a couple of pints. I glance at his waistline and clock the overhang that looks as if it might slide into avalanche sometime soon and think that if one day I need him in a hurry I'm in trouble. I try not to wonder if some of the smell is sex and who knows if he did or didn't but one thing's for sure is he'll have to tell me if he did. I suspect he thinks he's doing me a favour, a helpful leg-up into the saddle as he'd put it. I don't need any leg-up. I don't need anything other than what I haven't got. So I concentrate on the door but it looks as if it's been frozen in time and has no memory of ever being open. Strange how such an empty little house can make so much money for those who don't even live in it. And the neighbours aren't complaining either – the warmth slowly seeping through the walls must have reduced their heating bills. If we had infrared equipment we'd probably see it glow like a Christmas tree. The windows are blocked out and I try to visualise the interior walls lined with reflective material, high-intensity lights hanging from the ceiling, the watering apparatus and the fans, it all looking like some domestic ecosystem from our galactic future.

All we need now is for Mr Big to arrive and then we'll collar him. In truth, by this time we'll consider any arrest a bonus because it's not starting to look good. And if George hindered by his paunch is slow to the scene and Mr Big or some accomplice shows a disinclination to have his collar felt, I'm thinking that I might give him a bit of a slap as payment for all the hours I've spent in the car waiting for him, because sometimes you hear a voice, an insistent voice, saying that a slap will make things better. No one comes but as drugs are this month's quartile target on some graph we're told to stay put. To be patient. That makes me angry – I don't need anyone to tell me to stay patient. A whole year I've been patient. But now George is working up to inform me about the sex I haven't got the stomach for it and so I tell him I'm going to get a couple of coffees and a walk round the back of the premises.

The mist-raddled morning air clings to my face and crimps the skin so it feels as if I'm wearing a mask. But that's good, I tell myself, because then there's less chance of being recognised as a copper and even though we always like to pretend to ourselves we don't look like one, the sad truth is we always do and it would take more than this skinny wisp of mist to disguise that fact to a villain's eye. There's a little shop on the corner of the next street where I pick up two coffees and a couple of sausage rolls, trying not to think about George's paunch and the slim possibility that before the day is out we might need to generate some speed.

The mist is slowly clearing but passing cars still have their sidelights on and I wonder to what worlds of work the drivers are heading and suppose that many of them are destined to spend a day staring at computer screens. That must need its own kind of patience. But if truth be told everyone who's watching is being watched – the who, the where and the when drawn incessantly into the unblinking eye of the camera, the grainy pictures processed and preserved. And if you want the truth the geek squad back on police computers, their pale striated faces bathed in the transferred reflections on their screens, probably catch as many villains as we do as they log the unceasing flow of the city's human traffic or trace mobile-phone signals – there's more on-the-run lags caught by ordering a pizza than by anything else. In fact the more I think about it the more I believe that in the future a camera will replace what I do, a camera that's cheaper and more reliable. A camera that's the perfect watcher. I think that's creepy.

The narrow alley at the back of the premises is like every other alley I've ever been in, mapped out by familiar contours of litter, a couple of wheelie bins, a supermarket trolley filled with sodden cardboard and the usual scattering of empty beer cans, and there at my feet amongst the fast-food containers a used condom. What sort of love takes place somewhere like this, what dreams are possible amidst the debris of human waste? It's my intention just to keep on walking past our house and then return to the car but the gate is partly open so I pause and look in at the back, keeping as much of myself as possible pressed against the pitted and cement-scabbed wall. And suddenly I feel the ridiculousness of having to make a potential arrest while holding two cups of coffee and two sausage rolls in a white paper bag so I set them down on top of a wheelie bin and hope they'll still be there when I return. I glance up at the blacked-out windows that make it seem like a house in mourning, hesitate for a second then decide it's time to take a look.

More of the leaves have fallen. Soon the bare branches will offer less of a covering for the car. It's a Thursday night and they've been swimming, their costumes and towels carried in a sports bag. The boy's hair looks a little tousled and spiked like it's been given a good rub with one of the towels. She's carrying a pizza box under her other arm. I can't be sure but guess it's a Margarita with possibly a portion of potato wedges. Time changes things. But only things that don't really matter. Then I reassure myself that the car is still scented by pressing my nose against the tree that hangs from the rear-view mirror. It is, but it makes me angry that they lose their strength so quickly. The lights switch on in the hall, the living room and on the landing. They'll probably eat the pizza on the settee while watching whatever's on the television. I wonder if he'll come tonight – he's been coming more frequently recently – always after the boy goes to bed – and soon I guess he's going to stay over and not just leave with a kiss on the doorstep, the open door a bright frame of inviting light behind her. I feel the coldness of the car but it's the thinking about it rather than feeling it that makes me shiver.

I step into the yard where in a corner the stripped-down carcass of a motorbike has spilled its oily guts and I do it the quiet way I'm good at and already I see that the back door isn't shut properly and the handle is hanging at a strange angle like a dislocated limb. I should call George but know that I need this moment to be mine alone and what I want on this autumn morning is to step into the sudden shock of humid warmth and smell the verdant sweetness of what's growing in this shitty little mess of concrete that not even the unbroken line of satellite dishes can make look like something that resembles home.

I want the rich flush of greenness and the release of any scent that holds a promise of something purer than what exists in this world. My hand rests lightly on the door and it opens as if longing for this moment and suddenly it feels as if the whole house is inviting me in, waiting to give itself up. My heart is beating a little faster and some of that is caused by excitement and some by fear.

It's dark inside and I switch on my torch, let it play over the kitchen. It glints on the tinfoil cartons that strew the table, the plastic forks still sticking out of them, then shines on the scrunched beer cans and the green wine bottle. I press the light switch beside the door to the hall but nothing happens and the thick shadows of the house are layered with a silence that seems to flow towards me so as I edge forward it feels as if I'm wading into an ever-deeper stillness. And already I know there's something wrong because every step I take is shrouded with a damp chill and what I smell isn't what my imagination has already created. The plants are in the front room, all right, but there's no soft glow of warming lighting, just a tangled mess of trailed-out wires, and what the torch reveals is a wilted crop of withered, shrivelled leaves. I go to touch one of the plants but pull my hand back. In a corner of the room is a ferti-liser bag and on the tables empty spray bottles and an electric fan knocked on its side. And the smell spuming up around me is of rot, of soil soured and failed. I turn off the torch and walk slowly back-wards, as if frightened that this dead thing will quicken and cling to me. I return the way I came, trying to stay in the safety of my own steps then somewhere far off, as if in a different world, I hear George call my name.

A court order is not something to be ignored but courts don't do understanding and neither does she. We could have talked it out if she had given me the chance. Did she really think that I might harm her? She knows deep down that I could never hurt anyone and I'm not one of those sick and selfish bastards who harm their child in revenge or even in despair. And she's careless, always taking things and people on face value – that's why she hasn't changed the locks. That's why she needs looking after. The house is silent, lit only by the streetlight that presses through the uncurtained windows. It smells just as I remember it, warm and milky and whatever else it is makes a family home, and I move through its spaces with the tips of my fingers touching things that release sudden charges of memory. And I desperately want to feel as if a piece of the puzzle is missing and me being there makes it complete again but there's only the steady purr of the fridge and a red spot of light from the television.

It's swimming night at the same pool where I used to encourage him not to be afraid of the water. His schoolbooks are on the table and I flick the pages and see the little stars that garland his work and I pick up his pencil case in which for some reason he still keeps the shavings of his pencils. There are two new neon fish in the small tank whose spines are a shock of electric blue and in the kitchen the fridge has drawings I've never seen but which are attached by the same magnets. I open the door and study the contents in the hope they might join together to make some story I can understand. The house suddenly creaks as if it's stretching itself into a new, more comfortable repose. A good house. She knew it was the one the first time she stepped inside. A house for life is what she called it but as I walk slowly through the rooms everything begins to feel different to how I remember and now everywhere in the spooling pools of shadows there are spaces opening that I don't know how to fill.

I climb the stairs and wonder what she really knows about this man? I've put his car registration through the computer and have an address so that's going to need some watching as well. I go into my son's room, lift his pyjamas from the end of the bed that still has the same duvet cover and press them into my face, absorb what lingers of him then fold them neatly and return them to the same place. Looking at the new posters on the wall I see he's an interest in the planets and solar system. Perhaps when he's older I can buy him a telescope then I wonder if he'll come to think of me as some remote planet strung out on the edge of a distant galaxy. Is that what she wants? I step into our room and look at the bed where soon she will bring someone who isn't me. I hold her slip and savour the scent that she's been wearing longer than I can remember. It's soft and I don't want to let it go and for a second I think of taking it with me but know I can't.

I stand at the foot of the bed and stare at where I used to lie. The trouble with Gina is she doesn't understand what's out there, has never seen what

I've seen. And we have a son and he needs protecting, someone to look out for him all his days. But there isn't much time now. They'll be on their way home from swimming, sitting upstairs on the bus as a treat for him. I need to go, slipping once more back into the shadows under the trees whose wind-worried branches are now black and bare, but I have to look and linger just for a little while longer. And if after all she were to come through the door and ask me what I was doing I'd try to explain it to her as best I could, tell her that I'm not watching them because if that were true it would be a creepy thing. That's not what I do. What I am doing is watching over them – it's a small word, 'over', but it's one that makes all the difference – and I'm doing it out of the love that compels me to hold them close through the long hours of the night. I'm watching over them because I've seen the world and know its truth. If I explain it right, maybe, just maybe she'll be able to understand, and then I turn and slowly go back down the shadowed stairs, gently caressing each of the steps into silence, listening for a key in the door.

The Strong Silent Type

I'M USED TO ATTENTION, being looked at, but this is something else. All that anyone's ever given me is their eyes. I've never had a relationship, not even when they've shuffled me close to one of the females in a sweet tableau of a romantic encounter, complete with props – picnic baskets, a bicycle, or even cruelly a child's pram. I've stared into their eyes all day and all night but their bald orbs of heads gave nothing back despite my outstretched hand that reached out invitingly to them. And when streetlights speared the glass I heard them cry because despite the perfect bodies that never grow old they weep invisible tears for their barren wombs.

So one night when the store has closed I am frightened to be suddenly carried in the arms of this young woman, who with the floor manager's help bears me through the back entrance into the coldness and towards a small car. She doesn't smell of the perfume counter but something for which I have no name and what must be the scent of flesh as she presses me tightly to her, my head lolling on her shoulder so closely I see the imperfections of skin.

'You're off your head, Abi. And I don't want your mother giving me hell when she finds out. Make sure she knows that it's nothing to do with me.'

'It'll be all right, Irene. I'll say I made you do it.'

'And look after him – these things cost money,' Irene says as they seat me in the front of the car and fasten my seatbelt. 'I want him back before anyone notices he's gone.'

Then we drive and she doesn't talk to me much, only checking that I'm strapped in properly, and when we stop at traffic lights she looks straight ahead and ignores the old man in the car beside us who's staring pop-eyed until I turn my head and stare back. When the lights change he stalls. On the journey I try to work out whether I'm on a date or being kidnapped but if it's a date she's not my type. For a start she's gangly and there's nothing much that's perfect about her. Her legs are shapeless and there's a light sprinkling of freckles across the bridge of her nose that makes her look like a thrush as she sings along to the radio. She has no cheekbones worth talking about and her face seems set in a permanent expression of surprise. But she does have an abundance of hair even if it's piled and coiled on top of her head in a kind of bird's nest with stray twigs poking out.

She looks at me for the first time and when we reach her home I understand we're to go in as quickly and quietly as possible. Her house isn't grand – a nondescript semi-detached with a stubby patch of front garden. I had hoped for better. She struggles a little with me as she tries to gently shut the door and a woman I imagine is her mother appears down the hall and says, 'What in the name of all that's holy, Abi, what have you got there?'

'It's for my art project,' she says. 'I need it to model some clothes I'm making for my coursework.'

'Making clothes? Since when did you make clothes? The only clothes I've ever seen you with have a Primark label on them. So now you're going to be the new Vivienne Westwood.'

But already she's lugging me up the stairs, pausing only to look at her mother's upturned face without saying anything in reply.

She has a little red-coloured boxroom where every available space on the walls is covered with pictures – posters, postcards and photos taken from magazines. There are some of her own drawings as well as a pillar of stacked books. She places me carefully on my back on the bed and sits at her tiny desk and I'm suddenly conscious of my nakedness. The throw at the end of the bed would lend me a little more dignity but now she's too preoccupied with talking to one of her friends on the phone.

'Yes I'm sure. Definitely. And I've gone to all the trouble of getting him,' she says, glancing over at me.

'Tall, dark and handsome and good as gold.'

'It's a load of cat's piss all this sitting round waiting to be asked like you're on a shelf begging to be bought.'

'I didn't want to go with him. I've never spoken two words to him all year. Jenny, I don't care who says he's all right, I'm not interested. And if you want to go with Peter that's fine. I'm sure he's very nice too but I've made up my mind.'

She walks to the bed with the phone still pressed to her ear and drapes the throw over me. I begin to wonder if she can read my thoughts.

'I don't care. The whole bloody thing has turned into a steaming pile of horse manure. What some people have spent on their dresses, dresses that they'll probably never wear ever again, spray tans, nails and hair! It's brain-dead *X Factor* shit! I'm sick of listening to it and sick too of those witches sitting round their cauldron in the common room pretending to be big-hearted by operating a match-up service.' She kicks her foot at something invisible and rolls her eyes before saying, 'Yeah, appreciate it, Jen, but I'm not changing my mind.'

I get stowed in the narrow space between the wardrobe and the desk and watch her undress in the mirror above it. Naked makes her even more different to all the other women I've ever known and I'm not sure at first if I like it because it's not the way things are supposed to be but there's something about it that holds my eyes. So I notice the little ripple of flesh around her hips, the way her breasts aren't perfectly sculpted images of each other, the exploding cascade of her hair when she pulls the pin. And her skin is white, not white like snow but like the pages of a second-hand book. I try to read her story but she slips on pyjamas and tumbles into the bed and under the duvet. Then the light goes out and I'm left with nothing but the thin sift of dreams where as always my companion reaches out her hand to meet mine and when we embrace I feel the flow of her warmth press against me and in that sudden flush our mouths blossom with words.

In the morning she comes to check me and then when she's about to leave pats my head but the touch of her hand only makes me feel like a child. And I'm alone for the rest of the day until much later the door slowly opens and her mother comes in and she looks a little furtive. I watch her tentatively touch things around the room and she is curious about everything but her touch is a light fingerprinting of what might be love or loneliness and it's as if she is frightened of moving something out of its set place, stirring things out of their proper orbit. She looks into my eyes but doesn't speak, only shaking her head slowly, and I recognise something and wonder if her womb too is empty even though she has a child.

When Abi returns there is a flurry of incoming and outgoing phone calls and her voice pretends exasperation but underneath it sings with a lilting descant of excitement. In between she does her make-up and paints and shades her face so it hides the limpid paleness of her skin and makes it closer to the colour of mine. She spends even longer on her hair, piling it up and pinning it in what looks like coiffured coils of serpents. Sometimes she stops and inspects herself in the mirror and then swears softly and for a second it sounds as the serpents in her hair are hissing, before she starts all over again. Then carefully she puts on her sparkly turquoise-coloured dress. When it's done she turns to me and asks me what I think and I want to tell her that she looks great, that she looks almost beautiful, but my silence seems to fill her with new doubts and she returns once more to the mirror, presenting herself to the glass at different angles. And I want the glass to tell her what I can't.

'Now it's your turn,' she tells me and produces what I am to wear from the wardrobe. I'm flattered, of course, but I'm not skilled at dancing and I start to think of all the things that will probably go wrong. Just as her friend did, I want to ask her if she's sure, whether she's thought this through. But as she dresses me she's giving my appearance almost as much attention as she gave her own. So I'm in my white shirt and tuxedo that smells of must and I guess has been hanging in some charity shop and she's pressing the jacket smooth and then, placing her hand kindly over my eyes, sprays me with scent. And it's like we're going to do a three-legged race because she attaches us at the ankle with a tie and at the wrist with a corsage. We look at ourselves in the mirror and I can tell she's having second thoughts and she's saying 'shit' over and over in a rising note of something that might be worse than doubt. But then she stands herself as straight as her skinny legs will allow, takes a deep breath and we practise walking round the room and when I see myself in the mirror I think that I look handsome in a James Bond sort of way and as a couple we might just pass muster.

The stairs are a little tricky and we almost tumble into chaos when her waiting mother startles us by shouting a summons to Abi's father to come and witness what she has already suggested must be the product of 'her eyes deceiving her'. Her mouth gapes open like a hooked fish but when Stanley appears he only laughs and when he is rebuked and instructed to tell his daughter that she can't go like this he says, 'It's only a bit of fun, it's only a bit of fun,' then comes to the bottom of the stairs and tells Abi she looks great but suddenly stops laughing and asks her if she's sure.

'I'm sure,' she says, but I feel her body give a little shiver.

'Then it's only proper that you introduce me.'

'Dad, this is ...' she hesitates, looks at me as if expecting me to tell her before saying, 'this is Simon.'

'Pleased to meet you, Simon,' he says, shaking my hand. 'And, Simon, I expect you to take good care of my daughter – take good care of her or you'll have me to answer to.'

It's strange having a name but I nod my head and he seems satisfied, ignoring his wife's assertion that he is as mad as Abi.

The taxi-driver is called Barry and a friend of Abi's father. They exchange words at the open window and I hear him whisper that his daughter marches to the beat of her own drum while Abi concentrates on getting me sitting up straight. Barry watches us in his mirror as he drives and it worries me that we might crash.

'What's he called?' he asks and when she tells him he repeats my name. 'I wish all my passengers were as good as him,' and then he tells stories of his most recent nightmares that involve vomit, sex and runners. 'I've seen it all,' he says, 'and then something more. But at least the Troubles are over.'

Abi says, 'That's right,' but it's as if she's not really listening to him and she's heard it all before.

Barry doesn't seem to care because he doesn't like silence in his cab and I wonder how he would survive a night in the store when it's as if the stillness has frozen into ice so thick that it can never crack.

'We should have got medals,' he says mostly to himself. 'We kept the city open even through the worst of it and never got so much as a thank you. Sometimes when you were sent out on a call you didn't know if you were ever going to come back or whether you were delivering yourself up to some psychos like fast food. And the things I've seen – you young ones don't know you're born.'

When he looks in his mirror Abi nods her head as if she's listening but at the same time she's patting her hair to check that it's still in place. And I want to tell him that he wasn't the only one to have seen what he's seen because we too were in the frontline. And when the car bombs went off in cleared city streets we were the ones they left behind. Left behind plates of glass that would shatter into shards and afterwards, when the white-coated forensic people would move like walking snowmen, I've seen body parts, severed heads, roll about their snow-shod feet. So don't tell me about what you've seen because I've seen it too and known the terror of the empty street, the silent minutes of waiting for it to happen and not being able to close your eyes or turn your face away.

Perhaps he's right – the young ones don't know they're born – but I have no memory of ever being younger than I am in this moment. I have no childhood to be nostalgic about.

'Would you look at the state of that,' is what Barry says at regular intervals and it always involves some short skirt or skimpy top. 'Does your mother know you're out?' he asks no one other than himself. And when Abi gets him to stop at a garage so that she can buy a bottle of water he starts to talk to me man to man and he's telling me, 'The secret of success at these things, son, is to stay sober for as long as possible – pace yourself, like. Because just about all these little twats will be throwing it into them like there's no tomorrow and before very long they'll be out for the count or puking up their guts in the toilets. And that's when you, my son, are the last man standing and can have the pick of the bunch.'

He's not looking at me when he's talking, not even looking into his mirror, because his eyes are scanning for anyone who will cause him to say, 'Look at the state of that.' And because he can see Abi standing in a long queue he proceeds to tell me a dirty story to fill the time.

'Take her to Larne, she says. Bloody Larne. So I look at her in the back seat and ask is she sure and she tells me she's sure so off we go. And I keep my eyes on her in the mirror because I have my doubts about her – when you're doing this job you develop a sixth sense. And she's fidgeting about and beginning to look nervous, almost as nervous as I am because Larne's a long way and the clock is climbing. So we're about ten minutes away and she tells me to pull over into a lay-by and when I do she tells me she hasn't any money. Naturally I'm not pleased about this and I'm just about to let her know when she says, "Maybe there's another way

I can pay you," and before you know it she's lying along the back seat and she has them off.'

I see Abi walking across the forecourt and the neon colours her hair and she's clutching a little bottle of water.

'And I look at her and say, "Have you nothing smaller, luv."'

He's still laughing when Abi gets inside and when she asks what he's laughing about he tells her, 'Yer man's a riot, a real bundle of laughs,' and she looks at me with questions in her eyes before she carefully reattaches us.

When we arrive at the hotel Barry nearly crashes his taxi because there's so much for him to gape at and the shock of it seems to bring him back to concentration and he gets out and with something of a show opens the door for us whispering to give him a call when we want picking up and he winks at me as if we're all men together.

So this is the moment and as we make our way through the double doors heads are already turning and there's bursts of laughter and phone cameras flashing but she doesn't flinch and we stand as straight and tall as is possible. And then someone I realise is Jen comes skipping towards us, one hand bunching up her dress so she doesn't trip, and we're formally introduced, shaking hands and nodding politely to each other. Then others are crowding round and Abi is smiling because everyone seems to think it's clever and cool but I don't like it when someone describes it as the best joke ever. Except not everybody's laughing and in a few minutes one of them approaches and I look with disapproval at the way his jacket doesn't fit and his braces and bow tie are a vulgar colour – if I'm in the window I only get to wear the best.

'You must have been desperate, Abi, to get someone to go with you,' he says and he's shaking his head, which adds to the fine sprinkle of dandruff on his shoulders. 'Pretty sad.'

'Pretty sad to come with a prick like you,' she says.

He looks at her as if he's going to spit in her eye and when he says, 'Spot the fuckin' dummy,' she raises her arm quickly to flip him the finger and before I know what's happening I've nutted him across the bridge of his nose and almost immediately a few drops of blood have dripped on to his shirt. He's swearing and shaping up but other hands are pulling him away and I think it's the laughter buzzing round his head that makes him take to his heels, one hand trying to stop the drip turning into a flow. Then other hands are slapping me on the back and reassuring me that he had it coming and claiming it was the funniest thing they've ever seen.

Nothing else goes wrong and we manage the meal and the speeches without incident and after the dancing has started Abi takes me out to the floor and we do a passable smooch to 'Careless Whisper'. She presses her breasts against my chest and I like the feel of it and it doesn't matter that they're not perfect echoes of each other or that already her hair is starting to slip. It's also true that I move a little stiffly, that I don't have a great sense of rhythm, so I have to rely on my partner and move according to their desires and all night long I have a series of different ones. They tell Abi that I'm a better partner than the one they lumbered themselves with and are queuing up to dance with me. In one thing at least Barry was almost right because it's like a race to see who can get the drunkest first and some of their dates are semi-comatose or collapsed in a corner blowing bubbles out of straws. And sometimes it's the girls who are unsteady on their feet and a few of them are a little forward with their hands and there's at least one who tells me that she loves me. Each one of them is a different size and shape, each one has a different scent, and up this close all of their skins are different. It's difficult to get used to when everything I know is always the same.

Sometimes I glance over at Abi when I'm dancing and she looks a little lonely and I think that now the joke has been shared and the laughs have been laughed she'd rather have something else. Someone whose body will yield under her touch, someone she can sink her need into. So I start to feel as if I've let her down. She's separated us and propped me on a chair beside her but when I get taken for dances I look over my partners' shoulders and watch her sipping slowly from her drink. And perhaps it's the swirl of the dance or breathing in the alcohol on my partners' lips that makes me wish for a crazy second that I could be the one she really wants – not to make a point or a joke but the one she wants to love. Now I'm dancing with my first guy who introduces himself by telling me that he's not gay or anything but is up for the laugh and he thinks it's funny when we do his idea of a tango and before long our legs tangle and we're sprawling on the floor. Then Abi's helping me to my feet and dusting me off and I hope it's not just because she remembers what Irene has said about looking after me.

Afterwards when it's all over she decides she's not going on to where everyone's supposed to go and is heading home instead. But when she phones Barry he tells her that he's broken down and off the road so we have to walk to the nearest taxi depot and join the queue. I've never been outside like this and the city is splashed with light and the night air is cool on my cheeks. I'm a little scared by everything at first, thinking of all the lies and loves that simmer all around us, of a multitude of lives being lived in a world where time winds itself both down and up. And I try to tell myself that I'll protect her if the need arises. But when we pass a bar where a group of smokers are hunched outside and one calls out, 'Need a real man, luv?' she gives him the finger and says to the cheers of his mates, 'I don't see a real man.'

The city has its own buzz and hum and I don't know if it's something burrowing insistently through the bricks and kerbstones of its history or just the circuits and grids that power what glows and burnishes all about us. We pass a couple of cops lolling against their white Land Rover and one of them offers Abi a pair of cuffs so there's no chance of me making a run for it, but she ignores them and I want to tell them to go and catch some terrorists but we don't say that any more. And it dawns on me that in this city everyone is a comedian even if it's their own jokes they find the funniest. I can't laugh or cry but if I had the choice I'd like to know what it feels like to have tears suddenly appear on my cheeks and find out whether they're warm or cold.

Our driver is another Barry and he tells Abi that at least she's had no problems with wandering hands and proceeds to tell her of all the famous people he's had in his cab. Everyone wants to laugh, no one to cry. Perhaps this is the thing that's wrong with us. And of course, as I think they all probably do, he gives us the time he claims he had the Beirut hostage John McCarthy in the back and asked him if he wouldn't be more comfortable in the boot. But in the face of our silence he eventually runs himself dry and we're left with country-and-western on the radio weeping about rodeo girls and silver moons.

We get out at the end of her street. Darkly rest the houses, the stars jittery and trembling at the brush of my eyes, seen for the first time without the separation of glass. Our footsteps tinkle against the silence. Now she's crying softly and I wonder again if tears are cold or warm and if I could I'd touch them with my fingertips. But my hand is stretched out vainly forever in a window. I want to apply words to her hurt like a salve as all the things I need to say course uncontrollably through my being, rising and falling on a whelming tide of love, but no matter how hard I try, none can breach the sewn seam of my mouth.

The Painted Cave

ADOLPHO PAUSES BRIEFLY AND stares down the valley. The white-walled houses and yellow spire of the church seem to blink at him in the final flush of the day's light. He wipes his brow and then taking a bottle of tepid water from his rucksack sips slowly. The water must last but he doesn't know for how long. A couple of days – a week at worst – just long enough for the heat to blow over. He's out of condition – the two-hour climb has confirmed that and there's another hour to go before he reaches the cave, the cave of the pictures. He first came to the mountains as a boy charged with herding goats and it's an environment to which he no longer belongs. The narrow path that languidly winds its way upwards through the scrub and white rocks feels as if it resents his presence and as he starts to walk again the sun on the back of his neck seems to accuse him of faithlessness. He has come back here the way when faced with crisis the lapsed believer calls on the God he has scorned for decades.

He stumbles a little on some straggling roots and the accusations make him angry. What was he supposed to do? Herd goats for the rest of his life or like his father labour in a backstreet garage, welding and repairing rust buckets of cars that were fit for nothing but the scrapheap? Their ancestors were blacksmiths and his father spent his life beating out a miserable existence, illuminated by nothing more than the momentary flare of sparks. So he had no choice, he tells the mountains. No choice but to do whatever things a man needed to do to make his way in the world.

The air is thinner here and his breathing is laboured. He towels his hand across the back of his neck and feels the warmth trapped in the furrows of his skin. He will need this warmth because he must sleep in the cave and although it is many years since he did it last, he remembers the coldness that woke him just before dawn. Maybe in a different time and place he could have been something else – a lawyer, or an architect perhaps.

His name means a noble wolf but as he pauses again and stoops forward, both hands resting on his hips and tries to fill his lungs with air, he feels no sense of nobility. And if his name was meant to inspire his future all it did was describe what he has been reduced to. For he is a scavenger, his days given to trying to make something from nothing, living off his wits and always in search of some scheme that might help him escape the confines of poverty. He thinks the world cruel to be always flaunting what the eyes desire but never providing the means to achieve it. He had no silver spoon, no inheritance to make those desires possible, and so there was no other way than to find his own.

The scrub around him looks tinder dry but is splashed by the colour of rock lavender in its stony outcrops. A buzzard with serrated wings and fanned tail, all held perfectly still, drifts effortlessly above, its weightlessness on the cool currents an unwelcome reminder of the soreness of his feet and the pain slowly spreading across his forehead. He needs to smoke soon but tries to find motivation in the promise to himself that he will only do so in the safety of the cave. He plucks a little head of lavender and holds it to his nose as a kind of substitute but takes little pleasure from it. And then he thinks of Sabrina and in the crushed petals on his fingers tries to find some memory of her scent. But he can't conjure her any more without those final images overpowering and irrevocably tainting what it is he wishes to recall. He brushes his hand clean.

She knew what she was about, right from the start on that bouncing, dilapidated bus to Tangier. Giving him the eye, letting her skirt ride up, and when they stopped for the driver to mysteriously and wordlessly disappear for fifteen minutes she had rolled her eyes, then smiled in an invitation to him to make his move. They had shared the rest of the journey and when they eventually reached Tangier she had invited him to her home. Nothing is as easily exploited as a man's ego. The memory of the scam, despite everything, almost makes him smile and when he found the address beside the bakery and spice sellers, just as she had described, he discovered himself looking not at Sabrina but her two brothers who pulled him into a deserted courtyard and accused him of dishonouring their little sister and demanded appropriate recompense. Perhaps it was his laughter that threw them, even when the sharp edge of a knife was introduced into the conversation. Perhaps it was the realisation that he didn't have enough of what they wanted, but he likes to think it was because they recognised him as one made in their own image.

So it wasn't very much later that he found himself sitting in the same courtyard sharing a plate of sardines and anchovies, followed by thick black coffee and the best hashish he had ever smoked. Smoking and making deals. Sabrina had joined them by then but with no trace of embarrassment or even the inkling of an apology.

'Americans are the easiest,' Jamal had said, passing him the joint. 'They think everyone like us is in Al Qaeda.'

'Think they're going to be in a video having their head cut off,' Hasan added.

After they had inhaled they passed it to him again, missing out Sabrina until she angrily grabbed it and remonstrated with them in words he didn't understand. She had the darkest eyes, the blackest hair he thought he had ever seen and skin the colour of the hashish. He wanted his lips on her skin, to slowly inhale all of her, take the hit and know the lingering, exquisite pleasure.

'Can you get more of this?' he had asked as he tried not to let her see how much he was looking at her.

'Of course.'

'Lots of it? At a good price?'

'No problem.'

And before the evening ended they had agreed a deal. Shaken hands. Smoked some more. It made the stuff sold by the Albanians, who dominated the market at home, look like the third-rate shit it was, bulked out with who knew what. And so as he sat in a little courtyard, at a blue-tiled table under the cooling shelter of an orange tree with the sounds of the medina shut outside and drank the mint tea laced with sugar that Sabrina had prepared, his head filled with dreams and a renewed optimism. Even the burdensome logistics – how to get a boat to ferry it the twenty miles across the straits – seemed to fade into little more than temporary inconveniences. Jamal knew someone with a fishing boat who regularly transported illegal immigrants and a little more cargo wouldn't make any difference. But did he have the dealers? Of course, he told them, a network ready and waiting, even though he barely knew a handful of possibly interested acquaintances who like him hung out in his home town waiting for a change of fortune. They'd start small, build it up and then make the killing that would change everything for all of them. It seemed the easiest thing to set in motion. The easiest thing in the world.

When her brothers had left to do some business elsewhere, she asked him if he wanted to see the sea and as dusk settled and in the shadowy distance camels slowly fretted the white-edged trim of the waves she let him dishonour her. She allowed it with so much enthusiasm and experience that he could barely retain any sense of his own prowess and when at the end she grabbed him hard by the back of his hair her cries were subsumed into his own. That first time, if he had known how to do it, that was the moment he might have fallen in love with her and as he rested his face on the pillow of her shoulder she pulled him back to look at her, then with a smile on her lips blew a stream of breath as if to cool him and even though she spoke good Spanish whispered in a language he didn't understand. Perhaps it was the hashish, perhaps it was because he felt the stirring of something that might have been love, that made it seem better than any other time he had ever experienced. Maybe because she was saying things to him that had the mystery of the unknown and so he was able to make them into what he had always wanted to hear. Of course he craved more but he understood already that she knew she had him hooked and so it was not to be at his desire but hers that anything else would be given. There was no disguise either in her vision of her future.

'We'll make money – lots of money, yes? When we have it you take me across and we buy a big house and then we'll do this as much as you want. Yes?'

'Yes,' he had told her. 'Yes, lots of money, a big house looking out over the sea. With a pool.' And then he added a list of other things in the hope that she might accept them as down payment on a second dishonouring but already she was brushing sand off her denim skirt and leading him up to where the lights of sea-front bars braided the night.

All his life has been lived in the sun. But as he climbs higher he thinks of the shadows on the beach, her eyes and hair so dark that she seemed part of the night. He wants the shadows of the cave now, wants to be out of the burning sun that has never warmed anything other than the surface of his skin. He does not want to think of Sabrina any more and tries to distract himself by calculating the time it will take to reach it.

Once when he was a boy his mother got a job cleaning the house of a big-shot businessman. By chance he shared the same age as the man's son and for a time they trained with the local football club but he couldn't look his teammate in the eye without feeling the humiliation of knowing what his mother did. And soon after he packed it in – he would never have made it anyway, too many bad habits even then. The old humiliations course through him again and add themselves to all the others until he shouts out a stream of swear words but the mountains smother them and give back no echoes. He tells himself that everything has been a mistake, that his life cannot be written like this, and that if only he can retrace his steps then some story that makes more sense will print itself on the page. And he has started to know what fear feels like. It's spreading inside him, loosening everything that he thought was secure and tightly fixed. Sabrina had no fear except of being poor. He needs to smoke but knows if he is to stop and take it there, he will risk losing all impetus, will be overwhelmed by his weariness or trapped in the paralysis of self-pity. And he must reach the cave because he'll be safe there. He has started to think that Sabrina will be waiting for him and they'll light a fire and warm themselves beside it and the flames will spark the darkness of her eyes into a new and fierce life.

He stops to look down again into the village. Its whiteness is slowly fading together with the earlier intensity of light. When they had finished with his father they beat his hands with the hammers he used in the garage. The old man should have told them sooner what he knew – he didn't owe his son anything and the little he knew might have been enough for them to let him go. But he understands too that these people are not like others, that they need no excuse to inflict pain. It is their reputation as well as their territory that they must protect. And so they take some pride in it, are always looking to enhance it with some flamboyant gesture. In a different story he would have gathered up all his men and taken his own bloody revenge but that story will never be written, because the truth he now inflicts on himself is that he is a small-time hustler who found himself hopelessly out of his depth. He sips slowly from one of his three bottles of water with unaccustomed discipline because he tells himself that his only chance of surviving is to throw off all his old self-indulgence and try to stay strong. He knows that more than anything he needs to smoke but also that there is not much further to go.

Other memories belong to the cave apart from the ones he is about to bring. A shelter in storms, a den where they came as young men and talked about women and drank beer. A hiding place when they were in trouble. The place to which they tried to entice girls, supposedly to see the paintings, playing out the fantasies in their heads again and again but in the secrecy of their single beds they came only in their hands. He had managed once to get a girl there

94

when he was seventeen but had got nothing more than the briefest glimpse of her breasts in the shadowy dance of the firelight. Afterwards she had acted as if they were betrothed and when he gave her the cold shoulder her brothers had come calling so that it had almost erupted into a family feud. His father had slapped his face in front of them, then, lifting a spanner and spitting on the oil-stained garage floor, told them never to come back and to take better care of their sister.

He thinks of Jamal and Hasan. They will know by now. And they too will come across the water with one thing in their hearts. They let her play the whore but this is different. Family honour will demand it. His father is an old man and his shattered hands will never hold a spanner again. His brothers are long gone. He is on his own. A lone wolf looking for a cave in which to hide. This is what it's come to.

It's not so far now. The sun is lower in the sky. The scent of the lavender and rosemary shaken loose by the lifting breeze sifts through his senses and speaks comfortingly of what is soon to come. It is the only thing that holds him together. But as he gets closer to the cave he begins to panic. What if he can't find it because his memory is as unreliable as every part of himself or because the mountains have themselves altered through the years? What if some landslide has covered the entrance?

He hurries on, trying to ignore the soreness of his feet and legs. The provisions in his rucksack are pressing against his back. His mouth is dry, unable even to muster a spit. Every part of him wants to stop but he tells himself that he must be nearly there – just a little further, that's all it needs, and the prospect of safety makes him labour the last of the way. And then a few minutes later it's there and all the disconnected fragments of his memory form a complete whole before his eyes. There is the marker of the sharp-edged sentry rock that stands almost upright in front of the scatter of softer and rounded boulders that hide the entrance. He clambers excitedly up the slope, the rucksack beating against his back, and finding the narrow entrance slips the bag free. He must drop it first then climb down the few metres that lead into the cave itself. There are ridges for his feet and handholds worn smooth over the years. For a moment he feels like the youth he was the last time he made this same descent.

There are two caves, a smaller one leading into the larger which is on a slightly higher level and has the ancient drawings on its walls. Neither cave is completely dark because strange, turning funnels of grainy light shaft at intervals through circular clefts in their roofs. And although it is much cooler, some small part of the day's warmth has still managed to inveigle itself inside. But he knows before he can rest he must gather some wood for a fire if he is not to feel the night's coldness nag at his bones and so, taking the torch from the rucksack, he inspects what the cave might hold. There are the charred remains of a fire surrounded by a blackened hearth of stones but not much wood except for a few skinny remnants that will serve for little more than kindling. His feet kick empty beer cans that tinkle and echo as they tumble. Wreaths of cigarette butts litter the floor like some animal's dried-up droppings, a few pages of a year-old newspaper that will help him start the fire, but little else until in the bigger cave he finds a pile of gnarled wood hidden behind some rubble that looks like it has been scavenged from a lightning-shot tree.

Soon the fire is lit – he keeps it small for the time being because like everything else the wood must be rationed. But he wants to get it going before darkness makes the task harder. He crouches beside it then suddenly lifts his head to look for Sabrina but there is only the tremble and squirm of shadows. Despite her fierceness, the way she would slap his face when he wasn't concentrating or did something stupid, there was something childlike in her total belief they'd be rich and she liked nothing better than to search the Internet, making her choices in advance. So these were the shoes and this was the car. This was the dress and this the Pomeranian puppy. Pay attention, she would tell him as if he was supposed to commit the list to memory and when the time came make each a precise reality. So he's trying to show that he's paying close attention as they lie on his bed in the apartment he's just started to rent with the first of the profits and he wonders if his feigned enthusiasm will encourage her generosity. The sun is slinking through the thin white sheet that is acting as an improvised curtain and reaching the end of the bed. It is an image of a necklace she is showing him. He could manoeuvre her down the bed so that her face rested in the sun and perhaps its rays might ignite the tinder of her hair, flame her into passion.

'Do you like it?' she asks, holding the tablet closer to his face.

'It's very beautiful,' he tells her, resting his hand on her bare thigh. He is always surprised at how soft and smooth her skin feels – he expects it should have some of the toughness of her spirit. 'Perhaps not much longer,' he says, moving his hand higher.

'We go too slow. It's too small. We need to bring more across, move into the cities with bigger markets.'

'We don't have the capital,' he tries to tell her but his negativity makes her brush his hand away. So then he starts to talk big, outlining all sorts of crazy ideas about how they might raise more money.

'I want this,' she says, pointing to the necklace. It is a gold chain, laced with a filigree and flurry of rubies.

'Soon,' he tells her, 'very soon,' and when he places his hand on her thigh again she does not make him move it.

It's stashed in the front pouch of the rucksack and carefully and slowly he opens the cellophane covering to reveal the blond Moroccan, grown and harvested deep in the Rif. All his senses anticipate the first hit and his fingers fumble a little into a spill until he forces himself into steadiness and follows the rituals that although so familiar still hold a sense of intimacy. But despite the restraint he tries to impose on himself his fingers hurry and again spill a little and then he's losing all finesse and tumbling into the moment he needs so much – the moment he wants to begin by taking away all the pains and stiffness of the climb, then find an escape from everything he longs to forget. He uses one of the pipes she gave him as a present. The milky blue smoke puffs softly in front of his face before being subsumed into the smoke from the fire. What was the name of the girl he finally managed to bring here? The one who thought she had given him so much by sharing the briefest glimpse of her breasts. He struggles to remember and has to convince himself that his memory of her little pink buds of nipples is not a work purely of imagination. He empties the rucksack, stores the contents, then scrunches it into a canvas pillow and rests his head on it. Carla – her name was Carla. And in the same instant feels the slap of his father's hand on his cheek, pictures the way her brothers walked backwards out of the garage, their eyes fixed on the spanner tapping slowly against his father's thigh, pausing only long enough for one of them to warn him never to go near their sister again. But then as the effects begin to course through the furthest and most arid reaches of his self he shrugs these memories away and drifts on the warming currents that carry him once more to that first time on the beach.

So there is a tautly stretched frieze of stars and the soft break of the sea when her hand takes him as if impatient with his hesitation and her eyes are wide and black as they look up at him and he does not understand the words she is whispering in his ear but they are part of the mystery. And then all his sense of male mastery is consumed by her and he wants to tell her to slow down but there is nothing now that can stop the urgency of mutual need and all too soon he is spilling his desire helplessly like someone newly fledged. She is smiling up at him, teasing him by blowing her breath against his face. He does not know if he loved her. In the past he thought of love as a weakness best avoided, a distraction from the things that were more important, so what he felt in that moment was strange to him and not easily grasped.

He thinks of the buzzard, weightless and patient as it drifted on invisible currents. She wanted everything too quickly. That was why he had borrowed heavily from the Irish even though he knew they were dangerous people much given to the singing of sentimental songs in the chain of shamrock bars they owned along the coast before they shot each other. Sabrina had crossed the straits on that last journey carrying the goods personally in an overnight bag. She had shared the boat trip with six young men, all excited at being on the cusp of what they imagined would be a better life. She had tried to make him jealous by telling him how interested they had been in her, chatting her up as if believing she could be the first of their new life's benefits. He puts one of the bigger pieces of wood on the fire because slowly the importance of rationing is diminishing and the heat and the hashish will help clear his mind, ease away the frets and tangle of thoughts that afflict him. He thinks he should go to one of the islands. La Gomera, perhaps – he knows someone with a small bar there who might put him up but then discounts the idea, telling himself that islands have few exit doors. Better to go to some bigger place. Better to go to a city.

The aches and pains begin to fade out of his consciousness and for a few seconds he watches the turning funnels of light. They are flecked and aqueous so it feels that if he were to dip his hand into them he might clutch the stirring particles. When he was a boy he would sometimes fish in the river that bisected the town, standing on one of the bridges or clambering down to one of the narrow paths that bevelled its banks. He never caught much and mostly he would get bored – it was an old man's sport, one that allowed them to sit in silence and dream their dreams. He will go to a city. Barcelona perhaps. But not because he has a brother there, a brother who works for a shipping company and whose embrace of respectability will prevent him offering anything much more than a bed for a couple of nights and a sermon about the need to get his act together.

He holds out a hand to the fire and, staring at its changing colours, wonders again at how soft her skin felt. In the cave Carla would let him look but not touch. He wonders where she is now. Sabrina gave all of herself and then something more. Sometimes it felt as if she was not making love to him so much as her future life, believing if she held anything back it would slip out of her reach. He puts another piece of wood on the fire and sees it spume up in a fretwork of sparks, imagines he hears her whisper again in a language he does not understand. The Irish will expect their money back soon, complete with its thick slice of interest. And if it fails to arrive and it becomes obvious that it is never going to arrive then a telephone call will bring some professional on a flight out of Dublin just for him. He spits into the fire. Let him join the queue.

When he met her off the boat that came ashore late at night, for a second he hoped that they might repeat that first time right there on the beach but, as the young men were bundled into the back of a van, knew they too had to be gone. She was more excited than he had ever seen her as she told him she was never going back, that this was the start of their new life. And when he began to talk of her brothers she spat at his feet and called them 'worthless' and 'dreamers' who would waste their lives ripping off tourists and in small-time scams. Later, back at the apartment, they had smoked together, suggesting to each other that it was a necessary part of quality control and celebrated with cheap champagne.

The beginning was only a day away from the end. He stands up and taking his torch goes to the mouth of the second cave. Somewhere deeper are the drawings made by the first people who knew this place as their home. He struggles to see them. Faded now so they are only visible with bright light and close up, the charcoal outlines creatures like bison that are coloured with red ochre. He does not want to go nearer because it feels that if he is to do so he will encounter other images painted there on the rock. At this distance the ochre looks like a smear, a random stain daubing the stone. Switching off the torch he goes back to the fire and the pipe. All his life he has needed something to take him beyond himself.

He had been a fool to believe that the principles of free enterprise ruled in this world into which he had stumbled. So when the Albanians asked to meet them he had thought that perhaps they wanted to set up some fraternal and mutually beneficial arrangement.

It took place in a flyblown back room of a café close to the harbour and there with the minimum of social niceties they were informed that they needed permission and protection to operate and to receive it would require half their profits with a significant sum paid upfront as a gesture of 'goodwill'. If Sabrina had let him he could perhaps have talked their way out of it, given the impression that it was a done deal, but as soon as she understood what was being demanded she was swearing at them, shouting and waving her hands in the air. One of them slapped her and then looked to him as if he was her keeper and it was a humiliation on all of them to allow a woman to behave like this but before he could say or do anything she had stabbed her attacker with a knife lifted from the serving counter. The terrible screaming, the clattering of thrown-over furniture – all of it thunders again in his head until it feels only his own screams will silence it but he thinks that if he were to release them his brain might explode. And the one thing he thought about was making his own escape through the open door leading into the alley and if he hadn't half-turned his head he wouldn't have seen, would have spared himself what he knows he can never smoke away. So she has her precious necklace now, the red rubies slipping across her skin and bleeding on to her white blouse. He tells himself there was nothing he could have done except escape the same fate then holds his hand close to the fire as if inviting its punishment. But when the first pain flares he pulls it back and rocks himself gently.

The funnels are still now and there is only the light afforded by the fire. He smokes again. He will go to

Barcelona until everything blows over. There will be other girls, other opportunities to pursue. The smoke calms him. He puts more wood on the fire and stretches himself as close to it as feels safe. He wants to drift painlessly into the deep forgetfulness of sleep. Eventually it comes, slowly unravelling over him like when he was a child and his mother would put him to bed and tuck the blanket under his arms so he couldn't escape even if he had wanted to. Now he never wants to escape, never wants to wake from this unburdened state of ease. His closing eyes hold a final image of the fire, its violet and yellow flames smeared lightly across his senses.

He doesn't know how long he's slept but the fire has surrendered into a red smoulder. His mouth is dry. Something has wakened him. He closes his eyes again to make sure that it's not part of his dream. But it's still there and it sounds louder – a dull drumming and at first he isn't sure whether it comes from inside his head or somewhere else. What is the sound? His father beating a hammer against metal? The breaking of bones? By firelight hands engraving the image of the bison with flint tools, then outlining them in the blackness of charcoal? Sitting up he looks around him, sees the first opaque shafts forming from the circular clefts but which are still held motionless by the strength of the shadows. Hurrying human footsteps? Some animal scavenging at dawn? He stands and listens, tries to shiver himself alert, then looks to the entrance of the cave and for a second hopes that he might see Sabrina clambering down and it won't matter if she slaps his face and screams at him for leaving her. Nothing will matter except she isn't wearing the ruby necklace. Nothing will matter ever again. They'll both go to Barcelona, pickpocket if they have to until they snatch the dreams that fill her head. But the entrance is only a darkened well and he has registered already that the drumming is coming from the second cave.

He doesn't want to look but knows he has to and so he takes the torch and edges towards the upper cave whose entrance arches like an open mouth that might swallow him and leave no trace. The drumming gets louder with each step he takes, echoing and repeating itself, and into its insistent thundering flows what sounds like the wind and then fractured human cries that splinter against the greater power. He is frightened to go further as he stumbles a little over the debris of stone and shale layering the floor but understands he must. The sound is trapped somewhere deep in the cave and as he lets the torch range over the painted walls he sees the bison, once singular, now coming together in a vast herd that moves across the earth and the drumming is their hooves churning up the dust that flurries against their ochre flanks. Their movement is whipped ragged by the wind that streams against them and their steaming breath curdles about each charging head. Their eyes are sparked with fire. He wants to cower before them but with a shaking hand continues to shine the torch on their sinewy flanks that glisten with the heat of their fury as they cross the plains and valleys of the earth. Then there are stick men coming from behind rocks to throw skinny wooden spears but they bounce off the flanks of the stampeding herd. Nothing can withstand them, everything falls before the fierce toss of their heads and the terror of their hooves. Fearful that he will be trampled into the dust he plunges the cave into shadows before falling to his knees and making the sign of the cross. The drumming pounds even more, so loudly it feels as if it will drown out the whole world, but then as if it has passed over him begins to fade into the hidden depths of the rock. He whispers Sabrina's name again and again and, as the funnels of flint-flecked light begin to slowly turn, promises her that one day they will find all their eyes desired.

The Bloggers

THE DIVORCE DIDN'T GO well, as might have
been expected from how badly the marriage
went. It had taken only three years for us to understand that we were hopelessly incompatible but
even that realisation brought no amicable, let's-stay-
friends resolution, because from my point of view at
least, it looked as if there could be no final dissolu-
tion that didn't involve me accepting the exclusive
blame for our mutual failure. And again from my
perspective it looked as if ultimately what I was
supposed to apologise for really came down to being
born a man. So a genetic disposition to insensitivity,
an unwillingness to address problems constantly by
talking about them and not being finely attuned to
her needs in the various spheres of our life, all
appeared high on Romaine's charge list. And of
course in situations like this you start to keep score
so when provoked I would itemise her failings with
equal gusto, referencing her capacity to spend our
money on expensive fripperies – I later discovered
she kept a secret bank account despite us having

agreed a shared one; her inability to sustain a consistent stability of emotion; and the frequent hinting that her father was the only decent man the world had ever produced. And these were only for starters.

I suppose we might have dragged it out for a few more years if she hadn't created her blog and Twitter account. She wrote a blog to augment the reading group she hosted in our flat once a month and which I refused to join because her idea of a good book is light years away from mine, then grew disillusioned with the blog when she discovered that a new one launched itself every day of the week and too many of them achieved a level of intellectual pretension that she couldn't quite match. So after some thought she changed the subject of hers to what she described as 'women's issues' and called it Suffragette City. Within a month she had five thousand followers on Twitter and visits to her blog from every part of the world, all passionately contributing their views on everything from breastfeeding in public to being whistled at in the street, and all fired up with what seemed to me an incendiary level of anger against the male patriarchy that rules the world and seeks to keep women tethered in passive submission. So soon it wasn't possible to do anything – eat a meal, watch a film, or even on those increasingly rare occasions when we made love – that wasn't accompanied by a constant pinging demanding instant attention and, although thank God we never had any, she responded to them like a mother whose children claimed an urgent need of her. The blog and the virtual world expanded to fill all the available space in her life until, and if I have to admit it I will, I sulked at what I saw as my increasing neglect in the real world.

Sulking of course, as she informed me, was just another symptom of male selfishness and a mean-spirited resentment of her newfound freedom of expression. And on that she may have been right but as far as I'm concerned it didn't compare to the meanness of spirit she displayed when it came time to share out our worldly goods. After I finally, and probably too late in the day, decided to employ a solicitor to counter her endless demands, he suppos-edly justified his fee by explaining the reality of my situation, telling me in a tone of voice that suggested he was doing me a favour, 'You're a man, you're screwed.' So there I succinctly had it and screwed I was, apparently from the moment genes and chro-mosomes do whatever they do, screwed right down to her claiming things I knew she didn't want but insisted on having to spite me. So when compelled to split the DVDs, for example, she chose *Fight Club*, the complete *Rocky* series and *Pulp Fiction* amongst others, leaving me with a collection that included *Mamma Mia!* and a full set of *Harry Potter*s.

But the straw that broke the camel's back was when I started to appear in the blog. Always anony-mous of course but the frequent allusions, however oblique, were enough to let me know that my char-acter and behaviour were being used as exemplars in various scenarios she constructed for her online audience. I came to think of that audience as small birds who perched on the wires that traversed the Web and with every reference to me, no matter how veiled, flocked down to peck at what I supposedly represented. The night before our best/worst and final row was when I read her piece about the male's selfish and predictable approach to sex that turns out apparently to be just another means of domination. She had finally got round to laying out my sexual inadequacies for the world, but was thankfully unaware of my recurring fantasies about the weather girl and her slightly breathless talk of warm fronts, and because Romaine never found out about my occasional use of the milder sort of pornography, the charge sheet didn't yet contain an accusation of the degrading exploitation of the rest of the universe's women.

Of course after the separation I should have moved on but as I continued to appear on her blog with less concern for my anonymity on her part I felt a bitter little swell of resentment. 'Can you ever be friends with your ex?' was the title of one piece with the answer being no, unless like some defeated nation in a war he had expressed abject remorse and made full reparations for all the damage he had caused. I momentarily thought of assuming an online persona and sending a reply that through its barbed sarcasm would ridicule her assertions but was frightened that if she discovered it was me it would be used to confirm my shameful inadequacies to her ten thousand and rising followers.

Now what I should have done with all the spare time I found suddenly available to me was join a gym, take up a hobby and start to rediscover the independent social life that marriage inevitably curtails. But I struggled against a physical lethargy that seemed to paralyse each of my best intentions, never getting further than endless Internet searches for cheap gym membership and the best running shoes. Only my thoughts were in perpetual motion and, despite my best efforts to restore the inner calm I value, they seemed to constantly circle round Romaine, and every new follower on her Twitter account or visitor to her blog was another stab of pain and a reminder of what had come to feel like her walkover victory. So I can't pretend it was anything other than a fit of immature pique that made me decide to start my own blog. I called it Spartacus and dedicated it to 'men's issues', imagining I would churn out a few pieces about football, home-made beers and encourage debate about things such as whether *The Godfather Part III* was the weakest of all sequels. But I chose to launch it with an insider's guide to divorce and a ten-point list of things to look out for and if nothing else I felt better for having written it.

During my first week online I received about twenty responses, all of which said 'I am Spartacus' – men can be such dicks sometimes – as well as several invitations to meet beautiful Russian girls and a couple to buy Viagra. And then it started to happen. Slowly at first men began to post pieces and to my real surprise none of them were about football or home-made beers. And yes there were the occasional offerings that were just piss-taking attempts at humour but gradually these were pushed aside by what I was reading. And if they were mostly anonymous they were also revelatory and slightly weird in ways that I hadn't ever anticipated.

The very first one to arrive was from someone who called himself Hamlet and the first part went like this:

> My father's been dead for a while now but he won't stay dead. So some nights, usually after midnight, he appears out of the mists in my head, or in shallow dreams, and he's always chiding me about the things I haven't done in my life. He tells me I've always lacked determination, am too ready to give up when the going gets tough and too willing to make excuses for myself. He tells me when he started the business he worked every hour God sent and did whatever he had to do and sometimes that meant getting his hands dirty and doing things that are better not talked about. And he tells me all I want are the rewards of the business he created with none of the sacrifice, none of the pain. Sometimes when he's angry he calls me lily-livered and not fit to lace his shoelaces. I want to tell him that he was never there for me, always off fighting some war he'd probably started, but the words never come. Sometimes I don't think I'll ever escape him and need to find a way of making him stay in the hell he deserves.

There then followed a flood of postings outlining tribulations with fathers, both dead and alive, including a pretty gripping one where a son discovered his benign and mild-mannered ex-serviceman dad had actually killed people in some half-forgotten conflict. My real interest, however, was mostly in counting the steeply rising number of hits and no I didn't get into any form of response, not least because I didn't know what to say to these outpourings and instead declared that I saw my role as a provider of an open space, a facilitator and occasionally a moderator of inappropriate content and arbitrator of arguments. A friend in IT who had started to visit the site offered to improve the visuals and very soon it was looking smartly professional.

There were plenty of course who wrote specifically seeking my advice. This, for example, arrived from someone called Timothy:

I have a problem, Spartacus. I fall in love with women. Constantly, hopelessly and instinctively. And if you ask me to explain the type of women I can't because there isn't a type and even though they're probably not beautiful they all seem beautiful in the moment to me. All ages, sizes, shapes. Absolutely, completely beautiful. A glimpse of the underside of a wrist, the curve of a neck, the colour of the eyes, even birthmarks and blemishes, the sound of the voice and always, always the smile. It happens, for example, in the supermarket with the women on the tills – I never use the automatic checkout and don't care how long the queue is if it means my purchases are scanned by Francis, Rosemary or Brianna. I don't even get to say much to them apart from probably a couple of comments about the weather or how busy the store is. And it's never about sex. Never, never. I pass women in the street, sit opposite them on the bus, have my library books stamped by them and think them so beautiful it makes my heart beat faster. When I was in love with Elizabeth in the library I read more books than any time in my life. She said I was one of the quickest readers she'd ever known – I always felt I had to read them in case she asked me something about them. But books are not the worst. There was Husna on the paint counter in B&Q. I did all the paint charts, got the little sample pots and repainted most of my house before I fell in love with someone else even though I hadn't stopped loving Husna and will never stop loving all the ones I loved before.

And mostly I never even get to say very much to any of them but I still feel my heart shiver with the pleasure of them, especially when they smile. I can't help myself and sometimes, like now, it's dangerous.

At this point I imagined Timothy had fallen in love with someone's wife or actually got round to declaring his ardour to some gangster's moll but that wasn't his current problem. No, not at all.

Right now I've fallen in love with the Italian woman who serves in the patisserie in the shopping precinct. She's called Daniela and I go every day and buy something. Every day for a month and I've worked my way through iced fingers, meringues, German biscuits, chocolate éclairs, custard creams and apple strudels. So naturally I'm putting on weight and my cholesterol is probably dangerously high but when she stands smiling behind that glass cabinet full of those fresh creams and colours, her beauty just makes me want to buy every bun in the shop.

What am I to do, Spartacus?

Well if it had been up to me I would have simply passed on the wisdom of my solicitor and without charging an arm and a leg for it, but thankfully I didn't have to offer my thoughts because a welter of responses flooded in, suggesting inevitably, amongst other things, that he should join a church or club – dancing and hillwalking were popular examples – where there were more opportunities to sustain deeper and longer-lasting relationships. Some urged him to clear his head by actually having sex while others wanted to explore the history of his relationship with his mother. Some sympathised and said they shared a similar problem – one man said he fell immediately in love with any woman who called him by his first name. And someone called Roderick from Nova Scotia attempted to enlighten Timothy on the benefits of a gluten-free diet after pointing out the irony of women sometimes being labelled the weaker sex when they had the power to turn a man's head so completely.

It isn't possible to fit every contribution into a category and some didn't make a lot of sense however often you read them and occasionally I had to shorten ramblings that looked like a stopper had been taken out of a long-shut-up bottle. But if I think about it there was a lot relating to marriage problems; sexual dysfunction; workplace issues – a couple by guys who realised they had spent their lives in careers they didn't like but had either left it too late or weren't brave enough to strike out in a new direction; loads from men who loved their wives but couldn't give up the chase; men who had chased and forfeited what they now realised was the very thing they needed and who didn't get to see their children much; gays who wanted to talk about equal marriage and some who complained that they felt marginalised by the site's allocation of space; men with anger issues. There was also an ongoing contribution from Mike in Sheffield who believed a PE teacher was victimising his son by repeatedly making him substitute for the school's football team when it was clear the boy was more talented than those being given first-team places. It appeared to reach a climax when Mike was dispatched from the touchline for inappropriate comments to the same PE teacher when he was refereeing a game. And good old Desmond of course who at regular intervals wanted to enlighten us as to the joys of model railways and was constantly asking if anyone had a Hornby 1930s LMS locomotive for sale.

It is indisputably childish to admit that I frequently compared my hits and followers with those of Suffragette City and nor can I deny the pleasure I found watching the gap diminish. She seemed to have reached a plateau and was levelling off whereas I continued to climb steadily. I had also started to receive enquiries about advertising and various offers; for example, a free trip to Prague to test out a travel company's stag-do packages – I turned it down. But because the blog was taking up almost all my free time I was happy to accept revenue from a company selling health checks for men where they tested blood pressure, cholesterol, blood sugar and carbon monoxide and offered acupuncture, massage and water therapy; a firm selling classic-car kits and one detailing a range of cosmetic surgeries with a

special first-treatment reduction for anyone mention-
ing the name Spartacus at the initial consultation.
To my surprise I was also sounded out by a men's
up-market glossy magazine as to whether I was interested in having a trial as a provider of advice on a
new problem page they were considering, but as this
clearly involved knowing what the answers were to
the kind of stuff I was being sent I declined.

Sometimes I got a little anxious about what I had
started and where it was all going to end but I don't
suppose I was ever quite as anxious as this guy who
simply called himself L.

> I am an anxious man, Spartacus. Have been since as
> far back as I can remember so I no longer know what
> it feels like not to be anxious. There are some things I
> know I'm anxious about and I suppose it's quite a
> long list. So there's dogs – I was bitten as a small boy
> so I guess there's at least some logic in that; planes,
> naturally, but mostly the taking off – I always sit in
> an aisle seat so I can't see out a window; people who
> throw their lit cigarette butt out of the car in front
> which potentially gets inside my engine and turns it
> into a ball of flame; all kinds of heights – I don't do
> any higher than standing on a chair to put the star on
> the top of the Christmas tree; guys with tattoos; guys
> with tattoos and dogs; people who knock on your
> door and want to talk to you about your soul and
> the afterlife; waking up and finding yourself exposed
> as a lifelong fraud and everything you've ever
> achieved being taken away from you because you got
> it under false pretences – that's a really big anxiety,
> Spartacus.

These are the ones I can put a name to but it doesn't explain the worst one of all. And the worst and the most permanent one that's always lurking under the surface of my life doesn't have a name – it's just this constant nagging presence living off my life like some parasite. It's even in my dreams and sleep. I don't know if I'm able to explain it to you or not. Sometimes I think it's like walking out over ice and thinking that at any moment it might crack.

Am I anxious about dying? Well maybe it might sound strange, Spartacus, but I'm not. It doesn't worry me at all, come to think about it. I might even welcome it when the time is right. Casting off your burdens, peace at last and all that. But even now as I dwell on it there lurks the final anxiety of them all. What if four days into your perfect sleep you hear the voice of some fresh-faced Christ in search of a crowd-pleasing miracle calling you back into the coldly glittering light of life? What then, Spartacus?

What then indeed? Sometimes when I read all this stuff I felt a little inadequate, a bit shallow, because at heart I think of myself as a pretty straightforward guy and if I wasn't deeply affected by much of what was raining in on the site I wondered if it was because Romaine was right and I lack a bit of instinctive sympathy.

Shortly after L shared some of his anxieties Spartacus went mega. Out of the blue a journalist approached me from the *Guardian* and wanted to interview me about the site for a feature article. His name was Stevie but when we met up at a local coffee shop Stevie turned out to be a very attractive young woman with a mass of black hair you'd love to press your face into, bright red lipstick you'd like to smudge and no doubt with whom Timothy would have immediately fallen in love. And I don't say I wasn't tempted, not so much with the love bit but the possibility of sex did cross my mind. I tried to concentrate on the answers to the list of questions she had sent me in advance and was now asking me.

'So why do you think the site has proved so successful?'

'I think it's because men don't really have anywhere they can talk about the things that are important to them. Women have always had places even if it was just a circle of close friends. All I've done is provide men with a blank wall and invite them to come and write about the issues they haven't found an outlet for.'

She nodded, moved her tape recorder slightly and pushed a thick swathe of hair from the side of her face. There was a little smear of lipstick on the rim of her cup. I tried to stop wondering whether her mouth would feel hard or soft and instead focused on her questions about how the site started, what were the most frequent topics and why I personally didn't offer advice.

'I see myself as more of a facilitator,' I told her, 'someone who acts as a conduit for the voices of others, and there are plenty of our users who are able to offer thoughtful advice, often on the basis of relevant qualifications and experience.'

'Has it surprised you what men are prepared to open up about?'

She wasn't wearing a wedding ring – not that it counts for much one way or the other any more – and I assumed that I was coming across as a sensitive soul and surely the type of man a modern woman was looking for until she said, 'And you don't think there's a danger of it all just being a chance for men to witter away like …'

'Like women?'

'No, like … like old hens,' she said and we both laughed.

'Well why not, if it helps them come to terms with the stuff that's troubling them?'

'And have you been surprised by the range of subjects that's been aired?'

'Yes, I suppose I was at the start but now I just accept whatever comes at face value and try not to have preconceived ideas or expectations about what men want to talk about.'

'You don't seem to post yourself any more. Why is that?'

I was conscious of a trace of her scent sifting through the smell of coffee and the way her eyes widened slightly as if the question was a tease. So I offered some vague justification and didn't tell her that apart from the pains and indignities of my divorce I felt no urge or need to share anything of my inner life and in fact was happier to draw a veil over it in case further revelation confirmed it as screwed up as I sometimes suspected. She seemed happy to chat on, insisted on paying the bill and after the article appeared in a Saturday-morning supplement, complete with my photograph, the site nearly crashed with the volume of traffic. I couldn't walk down the street without someone greeting me with 'I am Spartacus' or get a pint in my local without the guy serving me wanting to tell me some complicated story about his personal life. I also had to make a private arrangement with my postman in order to deal with the volume of post that flooded in – everything from newly released novels and films looking for the Spartacus approval, to invitations to give talks at festivals and sit in the front row of fashion shows. There was a welter of free samples – male-grooming products, obviously, as well as vouchers for spa weekends and balloon flights, and enough packs of exotically named condoms to cause the world's birthrate to plummet. I ended up persuading Eddie the postman to keep most of the stuff – I heard later he sold it on eBay and made a bit of a killing.

But soon something was happening to the site and the early posters started to complain that they were getting elbowed aside by those who submitted items motivated by poorly disguised commercial or factional interest. There was a danger of it becoming a marketplace and while Spartacus always had a soft spot for the eccentric and the slightly strange it began to attract unpleasant nutters. So there were the religious zealots breathing hellfire on gays, materialism and the sexually promiscuous; right-wing fanatics demanding a return to their vision of white British manhood; and individuals who can't be categorised but who offered crackpot philosophies on who was responsible for 9/11, the secret cabals who supposedly ruled the world and a guy from Skye who believed he had married a mermaid.

I actually wanted to reply to the guy from Skye and tell him he should watch the film *Splash*. But mostly I just felt depressed and so under pressure that if it hadn't been for the money I was making from advertising I would have been tempted to pull the plug, or whatever you actually do to close down a site. When I looked at Suffragette City I could see the tumbleweed blowing across the screen and I knew how tough it must have been for Romaine to see me in the media and Spartacus on the rise. We'd had no recent contact except a brief functional exchange about the payment of a communal bill. I didn't feel sorry for her but although I thought of it as karma the sense of victory didn't inspire any of the emotions I might have expected, and even though Stevie had given me her card I couldn't bring myself to ring her, unsure whether her interest in me was professional or personal. And if you want the truth my confidence with women was pretty shot after the separation. Failure isn't a good aphrodisiac and also, bizarrely I suppose, since creating the blog I had started to feel a vague responsibility towards my followers to be a thinking person. The very word 'followers' gives me the shivers because that was never how I considered myself but maintaining the site made me suddenly overly conscious about things. And I'm not good at this – I prefer just living in the moment, not thinking too deeply. Not worrying about the right and the wrong.

It was on one of those late-night furtive glances at Romaine's site that I saw the lead article and although it was anonymous I knew it was by her. In it she talked about the importance of reflection in life and the necessity of a period of quiet where you take stock of decisions already made and future plans. It wasn't so much what she said as the tone of voice. Most of the usual fire and aggressive assertiveness seemed to have drained away and for the first time I detected a hint of uncertainty. It made her curiously vulnerable and the strident, pecking voices of her acolytes at the end of her piece merely served to highlight the fragility of the lines above. And it made me go a little sentimental, remembering the way, for example, she was kind to my mother when she was ill and how she cried during a documentary about sick children. And not everything about our marriage had been bad – there'd been times when we'd shared laughter and others when she could be spontaneous and generous. I tried to balance out these slightly misty-eyed memories with a reminder of the number of ear-bashings my supposed failings had received and the scalpel sharpness of her solicitor's letters, but even then I was prepared to admit the possibility that some at least of these criticisms had been justified. If nothing else Spartacus had taught me life wasn't always black and white and that there were layers of complexity to which I hadn't generally been receptive. And a lonely bed has to be just about the worst thing in the world, no two ways about it when all you've got to hug is a surging emptiness that no brief sexual fantasy can remedy. There were times when I would have welcomed even the guy from Skye's mermaid.

But that night when most of the city was sleeping I started to write what was only my second piece ever and I felt my hands shake a little. I called it 'Second Thoughts' and did my faltering best to capture the same reflective perspective that I sensed had been present in her offering. I didn't capitulate or wave a white flag but I did pursue the tentative line of older and wiser, looking back at a period of your life when immaturity and faulty judgement meant that sometimes you came up short. I left the future uncertain and closed with what was probably a clumsy attempt to express a vague sense of regret.

By the morning I had received an influx of replies, the majority of which urged me in one way or another to keep the faith, some that shared similar stories of regret and a minority that responded to what I had written as if I had just betrayed them with a Judas kiss. Nor had it escaped my attention that Spartacus, well at least in the film with Kirk Douglas, ends up being crucified. I went on Suffragette City but there was only an argument about whether you could get breast augmentation and still be a feminist. I returned again and again but nothing. And then about a week later I had a phone call from Romaine telling me that she was thinking of selling the apartment and getting somewhere slightly cheaper and did I want to meet up to discuss the sale and the potential financial implications. She spoke neutrally at the start, and then slightly nervously as we politely enquired as to each other's wellbeing. When she congratulated me on the newspaper story I searched for some trace of sarcasm but finding none I responded self-deprecatingly and hinting at the problems it had created.

I hadn't been back to the apartment since the final clear-out of my stuff and it felt incredibly strange to be ringing the bell and waiting at a door I had gone through so often. When she opened it we shimmied towards a hug but ended up bottling it and instead gave each other the most polite of kisses where nothing really touched except the sides of our cheeks. I sat down in the living room, and although little appeared outwardly changed it felt curiously different, as if the furniture sat at new angles to itself and the spaces between had contracted, or in some places expanded.

We did small talk initially – personal health, work and family news – decorously waiting until each other had clearly finished speaking before responding and conscious of embarrassment when little silences extended too long. She'd had her hair cut and shaped in a different style but I hesitated to compliment her even though I liked it and it was soon clear that neither of us was going to let the words Suffragette City or Spartacus cross our lips. As she went into the kitchen to make us both a coffee I felt something slink across my ankles and found myself looking at a cat that jumped into my lap, curled itself into my contours and purred when I stroked it.

'You like cats?' she asked when she returned with the coffee.

'Yes, I like cats.'

'Could you live with one?'

'Yes, yes, I think I could,' I said as she set the cups down and came towards me and folded me in an embrace so tight that I didn't know where my body ended and hers started.

It was as simple as that. Five minutes later we were in bed but at the last moment I hesitated, suddenly mindful of my previously identified shortcomings and then there was a mutual indecisiveness about position, my head echoing with remembered accusations of domination. So we ended up spooning. It was the most exciting of couplings and all too soon I was trying to delay the climax by mentally listing Timothy's types of buns but not making it much further than chocolate éclairs and at the vital moment I had to make myself resist the sudden and hopelessly inappropriate urge to shout 'I am Spartacus'.

We didn't talk about the past and I think we both accepted we were starting from a different place and after we got rid of the cat – it turned out I was allergic – the first big decision we had to make was what to do about the blogs and Twitter accounts. It wasn't difficult – she was right when she said that kept on too long they all turn out to be just a case of howling at the moon, a case of diminishing returns, like one of those helium balloons with the air slowly escaping, but then as our absence from the sites saw them go into free-fall we had a rethink. I can't pretend it was my idea but I wasn't slow to see the potential of it. And so within a month of getting back together we had a new site up and running with the not entirely original name of Second Time Around, some media coverage, expanding advertising revenue and a rapidly growing audience.

Due to the volume of work Romaine was able to leave her job and work full-time on chronicling our first year back together. I was happy to let her and when we understood pretty early on that there was never going to be enough material to hold public interest – sometimes a television night in and a take-away pizza doesn't really cut it – we gave each other full licence to invent. And full credit to her – she turned out to be very good at it. So there were pieces about the delicate process of becoming partners once again, the issue of honesty about lovers who might have appeared in the period of separation (I hoped this was fictional – it was on my part at least) and some psychological babble about the benefits of time apart and mutual growth. She invented holidays, special events and did a soap-opera series on her supposed attempts to get pregnant – I couldn't quite get my head around some of the suggested methods but at least they gave us plenty of laughs, not least the one about having sex in a lift that's going from the top floor of a tall building to the basement without any stops, and the one that involved fish heads, oysters and full moons.

We got offered a book deal from a reputable publisher and there's even serious talk of an appropriately feel-good film. After some legal consultations we established various copyrights to become a kind of franchise and before long started to make appearances on morning television. We both know that eventually there will be a backlash – in the virtual world nothing lasts for ever – but by the time it happens we'll have made a killing and moved on to our next idea. And our marriage? Well I have to say that despite my initial reservations it's never been better. All the deep introspection, all the dramas and emotional turmoil happen out there in the hard drives and motherboards, in the connectors and memory slots. Real or imagined they play themselves out in the ether and in the ether everything exists in some parallel world that isn't life no matter how much it thinks it is, or wants to be, and so ultimately doesn't signify very much at all. In our other world we live quietly and without fuss and never having to think too much about stuff suits me right down to the ground. There's a rumour they've asked Benedict Cumberbatch to play me in the film.

Skype

H E DOESN'T HAVE TO record any data or collate measurements for another couple of hours and so he takes his customary walk into the village. He's glad of the exercise and glad too of the light because already the days are shortening and this far north there's no slow fade through the amber mutation of autumn, but rather a sudden collapse like someone's drawn a curtain or pulled a plug. He feels the first flinty hint of winter's breath on the breeze and he zips his fleece up to his chin. It's downhill to the village which makes the return tougher on the legs and lungs, especially when he's had a couple of beers in Anders's hostelry or is carrying provisions. But he has always believed that a man shouldn't live on an island without paying his respects to the sea at some point during the day.

And the village with its harbour and smattering of shops is where people are and when all is said and done no man is an island. So his stride is lengthened by the thought of Anna's strong coffee and the slice of pie that she will serve him hot, with the sweet apple slices slipping out the side of the pastry. He will enjoy it as much as he enjoys her smile and conversation and he will sit for an hour or so, read yesterday's paper and pass the time of day with whoever else comes in. Even though he is not a man given to small talk he likes to listen and when the mood takes him is happy to supply the prompts that allow others to lead the way.

Perhaps he talked himself out in the years he was the island's schoolteacher – or, as some of the older islanders still call him, the Master. The school was a single room then with a tin roof that rattled like gunfire under hailstones. As he walks downhill he can see the shiny replacement building with its three rooms and inside toilets. There are two teachers now and they get regular visitors from the mainland who offer assistance with particular learning difficulties. They also have the use of the new community centre for physical education and special events such as concerts. At the last count he thinks there were about thirty children. But it's never enough. Because, of that thirty, most will eventually take the two-hour ferry journey to the mainland and not return. They will go to work in the bars and hotels in the towns and cities along the coast; some will spend their lives on board the cruise ships that explore the fjords and others will sink steel foundations in the polders and think of their island with sentimentality only when late-night alcohol flows.

In their place will come the blow-ins, some of whom will stay a lifetime, others who will not survive the first winter. They all arrive with their Arcadian dreams of escape from the complexities of the modern world – a few even believe they shall find a return to innocence and then too late realise that they are no longer sheltered from the raw extremes of nature and cower like abused children before its unleashed cruelties. And there are strict planning laws in relation to new-build – permission is rarely given so those wishing to move to the island must wait until an islander dies, until the family line dies out except for some child long gone who wants a quick sale of the property, and then the outsiders outbid the locals and renovate into oblivion all trace of the house's former life. The locals think of them as standing in dead-men's shoes and offer little in the way of an easy welcome. These newly arrived sometimes cause offence because they don't know the customs and try to do business in the manner it's done on the mainland, always expecting their money to give them what they need. And what these city folk have to understand is that they must bring something to the island – they can't just take. So they need to offer skills that are valued and be willing to lend their shoulder to the wheel when it's required and above all they need to give the island children. So let them not come in their midlife crisis, or even as a few have done in withered old age, when the first strong wind blew them ragged. The island needs the ripeness of seed, the swelling of a woman's womb.

In just over a month's time the first Arctic winds will arrive – the locals call them the Bear's Teeth even though there have been no bears on the island for over two hundred years and with them comes the first promise of snow. So let the newcomers have their roofs secured and their larders well provisioned, let them have their oil lamps and candles ready for when the generators fail, and above all let them prepare themselves for the darkness. As the year progresses the days slowly contract, the dawn and the dusk rushing towards each other like lovers, and some of those same newcomers feel themselves slowly suffocated, shut in with each other and whatever it was in themselves that prompted their retreat from the mainland.

He passes the old stone buildings shaped like bee hives which were once used for smoking the fish on which the whole island's economy depended. Some of the stonework has tumbled in on itself and other parts are papered over with lichen and moss. One of the entrances is blocked with webbed brambles. He quickens his pace. Soon he has a clear view of the sea as it chops at itself in sharp-edged breaks of white. He opens his lungs to it and inhales what he thinks of as its briny life-giving energies. And yet as a people they have mostly turned away from it for their livelihoods and the traditional pursuit of herring. Only the Bronstad brothers fish it for a living and only because they have a good deal from one of the capital's high-class restaurants which likes to boast to their well-heeled customers about locally sourced produce and their 'bespoke' menu. No one can compete with the commercial fleets that drag the hell out of the ocean, processing tons of fish every day and thumbing their nose at weather conditions that would send smaller vessels scuttling for shelter.

As always he likes to think it was the gradual wearing down of the winters that drove Birgitta away. Easier to blame the darkness and the flail of wind and snow than spend the rest of his life turning over their failures, replaying on a nagging loop the sound of their separating lives. Perhaps his parents had been right – he should have married an islander. But he had fallen in love with her at university and for over a decade she had seemed happy to embrace the island's life, content to work in the community centre as a social worker and in the dark months develop ideas for her novel. When she took the ferry and never came back she left him an uncompleted first draft in a spidery longhand and a daughter they had named Hanna. The last he heard of his wife she was living in a kibbutz and in a relationship with another woman. His job as the island's teacher, combined with help from his parents, had made it easier to look after Hanna but now a grown woman she too had left in search of work and the life she believed the island couldn't give her.

He's down on the level now where the oldest houses close to the harbour lean against each other for support and the line of their roofs looks warped and buckled under their canopies of grey slate. As always the ridges are white-spotted with gulls. Johannes passes him on his bicycle, at eighty years of age a rattling bag of bones that surely wouldn't survive a tumble, so when the old man raises one hand in greeting his apprehension shortens his own response to the point of curtness. He makes his way briskly to Anna's coffee shop and lifts one of the papers that hangs on a rack just inside the door, then ordering his coffee and apple tart takes a seat by the window where a pale wash of sunlight stripes the table.

'So how goes it, Gabriel?' Anna asks as she prepares his coffee. 'What weather are you predicting this week?'

Always they ask the same question and always with a teasing lilt to their voices. Since he retired from teaching he has earned a little extra money from a meteorological company who pay him to record various data as part of an extensive early-warning system for what's heading their way. They also supply him with an expensive laptop on which to record the information and forward it to them. The islanders enjoy making a joke about it because like all islanders their senses are intimately synced with the weather and they believe they can read instinctively the signs and are in no need of charts and spreadsheets. They trust their eyes, believe they can tell what's coming by lifting their faces towards the sky and seeing the formation of the clouds, feeling the strength of the wind on their cheeks and marking in which direction the birch trees bend. The older ones will claim to know what weather's imminent by the flight of birds, the restlessness of the sea or in the very whispering of their bones.

'Not so bad,' he answers and then, playing the game, tells her, 'the spinning wheels say the rest of the week will be much like this.'

'That's good,' she says. 'We can all sleep safely in our beds.'

The word bed makes him smile and look at her more intently. He'd like to sleep in her bed, know once more the warmth of a companion, and he cares not a shot that she has slipped into rotundity and that all the blonde in her hair is leaching into grey. Her very amplitude holds the promise of generosity. She has a pretty smile that sparks her eyes. He's no oil painting himself, his skin toughened and weatherbeaten into submission, his hair a wiry cap that still insists on curling even in its retreat from his forehead. She is the pastor's wife and so his thoughts are both shamed and thrilled by their fervour. And as Edgar preaches only sin and repentance, his voice as dry and sea-bleached as his character, he stirs himself by imagining how she might welcome his warm currents flowing into her.

When she brings the coffee and apple tart to him she sets it in the wash of sunlight. Her sleeves are rolled to the elbow and for a second the light catches the fine lattice of blonde hairs on her forearms. But he is too embarrassed to look up at her in case his thoughts are printed on his face and so he merely offers his thanks and moves the cup slightly on the saucer to angle the handle towards himself. He reads the paper with little enthusiasm for its tales of political manoeuvrings and threats of terrorism but dwells longer on the sports page, and as always feels a little nostalgic desire to see an ice-hockey match or a football game in the flesh rather than through the temperamental rusted satellite dishes that sprout like mushrooms from every roof.

'Anything interesting happening in the world?' Anna asks as she leans fully on the wooden counter. There is a little wisp of steam rising from the coffee machine behind her.

'Just the usual madness. Wars and rumours of wars.'

'That's one of the signs we're living in the final days,' she says, propping her head in the palms of her hands. But because she's smiling he doesn't think she believes it.

'If it's the final days then there's not much point me breaking my back on that new cladding I'm putting up,' a voice says from the doorway.

It belongs to Alfred who comes in wearing a heavily laden tool belt that sags low on his hips and makes him look like a gunslinger. There are wood-shavings in his hair. He orders a coffee and asks for it to be 'as strong and black as sin' then studies the various cakes before selecting an almond tartlet. Gabriel is a little disappointed to see that Anna gives Alfred the same smile as he received – he wanted to think that there had been something personal in his. Alfred collapses at the other end of his table and the light coming through the window reveals a veneer of white that lines the crevices of his skin and rests on his upper lip like a delicate dusting of snow.

'Hard at it?' Gabriel asks out of politeness.

'Another two days' work at least.' He glances over at Anna as if to check that she's listening, then asks, 'So will the weather hold?'

'I would say so, I would definitely say so,' he says, seeing how Anna is smiling as she runs a cloth over the counter.

'Well I'll take that as gospel seeing you're the weatherman.'

'I am indeed.' He sips from his coffee and when Alfred turns his head to see how his order is progressing smiles at Anna to show that he's happy to play along with the joke.

Other people arrive in the coffee shop. Each new arrival acknowledges the others already there. Alfred gives up conversation to concentrate on eating. Soon there is a little flake of pastry at the corner of his mouth. Gabriel glances outside and catches the Bronstad brothers sauntering up to Anders's hostelry for their first drink of the day. They are both dressed in blue overalls and rubber boots. It might be their first drink of the day but if they have landed a good catch it won't be their last. Once he was foolish enough to accept their invitation to join them and a full day later he climbed the hill back to his house with a hammering in his head that made him feel he was far out at sea in a full-blown storm. Never again, he resolved – he even had to invent the data for the missing day.

When Alfred is finished he wipes his mouth with the back of his hand and shakes his head as if he's just felt the cold shiver of the work that stretches in front of him.

'All right for some,' he says as he stands. 'No pension for me. And if I don't get this job finished it'll be a sorry winter with every wind that blows finding a way to sneak inside.'

Gabriel wishes him good luck with the work and as he looks at the light catching the metal handle of the holstered staple gun thinks for a second of offering his help, but stops himself because he knows his meagre skills and Alfred's cantankerous insistence on having everything done his way would prove a poor combination. He watches Anna lift her hand and smile in farewell and is torn between sitting on in the warmth and stir of people and the work he has to do. Not that many of his neighbours would call it work, this daily recording of temperature, barometric pressure, wind speed and rainfall, and most recently the ultraviolet index. But it keeps him occupied and the money helps because despite Alfred's gibe about the teaching pension it pays him very little because he retired early, not long after Hanna left the island.

'Another coffee?' Anna asks and he says yes just to have the pleasure of her coming close when she pours it. 'How are you?' she asks as she does so and her voice is quieter. He tells her what he tells anyone who asks and thanks her. For a second she seems to be thinking of saying something else but she turns away and he stops himself following her with his eyes.

A line of children walks past the window followed by Gudrun, one of the school's two teachers, and a couple of parent helpers. The children are all dressed in warm outdoor coats and hats and carry little plastic clipboards. So it is some outdoor lesson they are about to engage in. He still goes into the school on special occasions, and once in a while to help out with slow readers, but has reduced the number of visits because he doesn't want Gudrun to feel that he is shadowing her or trying to steer the boat from the shore. She has her own ideas and although sometimes they make him raise his eyebrows he knows that she is able and has the children's best interests at heart. He watches the last of them saunter by. This is the time before the teenage years kick in, when they think they will never leave, when their family ties and friendships are at their strongest. When the island is still an adventure.

The second fill of coffee tastes a little bitter. He looks up to see Dominic arrive and greet Anna. He's handing her a page of paper and they're going through whatever's written on it and then he realises it's to do with tomorrow night's party. It's a tradition. When a young person leaves for work or university the family marks the departure with a party to which everyone is invited. Once they were held in individual homes but now it is mostly the community centre that gets used. He did it for Hanna.

Dominic sees him and waves. He looks a little flustered, like a man who has forgotten something, and when he comes over he walks slowly as if trying to remember what it is. He stands at the end of the table but is so preoccupied that he forgets to ask for a weather forecast.

'Anna doing the catering?' Gabriel asks.

'Yes, but there's always some last-minute thing you need doing or have forgotten about and you know how it is, if anything goes wrong she'll say it's my fault,' he says then looks slightly embarrassed but Gabriel smiles and nods to let him know that no insensitivity has been shown about a departed wife.

'What time are you starting?'

'About seven. Will you come? We'll understand if you can't make it.'

'Of course I'll come and I hope everything goes well.'

Dominic thanks him and shuffles back to the counter to confer again with Anna. Soon his daughter Astrid will take the ferry and join all the others. She will come back for the first Christmas and even for a week in the summer but then she will only return like all the rest do, skimming through the darkness to form once more in the homes they grew up in, travelling through the hidden mysteries of circuits and signals, coming back to the island on Skype. It's how they talk to their children now, scanning their faces to search for any distance between what is spoken and what they're feeling, intently studying the surroundings for clues about their lives. So they listen to them talk in far-off rooms rented in blocks of cheap apartments or in the high-rise towers on the outskirts of the capital that now house the dreams of those who have travelled from even further afield. Sometimes as they exchange family news they run out of things to say and there is an embarrassed silence filled only by the cry of a baby, the chatter of a television or the wail of a passing siren. The conversations rarely exceed fifteen minutes and mostly they take place on Sunday nights in that empty space between the end of the weekend and the start of the working week.

The desire to share the little they have been given by their children ensures the word Skype has become as common as references to the weather in the islanders' exchanges.

He carries his empty cup and plate to the counter and takes his leave of Anna but even her farewell smile fails to lift his spirits. He walks to the harbour, the strengthening wind snapping at his face, and watches the small boats rising and falling on the swell. His own father fished until an accident drove him off the sea. He remembers the way his mother always referred to it as God's blessing in disguise and thought the fall in their income a fair price to pay for the removal of her constant anxiety. This afternoon the sea looks irritable, slowly working itself up into a brew, and it hits the harbour wall as if startled to find land's obstruction in its way. It's always been like that, he thinks, always the sense that nature resents the presence they have carved out for themselves and at every opportunity seeks to dislodge them.

There is no work for young people any more. The fishing industry's collapse took with it the jobs in the fish factory where many of the island's women found employment. There are still the cottage industries turning out, amongst other things, deliberately rough-hewn knitted jumpers and enjoying a momentary influx of orders thanks to some detective television series he's never watched, but apart from a small forestry business and some tourist-related jobs there're only small crumbs of opportunity. The thought of work jerks him back into the routine of his day and he knows he must head home and complete his data returns. So he inhales the smell of the sea once more and starts his walk up the hill.

He's not uncomfortable with technology although he came to it quite late but there's always a moment of surprise when her face appears. And because he's looking at her on the screen of the laptop, just for a second she doesn't resemble his daughter and then the rush of recognition takes over and as usual he raises his hand in greeting and as always she must find this funny because the wave she returns feels lightly ironic. These opening moments are the most awkward because until their conversation gets going there is always hesitancy, each meeting feeling like a new beginning, as if their separation has made them a little more like strangers to the other.

'So how are you?' she asks.

'I'm good, and you?'

'I'm good, everything's fine.'

She's wearing a dark hoodie that serves to emphasise the paleness of her skin. And with her hair pulled back her face looks thin. He wonders if she's eating properly.

'And are you looking after yourself?'

'Of course,' she says as she shifts on her chair. Behind her there is a Banksy print of a young girl releasing a heart-shaped balloon. 'So what's the news?'

'Nothing much to report.' He always struggles to think of a reply to this question and even when he prepares stuff it mostly sounds inconsequential and feels like a tacit admission that there was no alternative to leaving. 'Alfred's putting up new cladding – there's hammering day and night. I'll be glad when he's finished and we get a bit of peace and quiet. Weather's been settled and all the collecting gizmos are working fine. Apparently they feed it all into a giant computer – all the data from the weather stations and satellites – then get the magic answer.'

'You'd think by the time they did that the weather would already have happened.'

'Yes, but what they're trying to get are the short-term and long-term predictions. That's the bit they make their money from.'

'Strange to make money from the weather,' she says, pushing a strand of hair behind her ear.

'And, Hanna, money's OK with you?'

'Everything's fine,' she says, looking straight at him.

'Well if you need anything make sure you ask. If you get a big bill or anything.'

'I will.'

'So how's work?' he asks.

'Good. Keeping busy.'

'And the children are behaving well for you?'

'Not so bad – you always get one or two who don't want to be there and spend the day asking when their parents are coming to collect them. Sometimes the ones who cry when their parents arrive are the ones who have been happiest all day.'

'Children are clever – they always know how to get what they want.'

'And was I like that?'

'You were a good girl, Hanna, but you had your moments like every child.'

'It wasn't ideal being taught by your father. I always felt I had to be perfectly behaved and that the other children spent their time looking to see if I ever got preferential treatment.'

'Which you didn't.'

'No I didn't, in fact I got worse treatment. I used to think it so unfair. I got lower marks when I knew my work was better than others and I was never allowed to win a prize however small.'

'It was difficult for me too. It's good they have two teachers now,' he says as he sees her glancing at her watch.

'And is your replacement still making changes?'

'New broom sweeps clean,' he says. 'Hopefully anything changed will be for the better. She's young, she has her own ideas. It's only to be expected.'

They talk a while longer and then he remembers to tell her about Astrid. He believes she's going to work in a hotel while doing a part-time college course in hotel management. Hanna asks about the send-off and he fills in the few details he knows before they lapse into silence. It is always in these few seconds of final silence, just before the screen goes blank, that he wants to say something but never fully grasps what it is and so instead he merely raises his hand in farewell and tells her they will speak soon but already her image is fading into darkness.

Having shared his life with two people the house seems perpetually quiet in their absence and it's not calm or peaceful but something that is edged with the rustle of former voices and the daily sounds of lives brushing against each other. Now all he brushes against are memories and the rhythms he has had to construct to fill the spaces. He wonders if he was too hard on Hanna when she sat in his classroom, too concerned with appearances. He thinks about Birgitta and wonders what it's like to work each day with the sun on your face. He turns on the television in search of sport but there is only junk and the reception isn't good so the picture comes and then breaks into abstract patterns. He'll have to see Ditman about getting a booster for his signal or finding somewhere higher for the aerial. And he doesn't want to lose sight of Hanna.

She has encouraged him to find a new partner – someone to help see him through the winters was how she described it. But it's easier said than done. There are no unmarried women on the island of a similar age to him apart from the Folden sisters who are committed spinsters and Edgar's daughter who ran away to become a nun but was rejected as unstable and had to have her visions back at home. Occasionally a middle-aged widow comes on the market but they last no longer than the shortest delay that seemliness permits before they're snapped up. And because he knows he will never leave the island the only possibility is to use one of the Internet sites he's read about and hope that someone suitable might want to experience island life. But that way leaves too much to chance and good fortune and he is reluctant to experience a second failure. So he's always laughed off Hanna's advice, telling her that no one would want the fag end of him but been secretly pleased when she's insisted that he's kept himself in good shape and someone out there would see him as a good catch. About her own love life she's instinctively secret, hiding behind a vague humour, and he's always been unwilling to embarrass them both by pushing too hard. He wonders if something of the teacher–pupil still lingers in their relationship and she puts too much store on trying to meet whatever she thinks are his expectations when all he wants is for her to be happy.

He can't tell if she looks happy or not. There's something slightly preoccupied about her this evening and the room isn't brightly lit so on the screen her face is shadowed. And tonight he feels as if he's intruding. He tries to be light but wonders if he sounds like someone calling in on an elderly parent, or checking up on a child who's wandered off. He knows they won't talk long by the way she fidgets on the chair and doesn't stare intently at the screen but takes it in with glances that makes him think she must be bored. So they hurry through the necessary courtesies and exchange a lean list of news. The day nursery where she works is to have an inspection and there are policies and documents flying off the photocopier. He tells her not to be worried, that she's good with children and everything will be all right. Then he remembers his own last inspection.

'The inspector arrived on the Monday ferry, grumped about all day, questioning this and that, turning over stones in search of who knows what

146

and then when the storm came his return ferry was cancelled. You were young but perhaps you can remember him staying with us. The storm didn't clear for three days. He finished off a bottle of my best whisky and I don't know what he intended writing but when the report came it was excellent. I think he made it so good that he never had to come back.'

She tells him she's not worried about the inspection. The print of the young girl releasing the balloon isn't there any more and the wall behind her is completely bare.

'Do you still have Mum's book?' she asks.

'Yes, why do you ask?'

'I think I'd like to read it. Have you read it?'

'I don't think it's finished but yes I've read it.'

'And?'

'I don't think I really understood it. It was a little experimental.'

'Will you send it to me?' she asks.

'Sure. Have you heard from her recently?'

'A couple of emails every so often, not much.'

'Why do you want to read her book?'

'Just to know what was in her head, I suppose.'

He doesn't tell her that was his reason for reading it. He found no ready answers.

'I think it was the winters made her go,' he says after a moment's silence, because he doesn't want his daughter to ever think that she left because of anything to do with her.

'They're pretty tough,' she says and when she mentions the Bear's Teeth he sees her shiver a little.

*

When he goes to the community centre there is a small knot of younger men smoking outside the door so he has to pass through a fine veil of smoke that shimmers blue in the spotlight fanning down from above their heads. One of them says, 'Stub them out, boys, it's the Master.' There is a little ripple of laughter but someone silences it almost immediately and when they greet him with handshakes he acknowledges each by name before he enters the hall. He is met by the sound of music and in the cleared space beyond the crowded tables sees the island's oldest couple doing a slow and stately formal dance that bears no connection to the rap that's blaring from the speakers on either side of the stage. Streamers and balloons are hanging from the ceiling and projected on a screen is a montage of photographs of Astrid. On the tables are platters of food and bottles of wine. As he looks for a quiet seat he thinks it unfortunate that a competitive element has crept into the farewells, with some families looking to outdo the others in the lavishness of their hospitality. If it was up to him they would go back to having them in the home and neighbours would come and then leave again to allow others to take their place.

'Good to see you, Gabriel,' Dominic says and rests his hand on his shoulder then calls for his wife to pour a drink for their guest. They find him a seat at a table where he will feel comfortable and he's pleased when it affords him a view of Anna. She's wearing a blue dress with a white collar and her hair is pinned up in an elaborate arrangement. She looks very different to the person he sees in the coffee shop and he's not sure which appearance he prefers. Some young children get on the dance floor and kicking off their shoes start to slide on the shiny wood. He catches a glimpse of Astrid who is dressed in white and surrounded by younger girls who hope that their proximity to the centre of attraction will increase their own importance. At the table people pass him the platters of food and because he doesn't want to offend anyone he tries to take something from each offering. But he hangs back in the conversations, lets most of it float past him. He has come only because tradition expects it and out of respect for the family.

When he looks at the montage he sees the child he used to teach. Only a couple of years younger than Hanna and a good student who took her work seriously. He hopes everything goes well for her in her new life. Dominic's wife Katja has had a word with the DJ and the music has slipped into familiar and melodic pop and more people get up to dance. He preferred it when neighbours brought their own instruments and made music with fiddles and accordions, played tunes on pianos and tin whistles. The children are being ushered out of the way. Some couples from his table take to the floor. He is sitting on his own and he knows that he will leave as soon as the formal part of the evening is over. He's done his duty.

Eventually the music stops and order is called for. The younger children are summoned to sit on their parents' knees. Astrid and her father are joined at the front by the pastor who holds both his hands in the air until a silence falls upon the hall. He welcomes everyone and thanks them for their presence on behalf of the family. Dominic has chosen not to make a speech so the pastor does it all but speaking in a slightly softer voice than the one he uses in the pulpit as he reminds them of the solemnity of this moment. Astrid is to leave the island and he invokes God's blessing on her as she seeks to make her way in a world that will seem very different to the one she has known. A child at one of the tables asks his mother a loud question and gets a shush in reply. The pastor tells Astrid that however far she travels she must never forget her family and the place that has brought her into the world, that they will always be there for her and she must make them proud. He puts a hand on her head and leads the hall in prayer, calling on God to watch over her and keep her safe until the time comes for her to return to them once more. There is a loud rumble of amen when he finishes and then, as is tradition, Dominic presents his daughter with a necklace made from shells washed up on the island's shore and whose purpose is to protect and remind the leaver of their true home. He struggles a little with the clasp as Astrid holds her hair high to try and make it easier for him and then when he gets it the hall breaks into long applause.

It is time for him to go. He wants to leave before the raucous celebrations start after the pastor has retired and the youngest children have been taken home to bed. He has no heart for any more. But he doesn't announce his departure and makes it look as if he's merely about to go and talk to someone in another part of the hall. At the door he turns to see Dominic and Astrid sharing a dance and then just before he turns away he's conscious of Anna looking at him and he doesn't know how to read what's in her eyes but hopes it isn't pity.

Outside, the night has turned cold and the stars hang far away in the deepest folds of the sky. He starts his homeward walk, stepping out more quickly as the air nips at him but no matter how far he climbs he can still hear the sound of music from down below. As always he has left the front door unlocked and the lights on – no one wants to return to a shut-up house in darkness. He needs something to warm him but knows that coffee will damage his prospects of sleep so he pours himself a small whisky and sits close to the stove. He wonders if he should have stayed longer, done his drinking in company – perhaps too he's passed up the chance of dancing with Anna and for the first time knowing what it was like to hold her.

The laptop sits open on the table. He looks at it then glances away again. He wants to see her. On this night he wants to see her more than ever. But he hesitates and leans closer to the stove as if its warmth might satisfy the need he feels. He drains the glass. When eventually he dials he gets a number-not-recognised message but he stands perfectly still and stares at the screen until slowly, and faintly at first, she finally appears. Her hair is down and looks shiny the way it does when she's just washed it. Soon she's smiling at something he's said even though he didn't know he was being funny. And the print is back again behind her – the small girl releasing a heart-shaped balloon. He sees her once more as a young child carrying a candle in the procession to mark the winter solstice. Cupping the flame to protect it from going out. All the girls' white dresses shivered by the wind. Now she's asking him for the island's news and he never knows if she enquires out of politeness or because she's interested. Whichever, he pads it out and always tries to make things sound more humorous than they probably were and he likes to tell her about the foolish things he's done so that she will stop thinking of him as her teacher and start to see him as someone as hopelessly fallible as every other living soul. When she laughs he feels a surge of pleasure but now she's fading again and there is nothing he can do to prevent it. His hand raises to shut the laptop but drops to his side.

And in her place, forming out of the fractured meeting of memory and need, comes the journey to the mainland, the boat bucking through the waves and struggling to hold its head up in the slash of rain that makes it impossible to see any glimpse of the shore. The longest journey he's ever made. On the blank screen he sees again the little bedsit she rented in a cheap part of the city, small and dismal despite her attempts to make it cheerful. A few posters and prints on the wall, a Polaroid photograph of her with her mother. Beside her single bed her mother's unfinished book. He rubs the back of his hand across his mouth. It's time to stop, to close it down. But he knows if he doesn't watch it will come back even stronger in his dreams.

So here's the nursery. He stands outside and looks through the gates, sees how good she is with the children. They flock round her like little birds, their hands pecking at her clothes for attention. Afterwards they send him a copy of the inspection report that praises the high quality of care that the young staff offers and which is the foundation of the nursery's success. In a drawer beside his bed there is a card signed by all her colleagues and drawings of her by the children. But these are not what he will see now because he's walking along the underpass, the sodium lights glowing orange, the walls scribbled with black graffiti. A bunch of flowers tied to a metal stanchion. He closes his eyes.

He remembers her pain and confusion after her mother left. How once she ran away and he couldn't find her until he discovered her crying in one of the derelict stone buildings used to smoke fish. Remembers too the day she wrote a note for Birgitta that she didn't want him to read but how she allowed him to stand watch over her as she put it in a bottle and gave it to the sea. He pours himself another drink then looks once more at the screen.

But there is only the return journey, through a sea that's exhausted itself into a temporary calm despite the fine fret of snow. He closes the laptop, lifts the shell necklace and holds it to his lips, each shell washed and given by the sea, picked by his own hands. He will speak to her tomorrow when what's left of the year's sun might still shine despite its fading strength. Already the Bear's Teeth are sharpening. And he will tell her that while all the other ghost faces homing even now in the darkness come through cables and networks, hers has returned, borne aloft on his heart and carried by the snow-flecked wind's embrace and the pull of the currents.

Heatwave

THE CITY SIMMERED IN its own juices, a sealed cauldron of electrified, motorised and human sweat. The city wore half-moon damp patches under its arms and on the buses and tube trains commuters fanned their faces with the free newspapers and avoided pressing against each other in the fear that they would stick, flesh to flesh, an instant Siamese twin with a stranger. People clutched small bottles of water like sacred amulets and the glass of every touchscreen phone was smeared and puddled with fingerprints. On television endless experts talked about global warming while the DIY stores sold out of barbecues and garden furniture. Elderly people silently expired in lonely breathless rooms to a requiem of children's voices from back gardens transformed into lidos, complete with plastic inflatable pools out of which water sloshed and lurched over the parched grass that no longer needed cutting and which was slowly turning brown like the pelt of a dying animal. In remote quarries young men died swimming in waters that were too deep and cold until someone came up with the idea of dyeing the water black. And the riot police sweltered in their RoboCop suits as petrol bombs quivered around them like red-lipped air kisses and when rivulets of sweat and fear coursed down their backs they dreamed of holidays in snow-capped mountains or on secluded beaches where they could take off every stitch of clothing and plunge into the sea's cool embrace.

In their expensive, self-cleaning, triple-glazed and electricity-supplying glass-fronted house Marcus and Daisy sat in as few of their clothes as might be considered elegant and debated the purchase of curtains. It was anathema to Marcus who fought constantly to protect his sleek white-walled temple from his wife's cluttered weakness of character that saw her, in their first year after moving in, backsliding against their agreed purity of vision and attempting to surreptitiously introduce family photographs, small ornaments and decorative touches that he dismissed as sacrilegious defacement of their home's clean lines. As he had designed the house and supervised its construction in the hills overlooking the city, he took her betrayals personally.

'The glass was supposed to keep us warm in winter and cool in summer,' Daisy said. 'It's obviously not working.'

'It worked in winter. Have you any idea how much money we saved on heating? But this is a heatwave – the highest temperature in thirty years,' he said.

'So it won't work if it's as hot as this and it could be like this every summer,' Daisy said, lifting her leg lightly off the leather settee when she felt it sticking.

It was suddenly important to her to hear him admit a failure. When none came she ended the silence by saying, 'We need curtains.'

'They'd look completely naff – they'd be completely wrong.'

'I'm not talking about the sort of curtains you're thinking of. I don't mean heavy formal curtains.'

'So what are you talking about?' he asked, his irritation obvious in his voice as he stared at the huge windows that framed a cloudless enervated sky and down below the sweltering broil of the city.

'I'm talking of voile, something light and loosely draped. White obviously.'

He glanced at her to gauge whether her last comment was intended sarcastically but she had turned her face away to concentrate on her toenails which she had recently painted a bright red that he thought a little vulgar.

'Just don't think it would work. It would break the whole line of the window and damage the view.' He heard her make a snorting noise and in an attempt to appease her and escape even the possibility of curtains, 'I could investigate air conditioning, see if you can run it off the solar panels.'

'And in the meantime we're to sit here in an oven baking?'

'I think you're exaggerating; imagine what it's like down there,' and he walked to the window and gazed out as if attempting to see the suffering the heat was causing.

The light filtered through his linen shirt and matching shorts and she saw his slimness and a body toned by the hour every day he spent punishing himself in their basement gym, before he went off to his office at the far end of the glass corridor that linked the living and sleeping areas. She had given up the gym some time ago, preferring to do a yoga class in the company of others where there was always the possibility of a shared coffee afterwards and a conversation with adults.

Angelina brought their son Theo from the play-room. When Daisy looked at her she was unhappy that the heat allowed their Italian au pair to wear shorts that showed off her willowy tanned legs and a skimpy vest revealing the top of her breasts each time she bent over their son. But she didn't know how to complain or even drop a hint when both her employers were similarly dressed and she also resented the time, even though it was technically her own, that Angelina spent in the gym. The more toned and slender the girl became the more she felt undermined in her own house. She would have found an excuse to get rid of her except that they had come to rely on her excellence at everything, from childcare to cooking, and when all was said and done in a litigious age you couldn't sack some-one because they were younger and prettier than you.

Five-year-old Theo was in his underpants and barefooted. He had just emerged from an early-afternoon nap and Angelina was still holding the damp facecloth she had used to freshen him.

'He doesn't want to put his clothes on,' Angelina said, her shoulders shrugging in an apology.

'You're too hot, Theo, aren't you,' Daisy said, reaching out her arms but looking at her husband.

Theo clambered on the settee, bounced a little, then fell forward into his mother's embrace, one that lasted only a few seconds before she gently pushed him back, repulsed a little by the clammy pulse of his body. He scampered off again towards his father but after being reminded not to put his hands on the glass ran back in the direction of the playroom slowly followed by Angelina whose flipflops quietly lisped against the white tiles.

'We should go out,' Daisy said. 'We've been cooped up here too long. Let's go out and find somewhere we can cool off.'

For some reason Marcus thought of a giant refrigeration plant where frozen carcasses hung from hooks, before turning away from the window and asking, 'Where do you suggest?'

'Let's go out to the coast and catch some sea breezes, have a swim. We can bring the beach tent for Theo, head out to Graver's Point or the nature reserve at Drayling Springs.'

'Is Angelina coming?'

'No, let's go in the convertible, drive with the roof down. There wouldn't be room after we load all our stuff,' she said, thinking only of Angelina's tanned and youthful body displayed to perfection in the black bikini she had worn when taking Theo to the swimming pool.

'You don't think we'd be better in the Jeep?' he asked, also thinking of Angelina but secretly glad to accept his wife's choice of transport. They'd have to get rid of the girl as soon as he could think of some plausible excuse. It was too much of a torment having her in the house – he thought of her, as he frequently did, on the rowing machine, gliding towards him before teasingly sliding back, the little moan of effort playing on her lips, the perfect pearls of sweat on her forehead and the tops of her shoulders glistening in the light. He thought of how right she looked in the morning without make-up and devoid of artifice, her hair pulled back simply from her face. Never ever in your own nest – he acknowledged the indisputable wisdom of it – so saw no point in having to deal with these nagging thoughts on a daily basis. And yet aesthetically she suited the house – he couldn't have someone who was overweight or unattractive spoiling the lines, the carefully created perspectives. Perhaps he could design a uniform for future help.

He glanced at his wife whose make-up was increasingly too obvious and which never seemed blended properly so it looked to his precise eye as if she was wearing a caked mask that stopped abruptly at the side of her face. And the T-shirt she was wearing stretched a little tightly so that it hinted at the swell of her stomach and the fold of flesh hugging her hips. Why didn't she use the bloody gym? It had cost enough. Yoga was all very well for flexibility but it wasn't going to keep her in shape. He wondered if she really appreciated the house or all the sacrifices and effort that had gone into making it a reality and sometimes he thought she'd be happier living in some suburban development full of mock-Georgian façades and a social round of lunch parties, golf afternoons or whatever was the current fashion.

'Are you getting changed?' he asked, trying to quietly convey that he didn't consider her present attire a winning look.

'No, I'm just going to put sun cream on and find a hat for the car.'

'We'll have to make sure Theo's well protected. Don't put the cream on him until we're ready to go in case he sits on the furniture. Are you going to make a picnic?'

His wife raised herself incrementally off the settee, slithered in her sandals towards the open-plan kitchen and started to rummage unenthusiastically in the fridge. He stared down at the city again where a lid of smog was sealing in the humidity before calling out, 'Plenty of drinks, some cold cuts, nothing too elaborate.' There was no answer. 'Shall I ask Angelina to put cream on Theo?' There was a mumble that might have been a yes so he set off towards the playroom where Theo had tumbled large amounts of toys out of the concealed cupboards and Angelina was kneeling on the central square of carpet – the only one in the house – amusing herself by building a house out of Lego. He tried not to stare at how her legs that were the colour of honey seemed to go on for ever before disappearing into the tight rim of her denim shorts.

'Angelina, we're taking Theo to the beach, would you be able to put some sun cream on him?'

'Yes, Marcus. That'll be fun, Theo, won't it?'

Theo, who didn't ever speak much, merely nodded and then drummed a brief rhythm on his stomach that his father interpreted as an expression of pleasure. When Angelina led his son to the bathroom he knelt down and looked at the house she had built. It reminded him of something out of a fairy tale with its narrow windows and turrets. He thought of the house in the story of Hansel and Gretel that seduced the two children and left them oblivious to the danger within. Theo was laughing, the type of giggling laugh he used when he was being tickled. Setting down the house he walked to the door of the bathroom and watched Angelina lathering his son with sun cream. It reminded him of a Christmas turkey being basted and he laughed too when Theo squirmed and protested. He tried not to look at the jiggle of her breasts.

In the car all three of them wore hats as the roof peeled itself back and folded elegantly and almost silently out of sight. After making sure that Theo was safely strapped in the back with his lidded plastic cup of water, and having gone through a lengthy check-list with his wife, he looked up at the windows and tried to imagine what they would be like with curtains but what he saw was Angelina waving them off.

'You don't think we should take Angelina?' he asked, weakening.

'There's not enough room in the back with the coolbox and all the beach stuff. If we were using the Jeep she could have come. She'll probably be glad of a few hours off.'

'Just seems a bit mean.'

'Perhaps some time on our own with Theo wouldn't be a bad thing.'

He felt obliged to nod and as the car set off they caught the first breeze but soon the sun was strong on the back of their necks and they argued about whether they should put the roof back up. In the end they decided that they should and relied on the air conditioning to keep them cool. They skirted the edge of the city then turned away from it towards the coast but many others had sought the same escape route and soon they were snarled in slow-moving traffic. The air conditioning didn't seem to be working fully but when she lowered her window he complained that she was letting hot air in. It irritated him the way she liked to make a song and dance about anything malfunctioning as if everything was personally his fault or the result of some poor judgement on his part

So the journey to the beach took an hour longer than it should have and when they arrived the car parks were full and traffic trying to access them through the narrow entrance became gridlocked with cars trying to exit. On either side of the road vehicles had been simply abandoned and these too restricted the flow. It had been a mistake to come – he should never have listened to her and his irritation increased when Theo dropped his cup of water and then kept trying to get out of his seat. There was the sound of an ambulance approaching – probably someone with heatstroke, he thought, or even a drowning – its lights and wail forcing a way through on the wrong side of the road and as it passed he suddenly indicated and shot out in its wake then kept going when the ambulance turned down to the beach.

'Well that puts ambulance chasing into a new light,' Daisy said, shaking her head in embarrassment.

'If we hadn't got out of that jam we'd have stewed here all afternoon.'

'What if the police had seen you? I don't think they would have been too impressed.'

He didn't reply but when faced with an open road he drove quickly. All of them needed to get out of the car that had started to feel claustrophobic.

'So where are we going?' she asked as she flipped off her sandals and placed her feet on the dashboard.

'There's other, smaller beaches along this stretch of coast. We'll find one of those. And it'll be less crowded.'

He looked again at the bright red of her toenails and how the colour only served to accentuate the whiteness of her legs. He saw too how there were thin threadlines of veins on her thigh as if she had been scratched by a cat and it struck him that she wasn't going to age well. The thought made him nervous and he decided he would mention the gym to her at some point during the afternoon, perhaps float the idea of a proper holiday as an inducement to get in shape before she slipped too far and there was no way back. There was a small grease stain on her shorts – sun cream perhaps. As he drove the sky unfurled before them, featureless and stretched tight so that clouds and rain seemed a distant memory of a different era. He turned his head constantly to roads on his right in the hope of seeing something that would lead them down to the sea but all the entrances had Private and No Through Road signs posted in aggressive writing.

'Perhaps we should just go home,' Daisy said as she looked over her shoulder to check on Theo and found him asleep, his mouth pressed open in a little pout.

'Is he sleeping?' he asked.

'Yes, and he'll probably be in poor form when he wakes up.'

Then in desperation to avoid having to concede the expedition as a humiliating failure he turned off the main road and followed a laneway that apart from the thin central line of grass was rutted bare earth and which curved between fenced fields.

'Marcus, this looks like someone's farm to me. We shouldn't be here.'

'There was no sign and anyway there isn't any-where to turn. We'll just see where it takes us and if it ends up somewhere private we'll just apologise, and turn round.'

The car bumped heavily over some thickly baked ridges of earth and he slowed down knowing it wouldn't be a good way for Theo to wake. Feathery ferns brushed against the sides of the car and then they reached a clearing that had a metal shed, open at the front and which contained only a rusted trac-tor and a few bales of withered hay. He kept going but felt increasingly nervous as they passed a derelict cottage with its slate roof collapsed in and buddleia and willowherb growing out of every available crev-ice, then a widened section of lane that had huge tyres piled on top of each other on the verge and where the pointed tops of the creosoted poles were impaled with empty beer cans. But that nervousness was temporarily forgotten as the sea suddenly came into view.

'There you go,' he said, holding his hand out palm upwards to the windscreen as if making an offering of it to her while they slowly negotiated the pebbled entrance.

'If the suspension survives.'

'And all to ourselves,' he added while thinking that it wouldn't win any beauty awards.

The part-sand, part-shingle beach backed on to fields where the knots of barbed wire were tufted with shards of wool or shredded black polythene. A thick swathe of slimy seaweed spotted with washed-up bits of plastic shucked against the rim of shingle. He thought the aesthetics might improve if he drove further down and turned the car at an angle to their entrance but a few minutes later they stuck in soft sand. He tried to power out of it, the engine screaming, and when this failed attempted to reverse but if anything they sagged deeper. Turning off the engine he got out and with hands on hips studied the problem. The front wheels were bedded in sand and when he crouched down he saw that underneath the car it was rucked up close to the undercarriage. At that moment he could think of no better response than to walk a small circle of himself and repeat the word shit over and over.

When Daisy got out and viewed the situation he said, 'We should have brought the Jeep. If we'd brought the Jeep this would never have happened.'

'If you'd gone to a proper beach we wouldn't be stuck.'

'This is a proper beach. There's sand and sea. Sand and sea make it a beach as far as I understand.'

'It's not a proper beach,' she insisted. 'We're the only people here and it doesn't look clean to me.'

He wanted to say that perhaps he should have organised a team of environmental cleaners to prepare it to her satisfaction but instead merely stared at the wheels stuck in the sand.

'We'll have to dig it out,' he told her, waving his hand at a fly that flitted persistently about him. None of the heat had gone out of the day and instead of cooling breezes blowing in from the sea there was a broiling fury that mixed with the briny smell made him think he was standing beside a giant cauldron of steaming soup. 'Get me Theo's spade.'

'Do you want the bucket as well?'

He glared at her but it didn't look as if she was being sarcastic and when she handed him the blue plastic spade he dropped to his knees and began to scoop the sand away from the wheels. The spade was pitifully inadequate but he couldn't think of anything else to use and so he went on digging down and throwing the sand to the side. Then he started to use his hands. The surface of the sand was hot against his skin and the grit and grains lodged under his fingernails. Soon he felt a stripe of sweat down his spine and the back of his neck was getting burnt but he kept on clearing until opposite each wheel he had amassed a hump of sand. He paused only to drink from the bottle of water Daisy handed him, gulping it so quickly that some spilled down his front and blended with the spots of sweat on his shirt.

'Is Theo still sleeping?' he asked.

'For the moment at least but he's bound to stir soon. And he'll be as crabbit as hell.'

'We should have brought Angelina.'

'There wasn't room. Why do you keep on about her coming?'

'She could have helped to dig and push,' he said, emptying some of the water over his head and resolving not to mention her again.

Then when he had finished digging he told his wife to get in the car but not to do anything until he gave her the word. The single fly had been joined by others and he swiped at them with the spade in a way that made him look as if he was conducting an invisible orchestra.

'When I give the word, put it into second gear and steer towards the shingle. Don't accelerate too much – just gently until we're out but when it's out don't stop until you reach the stones.'

He went to the back of the car and got ready to push. The metal was hot against his hands, the reflected heat a flurry across his eyes. Daisy turned on the engine. 'Gently! Gently! Don't rev her.' Then he counted down and as the car moved forward slightly started to shove with both hands. 'Keep going!' As it came almost immediately to a stop Daisy pressed her foot harder on the accelerator but produced nothing more than a scream of engine and spinning wheels that flayed him with sand. 'Stop! Stop!' he shouted but it was too late and they had simply shifted a few feet into new and deeper sand.

He swore loudly and then hurried to the front of the car to survey the damage.

'I told you to go lightly on the accelerator,' he said, 'not rev it to hell.'

'It wasn't moving. You weren't pushing hard enough or we need more people to help.'

'We'll have to dig again,' he said and swore. 'And you'll have to help – it's too much for me to do on my own.'

She got out of the car as Theo started to stir then opened his eyes and looked about with an expression of confusion. He told them he wanted out and no amount of persuasion or bribery would convince him to stay in his seat. So Daisy lifted him down and together they set up the little beach tent a few metres away for him to play in and when he demanded his spade they had to explain that for the moment it was needed. Daisy used it to start scooping and dragging sand from around one of the front wheels and Marcus worked on the other, using his hands to dig, working frantically like a dog about to bury a bone. His shirt felt sodden with sweat, sticking to his back like a second skin. A fly rattled and buzzed in his ear. Theo was starting to demand his spade again. He thought of Angelina lying on top of her bed with her brown legs stretched across the white duvet and then on the rowing machine pulling herself slowly towards him, her eyes wide and her slightly open mouth letting out that little rush of breath.

'We need something to give the wheels traction,' he said, shaking his head free from the attention of the fly. Then despite Theo's protests he took the plastic bucket and started to fill it to the brim with stones before layering them in front of the wheels.

'What about the car mats?' Daisy said as she inspected a broken nail, trying to soften the edge with her teeth.

He shrugged as if dismissive of the idea but almost immediately removed them from the car and placed them on top of the bed of stones. He wanted to be the one behind the wheel but knew he needed to push and so he gave Daisy a rerun of his previous instructions. As he stood close to her he was conscious that either his or her deodorant had stopped working and her face was oiled with sweat.

'Do you understand?' he asked, already deciding that it would be her fault if they didn't make it out this time. He gave Theo his spade back, ignoring his son's complaint that he had bent it, and made sure the child was far enough away from the car. But almost as soon as they tried a second time the attempt collapsed into failure. It was never going to work. He knew then that the only way out was for more hands pushing, or a tow, but the beach was deserted and so he walked to the front of the car and slumped back against the engine.

'What are we going to do?' Daisy asked, blowing a strand of hair away from her face. A damp patch stretched between her breasts.

'We need help.'

'So where are we going to get it, Marcus?'

He took out his phone but there was no signal and when she tried, it produced the same result.

'We don't even know where we are anyway,' she said as she threw the phone on to the front seat. 'And, Marcus, I hate to tell you this but I think the tide's coming in.'

He straightened and stared at the sea in the hope that she was wrong and then registered where the line of seaweed bevelled the beach behind them. He repeated the word shit again until Theo started to echo him, beating his upturned bucket with the spade in rhythm even when they both rebuked him. Suddenly he felt washed out, drained of ideas and strength, so when his wife said she was going to look for help his only response was the briefest of nods. He watched her as she walked off, the initial energy of her stride soon hobbled by the softness of the sand until the laborious rise and fall of her shoulders made it look as if she was forcing each step. He went over to Theo and sat down beside him. His son was making sandcastles but had not yet succeeded in creating a perfect one, his impatience making him lift the bucket away too quickly so they slid sideways, and Marcus took the bucket from him and showed him how to compact the sand and press it down with the spade before giving the base a final spank and then slowly turning it over.

'There you go, look at that,' he said proudly.

'Build a house,' Theo said.

And so for the next twenty minutes they built a castle together, constructing four walls with turrets on each corner and an arched gate that they pushed through with their fingers so that it opened into the inner courtyard. There they formed an inner square building and decorated it with sticks for flags. At intervals he glanced up at the tide and wondered if his wife would ever return or whether she had simply walked into the great beyond in pursuit of a new life. He had the idea of decorating the walls of the castle with shells but decided it would look tacky. It struck him that things hadn't been good between them for some time and the truth was he only had her word for it that she was going to yoga or anywhere else in the afternoons for that matter. And if they did get rid of Angelina they'd save money and she'd have to spend proper time with Theo like a proper mother should.

'Where's Mummy?' asked Theo.

'She's gone to get help,' he said but the words didn't fully convince so it was with some relief that twenty minutes later he saw an open-back SUV bumping along the beach towards them with Daisy perched in the back and he assumed the young man's arm resting on her shoulder was to prevent her falling off. She waved and his gratitude made him feel bad about his previous thoughts. When he stood up to brush the sand from his clothes he almost trod on part of the house they had built until Theo's scream warned him off.

There were two men inside the SUV and when they got out he could see they were young – probably mid-twenties – and, including the one who was helping Daisy down, all hewn from the same block. Tanned and weatherbeaten, two of them wearing white vests, the one who had been in the back with Daisy bare-chested. One of them smoking. They stared at him and then at the car when he greeted them, not really responding apart from a cursory, almost imperceptible movement of their heads. Then the one who had been in the back with Daisy smirked at him and shook his head slowly as if he was laughing at a private joke while his dark eyes skittered about like the flies that circled them all.

He shuffled uncomfortably, not sure how best to handle it, so he started by making fun of himself before anyone else could. 'Pretty stupid,' he said, 'definitely not the best idea I've ever had. I appreciate you coming like this. We're in a bit of a hole.'

'You're in a hole all right,' the driver said, pressing his toe against the part of the tyre not hidden by the sand.

'And the tide's starting to turn,' the bare-chested offered, still smirking.

The smoker was touring the car inspecting it and Marcus felt increasingly nervous. It felt as if they were far from civilisation and he didn't like the look of any of these guys who were scrutinising him in a manner that wasn't polite. And if they weren't heavy-weights then they were tightly muscled in a scrawny way and he guessed they worked outside most of the year. He didn't know where this was going.

'The tide's coming in, guys. Any chance of a pull-out so we can get this kid back home?' he said, pointing to Theo.

'Kid looks happy,' the bare-chested one said but staring at Daisy rather than Theo. His skin was the same colour as the oiled wooden fence posts.

'There's a problem,' the driver said, pressing his foot harder against the tyre.

'A problem?'

'Yes, a problem. This is a private beach. You shouldn't be here.'

'I'm very sorry,' Marcus said. 'I didn't see any sign and I kinda got lost.'

'There's a sign on the road,' the smoker said, flicking his cigarette butt in a wheeling arc. 'Says "Private Property, Keep Out". Maybe you can't read.'

'I just didn't see it. I'm really sorry,' he said and he glanced at Daisy for help.

'The guys'll help us, won't you?' she said, smiling at them and her hand pulling the top of her T-shirt away from her skin.

'Well it's not straightforward seeing you're trespassing,' the driver said.

'We'd pay you for your trouble of course,' Marcus said, increasingly anxious to cut to the quick of the matter and already starting to take his wallet out of his pocket. 'Would this cover it?' he asked as he held up a twenty.

The driver shook his head before half-turning to the sea and saying, 'Another twenty minutes and your car'll be floating. And getting it out won't be easy.'

Marcus produced another twenty and a ten. 'It's all I have,' he said and then when the additional money failed to achieve a result asked Daisy what she had.

'Let's see your purse, Daisy,' the bare-chested one said, his skin sheened and leathery.

Going to the front passenger seat she pulled it out and frantically searched until she found a twenty.

'Seventy – that's all we have,' Marcus said. 'Will you do it for seventy?' And he held the notes in the air where they were immediately inspected by flies.

'Have to do, but you're getting it on the cheap,' the driver said, stepping forward and taking the money then stuffing it in the back pocket of his shorts. 'Put the kid in the back – when we pull you out don't stop until you're off this beach.'

Daisy lifted the resisting Theo into his seat and strapped him in despite the fact that he was hitting her with his spade and squirming like a fish on a hook.

'You get in the car,' the man told Daisy. 'When the rope goes taut put her into second gear and gently ease her forward.'

Daisy got in the car as ordered and then Marcus watched her bare-chested admirer lean in over her and repeat the instructions she had just been given while playing with the back of her hair. The smoker took a rope out of the SUV and attached it to both vehicles and then the three of them took up position at the back of the car, their bodies close as they taut-ened against the metal. He was in the middle and conscious of the smell on either side of him – he wasn't sure whether it was alcohol, the car's exhaust, sweat, or a mixture of all three. Perhaps the smell came from him. He wanted to be far from this place and these people, to be at home in his shower with its enormous head powering it all away. He wanted to see Angelina. He tried to imagine her but couldn't conjure anything but the briefest image.

There was the sound of two engines, a high-pitched whine of resistance as the back end of the car squirmed, threatened to stall then slithered bit by bit out of its trap and on to the firmer sand and the stony stretch of the beach. The connecting rope was thrown off and Daisy was heading resolutely to the laneway that had brought them there and as he stood watching her he thought that she wouldn't stop but leave him to his fate. A fly struck up a fascination with his eye. He tried to blink it clear but it persisted until he used both hands to beat it away. The two men walked slowly to the SUV and the smoker started to coil the rope over his shoulder. He couldn't see his car now but hoped it was waiting for him in the lane.

'Thanks, guys,' he called and raised his hand in what was supposed to be an expression of gratitude and farewell, then when it was ignored glanced down at Theo's house and was sorry that the tide would sweep it away even though he thought its proportions didn't look right. The walk to the laneway was lengthened by the sense of shame he felt and by the laughter coming from the SUV where his one glance back had revealed them opening cans of beer.

'Inbred fuckwits,' he repeated aloud to himself and a little of his shame was absorbed by the words and with each step he constructed spiralling scenarios that involved increasingly violent retribution and gibbering smirk-free pleas for mercy. He could see the car and hear Theo's cries that had inflated into a full-blown tantrum. His relief at seeing that she hadn't left him was tempered by an awareness that as soon as he reached her he would be confronted once more by his failures in all their humiliating reality. So his walk slowed into a trudge and he cursed the train of flies that followed him.

When he arrived at the car Daisy was behind the wheel and she didn't look at him or speak until as he stood waiting for her to shift into the passenger seat she said, 'I'm driving.' He walked round and got in, his shirt immediately sticking to the back of the seat, and he leaned forward as he put on his seatbelt. Theo had paused for breath before starting up another red-faced squall. They edged forward, the car moving slowly over the rutted tracks, and from time to time he glanced sideways at her but she stared impassively and silently ahead. He wanted to say something that would make it right but couldn't think of anything so just as they emerged on to the main road under his breath he said, 'Inbred fuckwits.' She braked hard, looked at him for the first time.

'Do you want to go back and tell them that?' she asked.

He didn't answer and instead squirmed back into his seat then tried to think of the coolness of Angelina's languid body but all that came was the image of a giant industrialised refrigerator unit with yellow, fat-seamed carcasses of beef dangling from metal hooks.

'I'm getting curtains in the morning,' she told him and she was telling him other things as well and her words buzzed around his head like the flies on the beach until gradually they got lost in Theo's crying. He wondered if the waves had reached the sand house they had built and were even at this moment ebbing away its walls. Then in his mind the ice-spangled carcasses started to move on their mechanical rails. And he was standing in the middle of the giant room on a concrete floor patterned with drains and when he reached out his hand as they slowly passed, there was only a frozen unyielding solidity and not a single trace of the softness of flesh.

Man Overboard

NO ONE WANTED TO take Dougie but each of us owed him and we all knew that. After our weekly five-a-side on the AstroTurf we could have chipped in the reasons for our reluctance, in between recriminations about who had missed a sitter or who hadn't bothered to track back and mark. But at the end of the day it all boiled down to the fact that Dougie was depressed and depressed people aren't the best company on a lads' weekend. Our annual weekend away had become a tradition and was generally taken in May unless something important intervened such as births, deaths and Champions League finals between certain teams. Dougie hadn't been on either of the last two trips and if I'm honest we hadn't missed him.

Me, Terry, Spencer and Dougie had been born on the same estate and attended the same schools. Only Dougie hadn't gone to uni but as we stumbled into dull careers in quantity surveying and the civil service he had been the one who seemed most securely launched into moneymaking. He'd caught a wave, striking out on his own building business just as the market went crazy, throwing up his houses ever more quickly and then reinvesting the profits in sites. When the recession hit, the sites were worth less than half of what he'd paid for them and before long the bank was knocking on the door of the Ponderosa he had built for himself and Charlene on the edge of Belfast. In the seeming blink of an eye he was back on the estate in the same street he had started in, his business collapsed into nothing more than whatever handyman work he could find. Maybe it was that heartbreak or the humiliation that brought on his depression – I don't know – but he never talked about it and I suppose we never asked. What we did at the beginning at least was try and help in other ways – encourage him to keep on the football, invite him and Charlene over to barbecues etc. But when eventually she didn't respond we stopped making the effort, glad of the excuse.

'We'll have to take him,' Spencer said as he examined a scrape on his shin.

'He was well late,' Terry offered as he too assessed the injury.

'The bastard makes a habit of it. But long runs the fox.'

'So you're doing a Jackie Charlton, putting his name in your little black book,' I said but more interested in the ache in my lower back than his reply.

We knew however that he was right about Dougie because there was no escaping the fact we all owed him. He had done the brickwork for my conservatory a few years back, loaded all Terry's furniture in his van on his frequent moves between various women and floored Spence's roof space. And although he'd never admitted it there was probably another reason why Terry owed him because if the rumours were right he had poked Dougie's wife in the guise of offering sympathy, which as far as I was concerned was kicking a man when he was down. But Terry was at least consistent in this because for as long as I had known him he seemed to believe that the answers to most of life's problems, including his own, could be found in a shag.

Charlene had asked my Anita if we'd include Dougie and the mixture of debts owed, a wife's urging and our collective guilt ensured that we'd do the decent thing. So on a Friday night we collected him from his house and tried to generate appropriate enthusiasm when he appeared at the front door. The first thing we noticed as he ambled towards us was that he had grown a beard – I'm not sure if he had made a conscious decision to grow it or he had simply stopped shaving but it made him look different and I didn't know if that was good or not. Charlene was standing at the front door waving to us like she was seeing her boy off on his first day at school – I guess the weekend break was as much for her as him – and as we waved back I tried to catch some change in Terry's expression but he's a professional and there wasn't a flicker of anything even approaching embarrassment.

'All right, lads,' Dougie said as he clambered into the back seat.

'All right, Dougie,' we chorused.

Then I broke the moment's slightly awkward silence by asking him how it was going.

'Pretty good, Phil,' he said and we all nodded our heads to show that was indeed good.

Then we started to talk but it was obvious that we were just talking to prevent a silence filling the car and it felt like the conversation you engage in while waiting somewhere with a bunch of strangers. Dougie mostly just stared out his window until we tried to draw him in. So did he watch the Clásico? Where did he stand on who was best – Messi or Ronaldo? Had he any work on? How was Charlene's new job panning out? All of which he answered briefly as if the answers weren't really relevant to him, almost as if he was talking about a third party. Then suddenly he said, 'I don't have a fishing rod.'

'No worries, Dougie,' Spencer told him, 'the hotel supplies them. It's part of the package, along with a temporary licence.'

'That's good,' he said. 'Won't catch many fish without a rod.'

We pretended to laugh and then I wondered should I put us out of our misery by turning on some music. But I let my hand fall away when Dougie said, 'Remember when we used to catch smicks in the park?' And then we all chipped in.

'We'd spend the whole day in wellies and catch them in jam jars.'

'What about the day Fat Sam tripped over an old bit of bicycle and fell on his face.'

We all laughed for real.

'A bloody tsunami it was and then he told his ma he had been pushed and she came round screaming blue murder.'

'The big wuss. He could spoof for Ireland.'

'What's he doing now anyway?'

'Last time I heard he was calling himself a pastor and had a church – mission-hall type of thing.'

'He'll be good for baptisms then,' Dougie said and we all looked at him and laughed with what I think was relief.

We sat back on our seats and I started to think that things might just work out OK. I was keen not to let it slip away. 'Do you remember when we'd caught loads of the buggers we put them in an old sink at the bottom of Mozzy's garden and when we came back his cat had done for half of them?'

It went on like this for a while until eventually our nostalgic reminiscences dried up and we lapsed into silence once more but the awkward edge had gone and so I settled back and concentrated on my driving. Every so often we played out the ritual game of threes we'd been playing for as long as I can remember. At random someone would say a name and a subject and whoever was asked had to name the best three, or sometimes the worst three. So our best three players of all time? Best, Blanchflower, Jennings. The three best singles out of the North? 'Teenage Kicks', 'Alternative Ulster', 'Moondance'. Sometimes someone would offer an answer that either deliberately or unintentionally provoked an argument. No one threw Dougie anything difficult and if I remember right all he was asked for was the three best James Bonds so he didn't have to think too much.

*

The hotel had direct access to the lake and before removing our cases from the car we walked along the jetty and stared out across the water that was still silver-plated by the day's sharp light. As was naturally expected when boys encounter water, we had at least one pretend shove off the edge and various references to *Lake Placid* and thirty-foot-long man-eating crocodiles. Everything felt good and I told myself it would all play out just as it always had done and we had the safety net of a shared past that we could drop into at the slightest encouragement or when things looked edgy. I wondered sometimes why we rarely talked about ourselves in the present and never in the future. But I suppose if we rehashed the same old memories and tales of derring-do and minor disasters it kept that bond secure and meant we didn't have to think too hard or drift into uncertain places.

Our booking had Terry and Spencer sharing a twin room – we had tossed for it and I had lost but in a concession to my disappointment and as a compromise to my request for a best out of three, they had suggested getting two singles for me and Dougie and telling him those were the only rooms the hotel had left. My room looked out over the lake and as the light slowly faded in intensity a thin mist smoked low over the water's surface. There was a small boat coursing towards the jetty, its spuming wake almost immediately consumed by the mist, and I was suddenly glad that our morning's fishing trip would be led by someone experienced.

We took our evening meal in the hotel's restaurant and everything was fine, right down to Terry flirting with the waitresses, and we'd already got the first few jars in.

'I'm not really supposed to drink,' Dougie said as he started his second pint. 'Not with the meds and all.'

'You're on your holidays,' Spencer said, 'and we'll look after you.'

We all clinked our glasses and then Terry proposed a toast to tomorrow's catch.

'It's a pity they don't come already battered,' Dougie said as he held up a piece of cod on his fork and as with every joke he made we did our best to show we enjoyed it.

After the meal the options were to book a taxi into town or take up residence in the hotel bar. It had started to rain lightly and, glad of the excuse not to venture forth into the unknown, we settled on the latter. Dougie seemed to have forgotten his earlier reservations about mixing alcohol with his meds and when I gently reminded him he simply said, 'In for a penny, in for a pound.' And so we sailed merrily on but Terry didn't even have the excuse of being under the influence when he decided it would be helpful to quiz Dougie about his condition and, assuming his compassionate face, asked in a plausible whisper of sincerity, 'So, Dougie, what's it like?'

'What's what like?'

'Being depressed.'

'For fuck's sake, Terry,' I said, remembering the time when we were seventeen and I had smacked him when he had crossed the line and wondering if I was going to have to do it again.

'No, it's all right, Phil. They keep telling me it's good to talk – I don't mind – and if anyone's entitled to know it's you guys.'

'You don't have to,' Spencer said and I nodded in support.

'No, it's OK. Ask whatever you want.'

'So what's it like?' Terry asked again, leaning forward as if he was about to hear confession.

'It's not good, Terry, it's not good.'

Terry nodded slowly, suggesting he understood, before saying, 'Sometimes I get pissed off, feel really down for a while, like that time I did the promotion interviews and lost out to some twat in accounts.'

'It's not like that,' Dougie said, taking a sip of his beer and wiping his mouth with the back of his hand as if preparing himself for whatever he was about to say. 'It's not like being pissed off or feeling down for a while – it's something else, something else entirely. Know what I mean?'

'Not really.'

Dougie thought a bit and I could feel my growing unease making me look for a safe way out but already it was too late.

'Think of an egg timer,' Dougie said, setting down his glass. 'One of those old ones that you turn upside down and all the insides slowly drain out. That's what it's like, Terry.' He lifted his glass, stared at it and for a second I thought he was going to let it drain over the table but instead said, 'When it all drains away there's just this empty space. Empty as fuck.'

'Shit,' said Terry and for a moment it sounded as if he might have understood.

'But the drugs help, don't they?' Spencer asked.

'Mostly, mostly. They're supposed to restore your chemical balance. But it's never as simple as that.'

'What do you mean?' Terry pursued.

'Well, every drug you stick in your body has side effects. And not always ones you wanted.'

'Did it make you grow that beard?' Spencer asked and we all almost laughed.

'For a start it kills your libido,' Dougie said and we stopped almost laughing.

I heard Terry say, 'Shit,' before he inevitably chased it like a greyhound after a rabbit.

'How bad?'

'Total blank. Gone AWOL – it's the drugs.'

'What sort of bloody drugs are those?' asked Terry, who looked as if he had just encountered his worst nightmare. 'Without exception?'

'Without exception.'

'Miss World in a thong?'

'No.'

'The Kardashian sisters?'

'All of them at the same time?'

'Yes.'

'Even if you added in the mother it's still a no.'

Dougie shook his head slowly and I could feel my fist clenching like it did that day before it connected to Terry's teenage chin. Why didn't he just come out and call him Mr Limp Dick?

'Terry, we get the picture,' Spencer said and there was a moment's silence as we all settled back to our drinks. And as the silence seemed even worse than what preceded it he offered, 'Churchill called it the Black Dog.'

'It's a bitch all right and it's had its teeth sunk into my arse. Arse and balls, all at once.'

There was nothing could be said to that and without even the distraction of needing to get in the next round we sat and tried not to look at each other. And in those seconds I remembered Dougie back in the days when he was light and his blond hair permanently tousled and a smile that seemed permanently pressed on his lips, never giving a toss about school or authority, always up for a laugh. On the last day of school doing wheelies across the playing fields on his patched up motorbike, its exhaust piping black smoke across the wide-eyed first years who had halted their game to stand motionless in their white T-shirts. Dougie who had once managed to progress to an old banger that let us cruise the estate and feel like young Springsteens, momentarily replacing bonfires and drumbeats with the dream of hot New Jersey nights. I wanted to say something to him but I didn't know what it was and each of us slumped back into the seats and held our glasses tightly in front of our chests like shields.

After a while Dougie said he was knackered and was going to bed so he could be up and fresh in the morning. We all nodded to signal that it was a good idea but when he stood up he was a little unsteady on his feet and so I told him I wanted to get my phone out of my room and with that lie was able to see he got to his room all right. At his door I touched him lightly on his back, felt the hollow between his shoulder blades and wished him a good night's sleep and when I went back down there was another round of drinks in and the bar was filled with the noise of a hen party that had just arrived.

'Dougie all right?' Spencer asked.

'Would you look at the state of that,' Terry said, glancing over my shoulder. 'They're already halfway gone.'

'He's fine,' I said, staring at Terry.

'They look like children, Terry. Except for the bride to be and she's a bit of a heifer.'

'An eight-pinter at least, Spencer. Maybe more in bright light,' Terry said. 'The town must be dead if they've ended up here.'

'How many pints have you had?' I asked.

'Just the four.'

'Perhaps a good time to stop. Booze and boats don't mix well.' And then looking round, I said, 'Anyone but not the bride to be.'

'And not in the room,' Spencer said. 'If you get lucky it'll have to be a knee-trembler.'

But it all felt a bit desperate. We were stranded on the wrong side of forty and the talk and the football seemed increasingly like a slightly sad attempt to hold on to something that had already slipped away. I was suddenly embarrassed for us. There was a scream of laughter as the girls played a drinking game and it sounded shrill, sharp-edged, and I wanted the calm quiet of the lake. And I knew that even if I had wanted to – which I didn't – I couldn't pull so much as a Christmas cracker. Not any more.

'I'm going outside for a breath of fresh air,' I told them, then finished my drink while declining the offer of another.

The lake or the lough – I never quite understood which it was and geography was never my strong point – had cast off its mist as quickly as it had come and the water was lulled into almost a still-ness, the gentle swell breaking against the jetty in no more than a whisper. And it was a stillness that I liked and which made returning to the bar a less attractive option. I thought we should have gone to Prague or Barcelona where there were plenty of things for us to see and do rather than this choice of venue where inevitably we were going to sit in one bar or the other, drink too much, and either turn morose or unnaturally happy. They were probably wondering what I was doing and I didn't have the excuse of having a smoke. I wanted to skim some-thing in the water but there was nothing I could use. In the distance were some of the islands that littered the lough and I knew from having glanced at the material in my room that on some of these there were ruins of monasteries surviving from the Middle Ages. A pair of swans skirted reeds edging the shore.

But I couldn't drag it out much longer and when I returned to the bar there was still the high-pitched squeals of laughter and shouts of encouragement as a young woman in a pink tutu and fairy wings downed some drink the colour of paraffin. Terry and Spencer sat watching them but they felt separated from the party by something greater than mere distance.

'Thought you'd gone for a swim,' Terry said but not taking his eyes off the young women the way a cat looks at a goldfish in a bowl.

'I saw two swans.'

'Listen to Bill Oddie. I hope this weekend isn't going to turn into bloody *Nature Watch*,' Spencer said. 'And what about Dougie?'

'He's OK.'

'We're going to have to babysit him all weekend,' Spencer said.

No one answered for a while and I knew it was too easy to think that it was Dougie who was scudding the weekend but already I suspected it was something else and wasn't sure if we'd ever go away again.

'I hear Cracow is a good trip,' Spencer eventually offered as if having read my thoughts. 'Cheap, good clubs and you can do a tour of Auschwitz.'

'Yeah and we'll take Dougie. A tour of a concentration camp will really help him see things in a better light,' scoffed Terry.

'It's history and history isn't always cheerful,' replied Spencer.

I wondered how long I would have to sit and pretend I was enjoying myself before I could safely head for bed without risking being called a fader, a lapper or something worse. I was starting to suffer a lower back pain and I didn't know if it was the football or the long drive to the lakes or a combination of both. And I began to think of the strange empty bed that was waiting for me and wishing I was in my own with the snuggled warmth of Anita pressing the pain away.

A male stripper dressed as a fireman arrived for the bride to be. Everything was a cliché, nothing had any dignity. But it was my get-out-of-jail card and I rolled my eyes and made my excuses.

In the morning we all turned up for breakfast on time and Dougie seemed perfectly normal apart from having the continental while we all went for the full fry, baked beans and all. Terry flirted with the waitress again and I suddenly realised he wasn't flirting with the young Polish woman serving us, so much as flirting with himself and how he wanted to think of himself.

'Spencer says Cracow is a very nice city,' he said as she delivered a second rack of toast.

'Very nice. Very old.'

'We're thinking of going next year. You want to come and show us the sights?'

'I'm too busy here,' she answered, smiling then reddening slightly before making her escape from someone who was old enough to be her father.

When we went outside the morning was already warm and we were all dressed pretty much the same – T-shirts, shorts, trainers and sunglasses. Spencer's red graze on his shin leered up at us like a lipsticked grin. I alone wore a fleece in respect of my back complaint. On the jetty we met our boatman/captain/guide who introduced himself as Alex and shook each of our hands. The old man and the sea all right – he was probably in his sixties, with a head of tight hair and every part of his exposed skin suggested he had been left out in the sun too long. But his boat the *Lucky Star* was pleasingly comfortable and as well as having baited lines ready for us there was an ice-filled coolbox with cans of beer and the packed lunches that were all part of the hotel deal.

On board he gave us a safety drill and told Terry off for scrolling through his mobile phone while he was talking. 'Best to give this your full attention,' he said, 'just in case you need to put some of it into practice.' When he wasn't looking Terry rolled his eyes at me and for a second it felt as if we were all back in school with a strict teacher. But it didn't dampen our enthusiasm for long and soon Dougie was asking Alex about his boat and grilling him about its engine as we headed out into the island-studded waters and it began to feel like an adventure – an adventure that might just render the weekend a success.

And despite everything we caught fish. It was almost like the hotel package had arranged for them to obligingly jump on our hooks. Fish are fish to me but as they walloped on board after squirming and threshing Alex identified them as brown trout and one scarily large pike before he unhooked them, allowing us to take turns holding them briefly for photos, then gave them back to the water. I didn't like the slimy squirm of them in my hands, wanted to touch them as little as necessary, but the boys were in their element, whooping loudly when they felt that tug on their line. And when Terry caught an eel – a slithering nothing of an eel – we all gave him stick, even Dougie, and when Alex wasn't looking we made it suitably vulgar.

The light was bright on the water as we enjoyed some cold beers and when Alex declined one Terry started to wind him up by asking what his three favourite-tasting fish were. After he answered with 'Wild salmon, hake and sea bass', Terry said, 'Surely, Alex, battered cod has to be in the top three.' Alex looked at him and squinted his eyes under his hooded brows before saying, 'You should have taken that wee skitter of an eel home with you and cooked it for your tea.'

I tried not to laugh out loud so it sounded like a schoolboy snigger, all slithery like the fish whose smell was still on my hands. Terry's non-response made it clear he knew he'd been done. Then after an hour when the fish had grown weary offering themselves up to our hooks we had our lunches as Alex toured us round some of the islands.

'I like it here,' Dougie said. 'It's really peaceful. Maybe I should get a boat, not as big as this, something smaller and cheaper. Sail it.'

We all looked at him but no one seemed to know if this was a good idea or not so we all just nodded vaguely.

'You guys up for it?' he persisted.

I guess stuck in a boat for hours with Dougie's depression didn't exactly appeal to us as ideal leisure time but not wanting to snuff out any glimmer of future recovery we did our best to echo each other's enthusiasm. Then as suddenly as this future enthusiasm had puffed up on Dougie's lips it slipped away again. 'Don't suppose by the time the bank's finished with me I'll be able to own so much as a rowing boat.'

'You don't need a boat to go fishing, Dougie,' I said.

'That's right,' Spencer agreed. 'There's lots of places you can go fishing at home – all you need is a rod.'

Dougie nodded in a half-hearted way, then after a few minutes went and stood in the bow of the boat.

We went back to scoffing our sandwiches and drinking beer, turning to look at the island that we were sailing close to while talking about possible activities for the coming evening.

'Dougie seems to be doing a *Titanic* re-enactment,' Terry said a few minutes later, 'without Kate Winslet.'

We all stared. Something wasn't right. I think it was the way he was standing, his body stiff and his shoulders looking as if there was still a hanger under his T-shirt. I called his name and he turned and waved to us, then just as in that second we relaxed he turned away again and jumped into the water. There was the splash of him hitting it and funnelled ribbons of white, the sound of a kicked-over beer can rattling round our feet as we all jumped up and the garbled blend of our swear words.

'I'm going after him!' Terry shouted as Alex rushed up to see what the commotion was about.

'Where is he?' I screamed. 'Can anyone see him?'

For about ten seconds I thought he'd gone under, his pockets weighted with the misery that we could never fully see or share, but then his doused blond hair appeared on the surface and for one crazy moment I wondered if I could hook him on my line. But Terry was already kicking off his trainers and starting to clamber up in preparation for diving until Alex grabbed him and pulled him back shouting that no one else was going in the water off his boat. While they were arguing we saw that Dougie was swimming towards the island and, realising that people who want to drown themselves don't do the breaststroke, we all stopped shouting at each other and at him.

'Bloody hell,' Spencer said. 'What does he think he's doing?'

'His brain is that fucking scrambled he probably doesn't know any more,' Terry said.

'And if anything happens to him how are we going to tell Charlene?' I asked. 'And we're going to be the useless bastards who were supposed to be looking after him.'

While we started to debate whether we were to blame or not Alex turned the boat and began to follow Dougie but clearly intent on keeping a safe distance. He was also shouting something about having to report what had happened but the detail was lost in the sound of the engine. By now Dougie had reached the island and was hauling himself out of the water and almost as soon as he had done so he disappeared. I urged Alex to get us ashore but he told me that he had to use the island's landing spot and so we sailed away from where Dougie had vanished. It felt as if we were leaving him behind and every minute threw up a new welter of disturbing images.

When eventually we got ashore we split up and shouting his name headed in different directions. I was the one who found him. He was sitting on the grass in front of something that looked like the ruins of a church, under a row of stone-carved faces all of which seemed to be leering down at him. He didn't look up at me even though he must have seen my approach. His hair was plastered to his head and for the first time I noticed that it had a few fine threads of grey. He had taken off his T-shirt and also for the first time I realised how much weight he had lost and how his ribs pressed against the tight stretch of his skin.

'All right, Dougie?'

But he didn't answer and when he did look up at me it was as if he couldn't see me. I searched for Spencer and Terry.

'That was a bit of a scare you gave us. Fancied a swim, did you?'

He stared at my feet but didn't speak. I let my arm rest on Dougie's shoulder and realised that in all the years I had known him it was the longest I had ever touched him.

'I like it here, Phil,' he said. 'I think I would be OK if I could stay here.'

I squatted down beside him, my arm still on his shoulder.

'I know, Dougie. I like it too. It's very quiet and peaceful.' Then I took off my fleece and draped it over his shoulders and the strangeness of touching him was eased by its familiar feel. 'If we take you back with a cold Charlene will give out some stick.'

'I don't want to go back, Phil.'

He looked at me and when I looked into his eyes I was the one who shivered because it felt as if I was looking into the empty space he had spoken of. I could hear Terry and Spencer but I knew we were faced with something very fragile and I didn't want the wrong thing said or done in case it crushed that fragility into pieces none of us would be able to put together again. So I held my hand up and they stopped running and walked towards us.

'Dougie likes it here and he wants to stay,' I said, desperate for them not to say the wrong thing.

'It's good here, Dougie, all right,' Spencer said as he too squatted down.

'I wanted to know what the water felt like. Wanted to be on the island,' Dougie said.

We nodded as if it made perfect sense.

'It would be a good place to live all right,' Terry offered. 'Right out of everything. No one to give you grief.' A moment of silence tautened into something that was weighted with uncertainty. 'Why don't we all come back here and camp out in the summer?'

'That's a good idea, Terry,' I said, almost feeling sorry that I had chinned him all those years ago. 'What do you think, Dougie?'

'I'd like that,' he said as he shook his sodden hair making little droplets skite into nothingness.

'Here, Dougie, I'd forgotten you were such a good swimmer,' Spencer said. 'Do you remember that time the school held a swimming gala in Templemore Avenue baths and they had to scoop a floater out at the end of a race? Apparently Old Man Mulgrew entered it in the results book as "Also taking part, A. Turd".'

Dougie laughed. We all laughed and helped him gently to his feet making sure the fleece didn't slip off his shoulders.

'Here, Dougie,' Terry said while all three of us kept one hand on him as if he might topple over without our support. 'Your best three mates?'

He paused for the required amount of time to show that he was giving the ritual the necessary respect before he said, 'Spencer, Phil ...' and then when he turned to look at Terry it was clear that he knew, that he had always known, but still he said, 'And you, Terry.'

Despite what anyone else might say I believed he'd called it right and I understood then that whatever happened in the days to come we'd look after him. Look after him as best we knew how. And not just because we owed him but for reasons we didn't need to put into words.

Gecko

B Y NATURE THEY WEREN'T given to elaborate or effusive romantic gestures and in the absence of a wide circle of friends with whom to share a celebratory party, they had decided to mark the achievement of reaching twenty-five years of marriage by taking a trip to see the Northern Lights. It was the generous present they would give each other.

He taught science unspectacularly to mostly uninterested teenagers, increasingly shadowed by health and safety considerations that left him reluctant to allow the students to engage in experiments, or any form of the practical. Boiling water, gases, chemicals, and adolescents with mischief bubbling in their hearts and high at the very best on unpredictable hormones, was not a combination he could bring himself to trust. So he gave them science mostly out of books, heard himself say 'Listen up' repeatedly during the day and tried not to be hurt by the barrack-room lawyers who complained at intervals that the newly arrived Mr Langley let his class do experiments. When he allowed the complaints to get to him he'd find a video about tornado chasers or let them help dissect a sheep's brain or a bull's eye, counting out the scalpels and counting them in again at the end of the lesson.

But one wet afternoon in October as rain streamed against the windows and in the playground birds scavenged on the discarded remainders of packed lunches, he realised he was bored by his own voice, realised he'd reached the tipping point and pondered how he was going to see out the five years that separated him from retirement. He didn't tell anyone in the staffroom about either having reached the tipping point or their proposed trip because he was embarrassed a little by both, and, knowing the romantic connotation that might be given to their celebration and the smiles it could have induced, had already resolved to present it in the vocabulary of science to anyone who found out. He wasn't indifferent to, or ashamed of, romance, and did his bit on Valentine's Day and other appropriate occasions but considered it to be a private part of life, best shared only with the loved one. She in contrast told all the people in the City Hall where she worked registering births, marriages and deaths and was pleased when her colleagues were much taken with the idea.

There was no guarantee of actually seeing the Northern Lights – it was printed in bold type in the brochure and he understood better than anyone that nature couldn't be timetabled. At the back of the lab a couple of Year 10 students were standing looking at the newly arrived gecko in its case. Kids were always buying them, then soon got bored because they didn't fetch sticks or do tricks and had the unfortunate characteristic of living for a very long time. So there were frequent occurrences of self-interested generosity on behalf of their parents who donated them to the science department. He expected the boys to tap the glass in their impatience to see some movement and then to hear himself rebuking them. But they continued simply to stare.

'Come on, men,' he said, 'you'll be late for your next class.'

'It's only Learning for Life and Work,' Anderson said.

'I'm sure it's an important subject,' he said. 'Preparing you for the world of work, making you think of your future career path. Et cetera, et cetera.'

'It just stares and stares.'

'Geckos can't blink – mostly they just clean their eyes by licking them.'

The two boys moved their heads even closer to the glass. Robinson had a little wet pellet of paper in the back of his hair. The lizard rested motionless on the wooden log with its head raised towards them.

'And they shed their skin regularly. Usually eat it.'

'A bit like picking your nose and eating it,' Anderson said.

'Not exactly.'

'Does it have a name?' Robinson asked.

'It's a gecko.'

'Yes, but have you given it a name yet?'

'No.'

'Can we give it a name?' Anderson asked, looking up at him through the smeared lenses of his glasses.

He hesitated. Experience told him that sometimes the seemingly innocent could lead to unfortunate consequences.

'Depends what you have in mind.'

'Call it Gordon because it looks a bit geeky,' Anderson said.

'Gordon the Gecko,' Robinson said.

'Gordon the Geeky Gecko,' Anderson added, shouldering his bag.

'OK, we'll call it Gordon. Now on to your next class – I don't want getting the blame.'

The two boys scampered out of the room and after the door closed behind them he told the silence, 'And, boys, some species are parthenogenic. So the female can reproduce without having sex with a male.' Somewhere in the distance there was the sound of a door slamming.

In a few more minutes Year 11 would arrive from PE, bedraggled and half-changed, their faces red and if the lesson was outside with hair windblown and ragged. It would take the first ten minutes of the class just to settle them. The only bonus was that they were always late, delayed by the search for missing ties and having to stow their PE kitbags in the cloakroom. He'd make them copy from overheads for the first half and then when the steam of their previous lesson had evaporated he'd try and teach them something about measuring velocity.

He knew that he'd have to dig deep to summon the energy to make it through the hour. Perhaps it was the long years of teaching that had wearied so much, drained away the rush of life and turned him into a time-server, regulated by syllabi and the daily ringing of bells. Perhaps it was the twenty-five years of marriage that had sapped his vitality with its endless give and take, its wordless accommodations and making the best of things. But whatever it was he knew at this watershed moment he wanted something on their trip to spark him into a fuller flow of life so that the last five years of his career might be taken in his stride and stop him labouring his deflated and breathless way to the finishing line. He had started to believe too that if he didn't find this spark then he'd slip into retirement with a whimper and almost immediately become an old man.

She was slightly subdued at their evening meal. The one thing that a long marriage ensured was an acute sensitivity to the other's mood. Without the necessity of words or gesture, some intuitive seismic register caught the slightest tremor of variance from the norm.

'A busy day?' he asked as she handed him the salad bowl.

'Fewer marriages, more deaths,' she said. 'It must be the weather turning.'

'Something difficult?'

'A stillborn.'

There was nothing that could be said and he simply nodded and gave her his attention so if she wanted to she could go on talking or, if she didn't, she knew it was all right to return to silence.

'It's the second time. Happened a year ago. I remembered her very clearly. Terrible to see her again.'

'Not easy,' he said, unsure whether he was referring to the bereaved mother or his wife and then decided he was speaking of both.

He poured her a glass of wine and then they ate in silence until he sensed that she wanted the cue to say something more so he asked her, 'How was she bearing up?'

'In pieces, completely in pieces.'

He nodded again. He suspected that she, as he was doing, probably contemplated the absence of their own child. Even when they started to scurry away the silence with discussion of the minutiae of their day he felt that this absence lingered in her consciousness. He believed it often opened there, a space that could never be filled. Deciding to let nature be the decider they had never sought to find out the medical reasons so the failure was shared equally between them and perhaps it was better that way. 'Just wasn't meant to be,' was the attempt at solace they offered each other despite knowing that it wasn't enough. And because they knew how deep the drop might be they never risked the fall by talking about it.

So he told her about the boys naming the gecko and embellished it to give the paltry story a brighter seam of humour. Told her about some new initiative that had just arrived with them on glossy paper and about the howlers he had encountered in the latest batch of homework. It was all standard fare but she listened politely and added in her own office news – a colleague's daughter getting married, an argument over restricted parking spaces with their manager, someone deciding to opt out of the lottery syndicate.

The meal was finished and they had re-established equilibrium so that after the plates were stowed in the dishwasher they were free to separate again into their own pathways.

After the constant flurry of school voices, and not least his own, he liked the quietness of looking at the stars through his telescope. Sometimes he didn't even do much looking but simply enjoyed the luxury of sitting in their loft conversion and staring through the specially constructed viewing window. Down below he could hear the television and then, as always, it faded from his consciousness to be replaced only by the occasional stretch of wood, the dripping passage of water through pipes and the confused mass of his thoughts. Most nights he saw nothing more dramatic than the passing light of a plane but it didn't really matter. Sometimes when he couldn't fully shake off the bind of the day he would find himself still teaching, answering their welter of questions. So yes, the star shines because of the fusion of hydrogen and helium that releases energy radiating into space. And how long does it take for the light from a star to reach earth? It all depends on how far it is away. It might take four years, it might take seven thousand. Why does a child die in the womb? He didn't know the answer to that. Stars too could die, exhausted of the things they needed to keep themselves alive. He knew that he would die when all his energy consumed itself and there was nothing left to fire the flame and he felt closer to that moment than at any previous time in his life. He had favourite words he liked to repeat and he said them now. Galaxy, constellation, cluster. Perhaps they would work themselves up into a spell and protect him. He thought of the gecko in the empty school, its opened eyes staring at the shadows.

An empty school was the most ghostly place he'd ever known. Once he had to go back for the money he'd forgotten to lodge with the school bursar and which couldn't be risked overnight. So much stir and movement stored up during the day slowly seeping out from the fabric of the building. Far-off noises, inexplicable groans and creaks. From behind the lockers or somewhere in a distant storeroom? He didn't know and nor did he know whose voices those were as they whispered down the corridors and stairways. Were they an auditory after-image of the children of that day or were they the lingering echoes of those long gone?

She called that his supper was ready. They never wanted much so he knew it was probably a little square of cheese on a couple of crackers or a round of toast but it was fine whatever it was and good of her to make it. He went to the viewing window and closed everything down, for luck touched his laminated star chart that was pinned to the wall. Too much light pollution in the city. Better after midnight but by then he knew he would be in the deepest part of his sleep.

'Will you be very disappointed if you don't see them?' she asked in bed, glancing briefly at him over the top of her reading glasses.

'Nothing's guaranteed. But we have a reasonable chance. We'll be far enough north to give ourselves a reasonable chance.'

'That's good,' she said, closing her book. 'We can still enjoy ourselves even if we don't get lucky, can't we?'

'Yes we can,' he said, closing his own book because she had, and then with the kindness they always showed to each other simultaneously reached over to turn off their bedside lights.

Nothing had quite prepared them for the cold and yet it was surely to be expected when you were this close to the top of the world. They had all the right clothes but it still unnerved them a little at first and she made a joke about Lanzarote as they stood waiting for their cases to be unloaded from the minibus that had brought them to the complex. He wondered if she too felt a little dizzy like he did, as if he had been shaken loose from the parameters of the familiar and, after a few hours in a plane and some more by road, deposited in what felt like the frozen edge of existence. There were about two dozen log cabins and some larger buildings nestling in a clearing and sheltered by a thick collar of forest. He looked up at the sky and was disappointed to see it clouded and sullen. Perhaps the whole trip had been a foolishness.

In the central lodge that held an administrative centre, a shop, restaurant and lecture room they were welcomed by two young women who with their blonde hair and Sarah Lund jumpers looked like they had been plucked from the cover of a Nordic travel brochure. Then after being checked in with their fellow travellers they were given a folder outlining the times of their excursions, instructions about safety issues and various bits of information about the centre. He wondered if they were sisters – they looked so alike – and listened while they emphasised the number-one rule that no one was to ever go wandering off on their own. For some reason he thought of the night he had found himself alone in the empty school and shivered.

Their cabin was a cabin only in name and soon revealed itself to be as comfortable as the brochure had promised, complete with a lounge area, a separate bedroom, an open fire and even their own sauna. The fire was already lit and there was a woven basket with kindling and a neat pyramid of logs to sustain it. She was pleased and he was gladdened by her pleasure and as they toured their new residence she sounded a little giddy with excitement. She made him open the bottle of champagne she had bought in duty-free and as they sat in what looked like deer-skin-covered seats they sipped it nervously and listened to the crackle and hiss of the fire. He went to the window at intervals and peered out but the sky retained its cloudy secrets.

'Relax – they'll contact us if there's any activity,' she said.

'Don't want to miss anything after coming all this way,' he said then returned to his seat.

'I think we should have a toast, don't you?'

'Yes, we should,' he said but looked to her until she told him it was his job.

He studied his glass that blushed with the fire's light and wondered what he should say. There were stupid, crazy things that ran across his mind but none of them made it on to his tongue. He knew the moment called for some form of the poetic, some expression of the heartfelt, but he couldn't muster it spontaneously even though he truly wanted to and so he simply said, 'To twenty-five wonderful years and to twenty-five more.' They clinked glasses and she held her mouth up for him to kiss and he tasted the champagne on her lips.

'Twenty-five years,' she said. 'A long time.'

'A long time.'

'Sometimes I look at couples registering to get married and I wonder how long they'll last. You think you can identify the ones that will and the ones that won't but really there's no telling who's going to make it and who isn't.'

He wanted to ask her if she had ever thought they were the ones who wouldn't make it but hesitated. And he felt strange, out of kilter with himself. He hadn't drunk enough champagne to give it the blame. Everything felt confused. He wondered if in the past people had disappeared into the wilderness and died from cold and exposure. It would be easy to get lost in the woods, your cries for help muffled by the thick choke of fir. He put some more logs on the fire and then poured more champagne in her glass.

'You'll be getting me drunk,' she said.

'Did you ever think we weren't going to make it?'

'For richer or poorer, in sickness and in health,' she said then sipped from her glass. 'Old-fashioned girl, I suppose. What makes you ask?'

He told her he didn't know then looked to the window again. He would have to find some student to take the gecko home in the summer holidays, someone who was reliable and would follow the instructions carefully. Perhaps he could ask Robinson or Anderson. What had made him walk round the empty school, lit only by the green exit signs and the orange outside lights that guarded the perimeter? Like walking in a different element that was at once strange and yet layered by the familiar. The small PE office with its scattered debris of sport – the rackets and shuttlecocks; the deflated rugby balls; the blue roll books; in a battered biscuit tin for valuables the left-behind inhalers, small change and mobile phones. The vast hollowness of the empty games hall with its blue rubber floor and basketballs trapped in the netting hanging down from the ceiling like a tied-back curtain. A world in which he had somehow got lost. Surely there were things to warm him. Children helped into examination success and careers. The days he had taught well. Days he had told them about the stars, held their interest. But these were mere sparks that failed to ignite any stronger flame and so there was only the echo of his footsteps on the corridor tiles and the whispering voices of faceless generations.

He hadn't always been sure they were going to make it. There had been a moment a decade earlier when he had felt something for someone else. A woman who worked in the school as a technician. He thought she had felt something too but neither of them had ever allowed those feelings to assume any form other than an obvious enjoyment of the times when their paths crossed and they allowed themselves to linger just a little longer than they needed to. If she had encouraged him what would he have done? He didn't know and knew that was a type of failure and its own betrayal. She looked happy as she sipped her champagne. But what about her? What about her during all those times when things had slipped into a rut? A comfortable rut perhaps but despite the absence of conflict or complaint a sense of merely drifting aimlessly through their shared todays. Sometimes as if both privately aware of the infusion of lethargy, the danger of their lack of momentum, they would try to quicken and renew what they had by a holiday or even something as simple as a meal out or a weekend walk. Sometimes they made love as a restorative and there were times when it seemed to work even though after twenty-five years what they mostly gave each other was comfort rather than deep pleasure.

'Put your coat on and let's go outside for a while. Have a look.'

She rolled her eyes but held her hand out towards him and, taking it, he helped her from the deep folds of the chair.

The sky was stretched black and taut above them. He had never seen the stars so clearly, their pulsing brightness so defined. It was as if the sky he knew at home had been washed clean of its ancient veneer of smog, like some old painting stripped of its clouded varnish.

'It's beautiful,' she said.

'Yes, it is. I'm glad we came.'

She was still holding her glass of champagne – he had left his inside – and she raised it as she said, 'To the stars.'

'To the stars,' he repeated, pleased by what she had said, and then she handed him the glass.

It was too cold to linger long and when they went inside their travel tiredness encouraged them to bed. They both knew they should make love and so they helped each other into the needed responses and afterwards in the silence they listened briefly to the fire's final surrender before they too fell asleep.

In the morning they went to the restaurant and with the other new arrivals had a generous breakfast. There was a range of morning activities open to them – everything from husky and snowmobile safaris to ice fishing. They had chosen to go on a guided cross-country hike and an hour later they joined a small group heading out.

They had come well prepared and layered against the cold and he was glad that they had invested in the necessary clothing and solidly laced boots but the wind still peppered his cheekbones and he was impatient to get moving. He hoped that the group would be made up of people similar to themselves, with no one clamouring for attention or being too raucous. There was a powerful feeling of stillness, as if the snow held the whole world silent, and he didn't want anyone to disturb the welcomed calm he now felt. Their guide helped them secure the short skis they had been given and after a brief demonstration on how best to walk in them and make use of the poles they set off cross-country along a smoothed path that polished itself under their movement. They both soon got the hang of it and as the little group followed in single file across the snow the only other sound was the wind and the hiss of their skis.

Their route took them towards the forest and at first he couldn't see where they were headed, but in a short while a clearing opened up allowing them a path through the thick swathe of trees whose scent seemed loosened by their passing. The branches were layered with snow and from time to time some of it would drift dreamily down. He looked back to see if she was all right and she lifted her right hand to signal she was. She was wearing sunglasses and he couldn't see her eyes.

Gradually the path started to slope gently downwards and he found it more difficult to control his speed. A bird spun squawking out of a tree leaving the branch vibrating and a spindrift unsettled in its wake. Then eventually the confines of the forest disappeared and they were stopping at an open vista, a lake stretching into the distance. They grouped awkwardly round their guide in a semicircle and listened while he gave them facts about its size and depth, the summer fishing, the thickness of the ice. Someone asked a question. Another took a photograph.

'How's it going?' he asked her as the group took a rest.

'Fine once you get the hang of it,' she said. 'Think my legs might ache later on, though.'

'I think I saw a sign back at the centre about massages being available.'

'No need to pay someone when you can do it.'

He stared out at the ice. The perfect surface was sheened by a narrow quiver of light that was eventually swallowed by the shadows of surrounding mountains. He told himself he felt lighter, cleaner, as if something was being slowly scraped from his skin. He didn't want to go back. But when the guide told them with a smile that they were going out on the ice his feelings were replaced by apprehension. How thick had he said the ice was? Images of global warming rattled through his thoughts. In school you couldn't take children on a nature ramble without filling in a risk assessment. He looked at her and she smiled in return but he still couldn't see her eyes.

There was nothing that could be done. He couldn't make a scene by refusing and he knew he wouldn't be allowed to find his own way back. So there was no other option except to carefully follow the person in front as they moved forward in file once more. It was difficult to see precisely where the shore ended and the lake began but almost immediately he sensed from the slightly different sound and feel of the skis that he was on the ice. Each of his forward pushes was weighted by the awareness of what was below him.

They moved slowly out across it. Was the ice strongest at its shore edges and weakest in its centre? They were walking down the narrow corridor of light. But where were they going? He told himself he heard a strange noise from somewhere far off and imagined it was the sound of cracking ice. And then just as he felt himself start to panic they came to a sudden halt and grouped once more around their guide as he told them that where they were standing the lake was 460 metres deep. He watched him dig his ski pole into the ice and for a second he imagined the sheet splintering and cracking like a broken pane of glass. Then the guide was kneeling and taking something out of his rucksack. It was a bottle and when small plastic glasses followed he poured each of them a drink. They toasted each other with what might have been schnapps and which slid warmly down the back of his throat. Then after posing for a group photograph they turned back the way they had come.

They enjoyed their lunch back in the complex and afterwards in the shop he bought some postcards and a poster of a sky illuminated by swirls of pale green and pink for his classroom wall. In the foyer he talked briefly to a couple who described themselves as aurora hunters and told him of their best sightings at different locations round the world. They had travelled to Iceland and Alaska as well as across Northern Europe. But when he asked them what they thought the chances were of a sighting in their present location they merely shrugged their shoulders and smiled.

Just as they were about to leave they were approached by one of the young women who had welcomed them the night before. She asked if they would be able to help out with something – a young couple were about to get married in the ice chapel and she was trying to round up a small audience. It would only take twenty minutes and they might find it interesting.

'We've been married for twenty-five years,' his wife told her as she offered their help.

'Cool,' the young woman said. 'Perhaps this marriage will last as long as yours.'

They followed her outside and along a path that wound behind the administration offices. Six other people were gathered round the doorway of a small building made entirely from blocks of ice and designed to resemble a miniature chapel. On either side of the door were sprays of fern and conifer cones decorated with ribbon and glitter.

'They'll be here soon,' the young woman told them and handed out little sachets of pink confetti. Almost before she had finished speaking a dog-pulled sled appeared with the bride and groom snuggled in the back under a fur blanket. As the driver stopped outside the chapel the dogs skittered on their lines then on the driver's command hunkered in the snow, their long tongues lolling and dripping. After clambering out of the sled the wedding couple removed their ski coats to reveal a traditional wedding gown and a dark suit. The bride carried a bouquet of pink roses and he wondered where in the world they had come from. As they were making last-minute adjustments to their dress the young woman from the administration centre ushered the witnesses inside and they filed into the ice chapel and took their places on simple wooden benches.

A robed woman minister stood in front of an ice altar decorated with a brass crucifix and two more displays of ferns. All around them the ice blushed with a blue sheen, the hidden uplighters intensifying the seamed striations of crystal. Music from some concealed sound system started to play and on the priest's gesture they all stood as the bride and groom made their slow and measured way to the front. He felt his wife lean her head against his shoulder.

'Maybe the City Hall should get an ice chapel,' he said.

'All the smokers outside the front door would probably make it melt.'

As the short ceremony played out he thought of himself as the groom standing on the edge of a new life. How strange it was to make a promise to love someone for ever when nothing else in the world endured or remained unscathed by the passage of time. He tried to recall his father's wedding-day speech when he outlined his advice for a successful marriage but couldn't remember any of it. What he did remember was his own heady optimism that the exchange of vows and rings would make his life different in ways that were better than how it was before. And as the bride and groom pledged their love in a language he didn't understand the words formed gossamer mists on their lips and the ice above their heads shivered blue. And it had made his life better because he knew that there was nothing colder than loneliness.

Fifteen minutes later it was all over and they were throwing their pink confetti over the newly married couple as they emerged from the ice chapel, before watching them don their outer clothes and climb in the back of the sled with the dogs scampering to their feet and barking out their impatience to be gone.

'She didn't throw her flowers,' his wife said as they watched the sled curve and then straighten its way into the distance.

'I guess with what they cost she wasn't going to let them go. Maybe it's not tradition here. And she'll probably need them for photographs or something.'

'She looked beautiful. The girls in work will be interested to hear about this,' she said as she took some pictures of the chapel with her phone.

'A bit of a contrast to getting married on a beach somewhere. But strange not to have family or friends there.'

'I'm not sure it's a bad idea when I think of some of the antics I've seen from family and friends in the registry office. Some are more interested in turning it into a circus than something serious and there's nobody more important than the man with the camera who acts as if he's directing a film, giving orders to everyone and asking for things to be done twice.'

'Do you regret not having a proper photographer at our wedding?'

'Sometimes, but we had both decided that it was best to have a modest budget and put the money into a first house.'

'Sensible, I suppose,' he said as they started to make their way back to their cabin.

'We've always been sensible,' she said but it wasn't clear if she meant it as a compliment or a criticism.

He thought again of walking out across the ice and how he had been frightened then asked himself what right he had to see the lights. Perhaps he had never been brave enough, content to wear his marriage like a coat that kept the cold away. He felt the sadness of this and knew that if they didn't see the lights it would be his fault. He wanted to make it up to her but didn't know how.

When they got back to the cabin she said she felt tired and was going to lie down for a while. He thought there was a sadness in her movements and so he said he would join her. They kicked off their shoes and got under the duvet fully dressed, shivering a little into the warmth of each other as he snuggled into her back. Soon she was snoring lightly and he pressed his face into her hair until she slipped away into her own heat. He wanted to fall asleep with her but despite his efforts it wouldn't come. By now her hair would be grey like his if she stopped going to the trouble of colouring it. He had read once that dying stars were very beautiful in their colours and shapes but it seemed to him that age slowly leached everything away. Perhaps that was why the lights were important, those charged particles sent spinning from the sun to be carried by solar winds and whose collision with the earth's atoms in the thermosphere produced the aurora borealis. If only he could see them they might colour his remaining days once more, bring them both into a renewed flame of life. He stroked her hair but knew he could never explain it. She was far away in sleep.

He imagined the sled with its lovers carving its way through the snow, the dogs yelping and straining on the harness and responding to the driver's calls. What future awaited them? Would what they felt in that moment slowly burn away until it was finally consumed, or would they find something that would carry them through the years? He slipped quietly from the bed without disturbing her. In their absence that morning someone had lit the fire and he placed more logs on then went to the window. The light was already draining out of the day. He suddenly thought that he wanted a gift to give her when she wakened, should have planned it before they came – a piece of jewellery or an unexpected extravagance. He tried to recall if he had seen something suitable in the shop but couldn't remember anything other than touristy items that weren't what he wanted. He rebuked himself for being too preoccupied with his own needs. But he tried also to find reassurance by telling himself that a marriage was not about the spectacular and might be kept alive by the countless small acts of kindness. Still it would be special, just even once, to feel it illuminated by something beyond what was comfortable and familiar and he didn't want to have to go back with regret for what might have been.

He thought of going for a walk but didn't want her to be alone when she woke because she would worry about him. Then on impulse he put on his coat and went over to the main building and spoke to the person in charge of the complex. When he returned to their cabin she was slowly stirring and he quietly took his coat off and hung it up. He made her a cup of coffee and carried it into the bedroom.

'All right, sleepy head?' he asked, setting the cup down on her bedside table.

'Coming all this way to go to sleep,' she said. 'It must have been that ski trip out this morning. Body's not used to exercise and all that fresh air.'

Her hair was bedraggled as if she had returned from a far journey and she looked older than he thought of her. He sat on the edge of the bed and handed her the coffee. She held it in both hands and he gently pushed a strand of loosened hair away from her face.

'Strange to be this close to the North Pole. Relatively anyway,' he said.

'If I were to send a letter to Santa, it wouldn't have so far to go then,' she said, smiling and offering him a sip of the coffee.

'Not so far. Did you send letters when you were a child?'

'We all did – it was part of the Christmas tradition – and you'd get a letter back supposedly from the North Pole. I think there was some part of the Post Office looked after it. Don't suppose they'll be doing much of that when they're privatised.'

'We just put ours up the chimney.'

She set the cup down and pushed a hand through her hair. Most of the afternoon light had drifted from the room. Through the open door they could see flames flicker in silhouette against the wooden walls.

'You couldn't sleep?' she asked, then taking his hand told him that he felt cold and bringing him into the bed held him tightly in her warmth. 'Is that better?'

'Yes,' he said, his voice smothered into a whisper as he nestled his face deeply into the fullness of her embrace. Then as his desire quickened she was taking off his clothes and slipping out of hers but trying to do it while she still held him close so for a few minutes they were a tangle of skirmishing arms and scrunching legs that momentarily reminded him of the awkwardness of long-gone courtship in cars. And when he kissed her, her mouth and everything immediately yielded to him but then just at the point of surrender she was kissing him, pushing him back and not stopping until he had to turn his head away from the full press of her mouth. And everything seemed to fall away, both uncertainty and all predictability, so that what he felt was an overwhelming sense of the moment's passion and he let himself be carried by it not caring where it was taking him and when it broke in a sudden rush he heard himself whisper words that he had no control over and he was telling her the stars were in her eyes and in her hair.

Afterwards they lay as if shocked and he wondered whether it was embarrassment that lulled them into silence until he heard her say, 'So you saw the stars.'

'Yes, I saw the stars.'

'And the lights – did you see them too?' she asked as she stroked his cheek with the back of her hand.

'I saw them too.'

'That's good. And you're not bored after twenty-five years?'

'Did it feel like I was bored?'

They lay without speaking for some time until they decided that they should get dressed. He let her shower first and saw how when she came out of the bathroom she had covered her nakedness with a towel. As she started to get ready they began to speak about inconsequential things. But as he watched her brush her hair, he registered for the first time the way she angled her head as she did each side, how when she had finished she did a final smooth with the palm of her hand; the almost cursory glance she gave herself in the mirror as if trying to avoid the impression of vanity. Now it was her turn to wait for him and she sat by the fire and held her palms to it as if gesturing her surrender.

Later that evening after their meal and when they had returned to the cabin he got her to pack her overnight stuff and when she asked him why he told her where they were going to spend the night.

'But it'll be freezing,' she said, shivering at the thought, even as she kneaded the warmth of the fire into her hands. 'You're joking me.'

'The igloo's made of glass. And it's heated. You won't be cold. I promise.'

He saw she wasn't convinced and was a little disappointed but knew that she hadn't fully understood. Eventually, however, she was persuaded and followed him with her overnight bag, then, after unlocking the door of the glass igloo and feeling the warmth greeting them, he turned to her like a child wanting affirmation.

'It's made from thermal glass. Doesn't matter how cold it gets outside, you'll be warm in here. And all mod cons.' They stood in the space that separated the two single beds and stared up through the glass at the star-splashed sky arching above them. 'And the glass never frosts or mists so you see everything there is to see.'

'Single beds?'

'They're all like this – it must be something to do with the design. We'll survive.'

They drank what was left of the previous night's champagne, lay on their backs on the single beds and stared at the stars. He pointed out the constellations but tried not to sound as if he was in his classroom. It felt intensely strange to be in a snow-blanched wilderness and yet be secure, separated from the universe outside only by the thinness of glass. It seemed too as if the whole night sky was vaster and yet closer than he had ever seen and that it was alive, not frozen or fixed, but alive and everything in it moving through time and space.

'Are you glad we came here?' he asked.

'To the igloo?'

'On the trip.'

'Yes, I'm glad.'

'That's good. And you wouldn't have preferred a villa with your own heated pool in Lanzarote.'

'Everyone goes to Lanzarote,' she said. 'I'll have plenty to tell the girls in the office when I get back.'

He didn't want her to share their trip with anyone, wanted everything to be personal to them, but he said nothing. They finished the light supper that had been left ready and went back to their separate beds but talked on into the night until conversation was exhausted and then fell into a comfortable silence. Perhaps it was the champagne or the strain she had been under at work that gradually lulled her into sleep. He fought against his own drowsiness because there were things he wanted to tell her and he could only do it because she was sleeping.

So he was the one who had come up short. Despite their agreement just to keep trying for a child and let nature make the final decision he had gone for the tests. So this child he knew she wanted so much was unlikely to happen because of him and, even though he knew she wouldn't have attributed blame, it had frightened him that he might have lost her because of it. There were things they could have done but he had denied her that opportunity because he knew that having a child was less important to him than to her, and because every day of his life he was surrounded by children and, although he had never admitted it, was content to have a part that was childless.

Looking up at the night sky he felt a renewed sense of that selfishness. He could never tell her now so it was a secret he would have to live with and all he could do was silently whisper that he was sorry. Above him the distances in space were so vast they could barely be contemplated. The light he saw had travelled so far that thinking of it increased his spreading weariness. So many dark spaces in a life; what could you do but try to fill them with a job, a family, a belief of some sort? Fill them with love. But looking up at the limitless depths it felt as if the spaces were too great, that even his best efforts were paltry in comparison.

For a second he imagined he saw the sky faintly edged with a smoulder of pink and green but then had to admit that he had imagined it. He remembered the pink confetti they had thrown in blessing over the heads of the newly-weds. Pink petals against the white of the snow. He made his way once more along the seam of light and out across the ice. He thought too of walking slowly down a darkened corridor where pleated shadows and children's voices laid claim to each of his echoing steps. In the other bed she was turning towards him and slowly wakening. She rubbed her eyes and asked him if she had missed anything. He told her no then stretched out his hand and she stretched hers, the distance between allowing them only to touch at the tips of their fingers.

Old Fool

THERE'S NO FOOL LIKE an old fool was the world's entirely predictable judgement. But as my human contact has shrunk since retirement to the voluntary staff who run the charity shop, a particular shift of supermarket checkout ladies, two female librarians who take turns to sign out my books, a few long-term neighbours with whom I exchange blandishments about the weather, and my always busy daughter who lives two cities away, this doesn't actually encompass much of the planet's population. But if you want to know the truth, it isn't the world's judgement on what it undoubtedly saw as my post-retirement, edge-of-senility, last-fling-at-life crisis that I worry about.

So although Gwen, the chief organiser in the cancer shop, gives me the cold shoulder and only speaks to me with weary disdain, constantly seeming to be waiting for either an elaborate and public expression of contrition, or for me to do what she undoubtedly thinks of as the honourable thing – fall on my sword and relinquish the two days a week I help in the shop – I've made the decision that I'm staying. I like working there and have done so for three years since my wife's death. At first after I retired it seemed a way of giving back something for all the kindness she received during her long struggle but soon realised I was doing it for me because it provided me with something to fill the otherwise empty stretches of my no longer working week. And as someone who had spent his career as a civil servant sitting at a desk shuffling figures and calculations about urban traffic volume and chasing the dream of perfect flow the way I imagine a surfer dreams of the perfect wave, I belatedly discovered I liked engaging with people, liked serving customers, liked working with others – even, for a while, Gwen – and for some reason I don't fully fathom found pleasure in arranging and sorting the donated clothes and bric-a-brac, the accumulated cast-offs of other people's lives. Of course there was always the sustaining comfort that, in arranging people's no-longer-wanted clothing, dusting their discarded ornaments, placing their crime-fiction books in alphabetical order and generally making an enthusiastic stab at ordering the incoming chaos, I was actually making a contribution, however small, towards a cure.

I find too that I have a curiosity about the lives of the people whose possessions pass through my hands. Quite often the owners are dead and a relative has gathered up their bits and pieces. Gwen lives in constant hope of discovering some rare and valuable heirloom but mostly, as now, when I find myself examining the contents of a cardboard box, it's a series of seemingly disconnected objects whose worth can only be measured in ways that are hidden from us. Sometimes I try to piece them together to form a story, even some vague impression of a life lived, but what can I make of these – three carved black elephants, trunk to tail, with some of their tusks missing; a child's tortoiseshell-backed hair-brush with withered bristles; an old 45 by Matt Monro; a tiny black and white wedding photograph in a circular ebony frame; and a small china bird that might be a wren, with a chipped wing. They nestle gently in my hands like mosaic fragments but I struggle to fit them into any completed picture or pattern.

Despite Gwen they can't make me leave because irrespective of her frequent bending the ear of Head Office apparently I haven't actually infringed any of the existing rules, so I haven't stolen money or goods, haven't procured any of the stuff that's daily dumped on our doorstep in black bags. I haven't bullied or made inappropriate sexual advances to any of the staff, not even to Sylvia who had started to convey a certain readiness to be advanced on and who now treats me as if I am guilty of breach of promise, although I think that offence no longer features in criminal law. I haven't engaged in racial or homophobic language so while they wanted me out they hadn't yet convinced themselves in a litigious age that they had a water-tight case. When I had a short interview with two very pleasant and slightly embarrassed young women who wore their names in clip badges on their lapels they asked me if I would like someone else to sit in with us. We drank a cup of tea, had a chat – it transpired that one of them knew my daughter from university – and after some wonderfully non-specific comments about the importance of maintaining the society's good reputation, sentiments with which I concurred enthusiastically, we had a civilised conversation. They were too kind and too sensitive to ask for the hidden details and as I didn't declare them they only had gossip to go on and in the absence of what might be considered a crime, as opposed to a lapse of judgement in my personal life, they eventually shook my hand, thanked me for my time and left.

When you retire time is what you've got lots of and there isn't that much generosity in giving it to someone – they're doing you the kindness by taking it. And after a working life the ingrained habits aren't easy to get rid of, so every morning I still wake at the same hour and my first flare of consciousness is always that there's no one in the bed except me. I don't suppose I'm ever going to be able to cast that off no matter how many years go by but as soon as possible I switch the radio on to try and chase away some of the silence that always seems to have arrived overnight and stares in at me whatever the season like a frosted face pressed against the glass. There's the same light breakfast with which I have always started my working day, only different in recent years by being finished with blood-pressure tablets and the fish-oil capsules Linda insisted on. Taking the globular fish-oil tablets feels like my final commitment to her and one that I can't bring myself to break. And was what happened a breach of faith to her? I wonder about that a lot and perhaps I'm fooling myself when I usually reach the conclusion that she wouldn't have judged me harshly. She never did when she was alive so why should she when she's dead? And it was never about the needs of the flesh because if anything it was the fragility of the heart and I think that Linda will take comfort, if comfort is needed, and know that it was her absence that made mine weak. I suppose she'll also grasp the not entirely admirable truth that part of me resents her going and leaving me alone in the phase of our life when we were supposed to be enjoying the freedom of our retirement and where you're increasingly conscious of the need for someone to help look after you in the years still to come. So if she can forgive me that selfishness then she'll probably forgive the rest.

The one thing I'm not good with in the shop is selling things when I'm on the till. There's a sign up that says we try to price everything as low as possible and aren't able to offer further reductions. But because most of the people who're buying the stuff don't look as if they're overflowing with money it's not as easy as it's supposed to be. I could of course do what most of the other staff do and absolve myself of any personal responsibility by simply pointing to the sign and smiling, or shrugging my shoulders in a way that says love to help you but it's the rules. My heart always sinks when I hear the question, 'Is this your best price?' or, even worse, the pointed personalisation of 'Is that the best you can do for me?' And because we have to log every single sale in the ledger that Gwen treats as sacred scripture, and because she has an instant knowledge of every item in the shop, there's no chance of cheating the price, so on those occasions when I can't bring myself not to offer some reduction I have to make up the shortfall out of my own pocket.

That was how I first met Georgia or Georgie as she preferred to be called. She'd come into the shop on a pretty regular basis and sometimes I thought it was just somewhere for her to spend time, of which, like me, she seemed to have too much. And she'd always have little Micah, her five-year-old, with her and to Gwen's disapproval he would scamper about the shop oblivious to his mother's half-hearted attempts at restraint and he'd do his best to impose chaos once more on the ordered rhythms of the place. She'd buy relatively little – a blouse she once described as 'retro', a long skirt and sometimes children's books or toys for the child. She never bought clothes for Micah and in truth he always seemed better turned out than her.

That afternoon when they came in out of the rain she was dressed in much her usual way that seemed to me to be a cross between retro and punk, wearing a long black skirt that stopped only to reveal laced-up red DMs, and a baggy navy jumper with what looked like a Victorian brooch pinned close to her heart. Despite the loose, rain-splashed clothes you could tell there was a skinny body hiding underneath. Her black hair was short and spiked with a blue and pink smear on one side that reminded me of the colour of petrol in water and her ears were weighted with a sequence of rings in descending order of size. She had a stud under her lip but the metal adornments served only to emphasise the delicacy of her features, the soft leafy greenness of her eyes. I guessed she was in her late twenties and everything about her seemed to say single mother with little money but there was also something that announced in quite a clear way that she didn't need anyone's sympathy. It wasn't that she was hard-faced or even hard-edged but she clearly possessed what my father would have described as 'spirit' – the highest and only compliment he knew to give to women.

So I suppose it was spirit that made her stand in front of me with some child's game and ask for a reduction because an important part was missing. She could even have been right – how was I to know?

'I'm really sorry,' I said, 'but we're not allowed to charge anything but the marked price. What's it marked at?'

'Two pounds, but there's a bit missing,' she insisted, little droplets of water beading her hair like seed pearls. 'You'd be breaking the law selling something you knew was faulty.'

And because she was saying it in a teasing and not a belligerent way and because, if I'm being truthful, she was smiling, and perhaps I'm imagining it, but because the rain still sheening her hair seemed to make her eyes brighter against the darkness of her clothes, I looked over to where Gwen was busy with a customer, rummaging in a cabinet for a matching plate to complete a set, and said, 'You can have it for a pound.'

'I think 50p would be the right price?' she said, smiling again and throwing a quick glance over her shoulder to where Micah was deep-sea diving in a box of toys, his head hidden under the surface.

'He's a bit of a handful,' I said.

'Keeps me busy. Perhaps a nice new game, even though there's a piece missing, might give him something to hold his attention, allow his mother a bit of a rest.'

I glanced over at Gwen again. Whatever contraption she wore to corset herself was pressing against the outline of her clothing so that it looked as if she had a metal cage for an undergarment. She was putting on her glasses that dangled from a cord on her neck and searching a pile of plates.

'You can have it for nothing if you know how to keep a secret.'

'I'm good at keeping secrets,' she said in a mock-whisper before asking, 'can I have a bag?'

'Why not?' I answered with a little splash of gentle sarcasm.

'You're very kind,' she said as she stretched her hand across the counter then, seeing my badge, added, 'You're very kind, Tom,' making a play of saying my name.

As she went to gather Micah I wrote the sale in the ledger and slipped my own money into the till, looking up in time to see her waving as she walked past the window, her head framed by condensation and raindrops.

When you live alone it's easy to let yourself go – there's no one to please any more or nag you when you need a haircut or your jumper is food-stained. I can see that but try to resist letting everything slide and working in the shop helps motivate me, keeps me in shape, and I've always been a walker with a metabolism lucky enough to burn off whatever calories haphazard, improvised meals and comfort-eating seek to impose. I've seen better days but haven't entirely gone to seed and even if my idea of sartorial dressing is buying a new V-neck jumper in Marks and Spencer I think I can pass myself if need be. And I've kept the house tidy as well, everything shipshape and spick and span, just the way Linda liked it. But it was even more painful than I had imagined to gather up the best of her stuff, put it in bags and carry it to the shop, taking care to avoid mutual embarrassment by suggesting that it was passed to me by a neighbour. So how does it feel when from time to time someone presents me with an item of clothing or a piece of costume jewellery that belonged to her? Depends on the particular day and how I'm feeling but mostly it's as if a little match has been struck and her face and her being momentarily flare into a brief quickening of life. And as I gently fold whatever it is, or place it in a bag, I give it my utmost care and then watch a stranger walk out the door with what was once part of her and after they've gone try to hold on tightly to the best memories of our life together.

Georgie came mostly in the afternoons after school was out probably for the same reason why she visited the library, the shopping precinct and the church drop-in centre, which was to get out of the house, use someone else's heating and possibly have a conversation with someone other than Micah. When she wanted to buy something she'd always wait until I was on the till and then inevitably it was 'Is that the best you can do for me?' and sometimes I'd help her and at others I'd dig in my heels and then she'd make a show of melodramatic disappointment but accept the verdict, either putting the object back or forking out the full price. It was a sort of game and sometimes when she wasn't interested in buying anything and just happy to put in some time browsing she'd ask me how I was and she'd use my name.

After she'd gone out of the shop once Gwen came up to me behind the counter and said, 'I think that one's well worth watching.'

'Why's that, Gwen?' I asked.

'Because I think she's potentially one of our customers, if you can call them that, who think charity starts at home – their home. So keep a close eye on her and when you look at the way she lets that child run amok you can understand where all those rioters came from.'

'I think you're being a bit hard' is what I said except I didn't and instead mumbled something that was designed not to rock the boat or highlight a difference of opinion that would lead to conflict because conflict is something I don't like and which I'm not very good at dealing with. Linda could sometimes brew up a storm and sometimes she brewed it up a little stronger because I couldn't respond in kind and once she complained that fighting with me was like fighting a paper bag. But now I think I should have countered Gwen and in my silence there was a sense of betrayal although what existed between Georgie and me at that point was nothing more than the flimsiest connection of two strangers, although I suppose a secret shared did mean that something, however small, had crept into tenuous life.

What happened took place on a summer afternoon at the end of August. It was that summer where there seemed more rain than sunshine and so on that particular day the surprisingly strong splay of sun appeared to galvanise the city and as I walked home from the shop there was an animated energy that pervaded every part of its life. So the cries of the fruitsellers on their stalls drummed out a rhythmic rap as they made spinning acrobats of their wrists and twirled the brown-bagged fruit they'd just sold with greater gusto. A skateboarder's skittering, clickety wheels scored the pavement in a blur of movement and all around me bare-legged women in short sleeves, or men with their working jackets draped over their arms like waiters, seemed to hurry to wherever was home, borne along by a desire to make the most of what time allowed them to spend on themselves.

It was Micah I saw first, holding on to his mother's skirt, something that was uncharacteristic of a child who always seemed intent on wandering as far from her as his short legs would allow. They were standing with their backs against a railing outside the station and a guy wearing a white singlet that even at a distance displayed heavily tattooed arms, the type that makes you feel the tattooist had an intense dislike of leaving any trace of white on the skin's canvas. And it was one of these blue-inked arms that was pointing at Georgie in a way that allows some men to transmit all their aggression into a gesture. As I got closer I could see that it was having its desired effect and as she pressed herself tighter against the metal railing her body was squirming away from his outreached arm and in that instant I knew this was the movement of someone who had been hit by the hand that hovered so close to her face. Closer still I expected to hear his raised voice but their conversation was drowned out by the traffic flowing a few feet away. No words were needed to understand the fear felt by Micah as he burrowed his face deeper into Georgie's skirt or that a young woman I thought of as spirited was cowering under the force of whatever was being said.

Now I don't think of myself as brave – there wasn't much need for it in a profession that required me to sit in an office and feed data into a computer and plot graphs. And if I found a kind of strength when Linda was dying it was only because it felt as if my feelings had been anaesthetised, slowly frozen because of the inevitability of the conclusion and a conviction that I needed to hold myself ready and be able to function through the drawn-out journey until I reached the prescribed destination. But when it happens – that thing you've played out over and over in your head – it's as if that part of you has been placed too deeply in cold storage so what you think is going to pour out feels like it hasn't had a chance to unfreeze and the days and weeks that follow are marked only by a kind of numbness that both sustains and frightens you in case it never goes away.

So was I frightened then as I walked quicker towards whatever was taking place? Yes I was but it was also true that having not so long before been in the presence of death made me bolder in facing up to life however shitty it might conspire to be and there was too a sort of protection in being what I felt as partially shut down, my future life starting up only in what my computer describes as safe mode.

'Hi, Georgie, everything all right?' I asked, simulating a casualness.

'She's all right,' he said, turning to look at me with ill-disguised disdain before adding, 'if it's any of your fucking business.'

'It's OK, Tom. Everything's fine.'

'That's right, Tom, everything's fine so why don't you piss off.'

'Are you sure, Georgie?' I said, ignoring him.

'She's sure. Now why don't you do a runner and keep your nose out of other people's business.'

I had hoped that in not addressing him I could sidestep the possibility of confrontation, as if ignoring the reality of his physical presence might somehow prevent my intrusion becoming a challenge to which he would feel compelled to respond. But as his anger broke against me, for a second I felt it threaten to erode whatever conviction I had tried to muster. I hadn't even fully taken him in so at that point he was not much more than a white singlet, his arms a blur of blue hatchings and shadings and only his voice that sounded aggressive and yet whiny at the same time registering deeply. He had dropped his hand away from her face and when he turned to me full on I had no choice but to meet his gaze and saw then that he was about thirty, his blond hair shaven so that it looked like a smear of yellow stubble and there was a little white seam of scar just above one eyebrow. Like everyone else I make my first, if not fixed, judgement on people by their appearance and in that moment his looked like the face in the newspaper sneering and gesturing out at you from the steps of courthouses, or caught on CCTV before being convicted of some late-night random, impulsive act of inner-city violence that shatters bodies and lives.

For the first time I felt truly frightened. I suppose that's why I chose to speak to him instead of Georgie and so I heard myself say, 'You shouldn't talk like that in front of children.'

'What the fuck makes you think you can stick your nose in other people's business and shoot your mouth off? So, old man, if you don't piss off like I've told you, you'll find yourself on the end of this,' and he brandished his knuckles to the side of his head at the same time as he angled his body towards me in a practised and perfected gesture that made me wonder how many times a day he offered it to the world.

'Please, Sean, Tom doesn't understand – he'll leave us now. Go, Tom, please just go,' and as I stared at her I saw the fear in her eyes and for a second, just for a second, it reminded me of how Linda had looked when a doctor, young enough to be her son and who had a turning mobile of silver birds hanging from his ceiling, gave her the inescapable verdict with a modern directness that was supposed to invite respect because it believed you were entitled to the truth. And that sudden memory fused a calm anger.

'If you threaten me again or touch me, the next time I'll see you will be in court and if you think you can hit me and get away with it then you don't see those watching cameras and all these people staring at you.'

He let his fist quiver in the air as if he was still contemplating using it to strike me but already as his eyes skittered over my shoulder I knew the moment had passed and then leaning forward almost as if to kiss my cheek he whispered, 'Next time, old man, next time.' And then he was gone, almost immediately hidden by people hurrying into the tube station. Micah was crying and she pressed his head into her skirt and fondled the back of his hair.

'You shouldn't have interfered,' she said suddenly, her face sullen, the way she held her head making the metal jewellery glint aggressively as if it was forged by some lingering residue of Sean. 'I know you meant to help but it's not your business and you've made things worse because he's pissed off now.'

That was the moment when I should have mumbled some apology or an attempted justification for what she saw as my interference. This was the moment when I could have walked away but instead I asked, 'Why's he angry with you?'

Her affection for Micah turned into irritation and she pushed him away from her telling him brusquely that he should stop crying and that they were going home. I knew in that moment I would never see her again and it frightened me a little as if it were another loss that might unbalance whatever equilibrium I had managed to establish so I asked again, 'Why is he angry with you?'

'Because I owe him money.'

'How much?'

'A hundred pound.'

I didn't ask why she had borrowed it – it wasn't my business – but it seemed a pathetic amount to owe if it necessitated experiencing fear. Fear's something else I don't like to have near me. Those few times I've felt its cold clamour clutching at me are enough to make me wary and know I want to avoid it as much as humanly possible in the rest of my life so it didn't seem like a grand gesture, so much as almost an instinctive act of self-preservation, that made me say, 'I'll give you the money.'

She shook her head and said, 'You can't give me your money.'

'Please,' I said as I touched her hand briefly, 'please, I want to. There's a cash machine on the corner. Just let's go now, just let's go now and get it.'

She hesitated, turning her head away from me as if distracted but clearly weighing up the offer before saying, 'I'll pay you back. I promise I'll pay you back.'

'No, Georgie, that's not what I want. This is a gift, a private thing that I want to do, and I don't want you ever to mention it again. Just do it for me.'

She nodded and with Micah in between us we walked on until we reached the cashpoint where I drew out £150 and when she looked at me and looked at the money in her hands I simply told her to put it away somewhere safe and that the extra was to make sure she didn't have to borrow again. She kissed me on the cheek and when I put my hands up and shook my head it was to help her understand that I didn't want any thanks and she apologised and then we both got embarrassed, looking anywhere except at each other. I told her I had to be going and after a moment's hesitation she asked if I would be able to do her one more favour. It reminded me of the time in the shop when after the price reduction she scrounged a plastic bag but after I asked her what it was she hesitated as if conscious of the inappropriateness of the request. She wanted me to mind Micah for half an hour while she found Sean and gave him the money. His flat was just round the corner from her and if she returned the money quickly then everything would be all right.

There comes a point in every story where different outcomes are possible, roads taken or not taken and all that, and if you want what I think is the truth I wasn't keen to do it – it felt like a step too far and already I wasn't sure if my impulsiveness about the money was a foolishness. And while we're talking about truth then I suppose I need to say that why I gave her the money was yes in part about side-stepping the press of fear – there wasn't any amount of money in the whole world was able to still its sudden flare we both felt at that young doctor's words and here it could be dispelled by a single cash-machine transaction. But it's also true that it made me feel better about myself and when you lose the one person in the world who somehow has been able to love you, there aren't so many opportunities to feel the approval of another. So I suppose that was why five minutes later I was following her through the door of a basement flat on Compton Road.

The room we stepped into was shadowed despite the brightness of the day and almost immediately she switched on the lights and then supplemented these by doing the same to the strings of fairy lights that hung from different places and which gave the flat a feel of Christmas. It was lightly furnished with a plastic settee posing as leather, an armchair that almost matched, a table and two skimpy chairs and a television with a bigger screen size than my own balanced precariously on a small coffee table. About the window hung gauzy strips of red and purple voile that were meant to serve as curtains and in one narrow alcove shelves holding Micah's toys and books buckled under the weight. The place looked reasonably clean but already even on this August day I could smell the presence of must and where one wall met the ceiling spun a black spider's web of damp.

'Sit down, Tom,' she said as she used a remote to turn on the television and within a few seconds it was pulsing cartoons, the room rendered even a little more plaintive against the sudden vividness of the colours. 'Micah will watch television until I get back. He'll not be any bother, will you, Micah?' But Micah was already oblivious to everything other than the screen and she took his silence as confirmation before smiling and telling me, 'I'll be as quick as I can and thanks again, Tom.' Then as she went out of the door she paused to call, 'Make yourself a cup of tea, just help yourself to everything.'

And then she was gone and although I tried to engage Micah with a few reassuring words about his mother not being long, he ignored me, stuck a thumb in his mouth and gave the television his full attention. So after a few minutes I went to the kitchen and filled the kettle. There were candles of various shapes and sizes but little of the predictable stuff that most of us have and only the child's drawings stuck to the fridge struck a familiar note. The contents of the fridge were as basic as everything else in the flat but at least there was milk so after making a cup of tea I took my seat again beside Micah, and then in an unexpected but curiously affecting movement he laid his head on the cushion of my thigh and still watching the television curled himself into foetal shape. I think I was cross with her then for leaving her child with someone she knew nothing about and then an awareness of the potentially haunting consequences of such an action made me uneasy and unwilling even to touch him in the most superficial way.

An hour later she hadn't returned and, his biological clock ticking, he suddenly sat up and told me he was hungry and wanted his tea. I told him his mum would be home soon but nothing I said was able to distract him from the realisation of his most pressing need so reluctantly I did another recce of the kitchen and twenty minutes later he was tucking into fish fingers and spaghetti hoops. He still had a moustache of orange sauce when she returned, scampering into the room at the same time as an apology tumbled from her lips.

'I couldn't find him so I had to wait until he came back,' she said a little too breathlessly while patting Micah on the head and telling him what he knew already, that I had made him his tea and he had eaten it up. Then as he left the table to revisit the television she rested her hand on my shoulder and said, 'You've been very kind, Tom, really kind and I'm very grateful.'

'It's OK,' I said, 'but I better be going,' and as I lifted Micah's plate away I heard her say, 'Please let me make you something. It's the least I can do,' and she took the plate from my hand and nodded at me in the optimistic entreaty she had perfected and which I recognised from our exchanges in the shop and when I thanked her but declined she urged, 'Please stay for tea – it'll be something simple that won't take me long.' Then when I hesitated, 'We don't often have a visitor so it would be nice if you could stay and have something to eat.'

'I don't want to put you to any trouble,' I said, not wanting her to think she needed to find payback for the money.

'I'll just put Micah to bed and then stick something on. Watch the TV.'

So I sat on the settee again and watched cartoons because I couldn't see where the remote was and didn't want to start rummaging around for it. After about ten minutes she reappeared and said Micah was worn out with all the earlier walking they had done and had gone over in an instant. There was something different in her appearance and I didn't know if she had changed her top or simply splashed her face but she looked fresher, lighter, as if she had cast off some of the burdens of the day.

'So he came back then,' I asked, 'and you gave him the money?'

'Yes, he came back eventually.'

'And there's no problem about the money or anything else?'

'No, it's all sorted,' she said, speaking from behind me as she busied herself in the kitchen.

I wondered what she was going to be able to conjure from the empty shelves and for a second thought of offering to get a takeaway but I think I knew there was a chance that if I went I probably wouldn't have returned because I felt an awkward embarrassment, the self-consciousness that prevents us from lingering after we have dispensed a little generosity to some homeless guy in a doorway or a busker on the underground. Drop the coins and move on, but never hang around as if expecting an effusive expression of thanks. The meal felt wrong but she had started whatever alchemy she was about to work and so it was too late to leave.

'Is anyone expecting you?' she asked.

'I'm on my own,' I said before instinctively adding, 'my wife died,' as I always find myself informing even complete strangers who don't need or want to know. Why do I always say this even when I've resolved to stop? I don't think I'm looking for sympathy so maybe it's my way of saying that Linda was once alive and living in this world. And maybe something else, which is that once I was loved because even though more time passes it's something I don't ever want to forget. But whereas most people shuffle through their embarrassment by either ignoring the statement or mumbling some quick expression of symathy Georgie asked me right away what she was called.

'Linda, her name was Linda.'

'When did she die?'

'About three years ago. She had cancer.'

'I'm sorry,' she said as she momentarily paused whatever she was doing before offering me a glass of wine that I was suddenly pleased to accept and in the next few minutes there was only the sound of the television and kitchen cupboard doors opening and closing. And then the meal of a microwaved potato filled with cheese and garnished with salad was ready and although she apologised for its simplicity I was conscious that it was the first meal I'd had served to me since my life became solitary and when I told her it was very nice I meant it.

'You must miss her,' she said as she refilled my wine glass.

'Yes, I do.' And then to break the settling silence added, 'But life goes on,' and was immediately ashamed of what felt like a betrayal. 'It takes a while to get used to it. Not sure if I'll ever quite crack it.'

'Children?'

'One daughter. She works in a law firm so she's kept busy.'

'Not too busy to see her father, I hope.'

'No, no,' I answered as convincingly as I could and beginning to feel as if I'd already revealed too much of my private life to someone I barely knew.

'That's good,' she said, holding her glass towards me and inviting me to do the same. In that faint clink of connection strange thoughts came tumbling out before falling away again and I tried to wipe away all traces by asking her if she had always been on her own.

'More or less. I lived with Micah's father for a little while but it never worked out,' and she shrugged her shoulders.

'Is Sean Micah's father?'

'No, he's just a friend who helps out from time to time.'

I thankfully resisted the temptation to make some cynical observation along the lines of with friends like that who needs enemies and for a few moments we lapsed into silence until as if reading my thoughts she said, 'You didn't see him at his best today and I'm sorry he spoke to you that way. He's not always like that and I've owed him the money for longer than I should – he needed it to pay his rent. He just ran out of patience, that's all.'

She said this looking intently at me as if to gauge whether her words had convinced but I focused on what was left on the plate and then the conversation turned to Micah and her uncertainty about whether he was in the right school. I told her about my former career but the more I tried to explain about the complexities of traffic flow, the more it sounded a curiously random and strange thing on which to have spent your working life. She told me a little about herself, about completing a degree in jewellery-making at art college and how it was her ambition to have a little shop where she sold her own designs.

After we had finished eating she offered me coffee but I thanked her and as soon as was polite told her it was time for me to be getting home. At the door she held my sleeve lightly and when she started to thank me for the money once more I raised my hand and stopped her, reminding her, 'The deal with the money is that you never mention it again,' before adding, 'I enjoyed the meal.'

She took her hand from my sleeve and rested it on my shoulder then raised her cheek to mine for a second and I felt both the warmth of her skin and the cold brush of metal. So what did I think when I walked back home? And what was it I felt? Well, as I passed the front gardens of suburbia and saw the displays of bedding plants in those that hadn't been turned into parking spaces, heard the snatches of family life ebbing from opened windows and at the corner of my street smelt the unmistakable smoke of a barbecue, what I felt was a more acute sense of loneliness than I had experienced for some time. All around me life was flowing from what was normally enclosed and private before merging openly with the languorous rhythms and scents of a summer night where all the exhausting light of the day had been burnt off and time was slipping painlessly and slowly towards a renewed sense of calm. I passed a corner garden where violet spears of buddleia were badged with an orange clot of butterflies and another where two young boys were playing cricket with their father, his run-up and bowling action a slowed-down, almost freeze-framed demonstration of spin.

When I opened the front door of my house for a second I felt a reluctance to close it as if to do so would be to shut out the world and close me in with nothing much more than myself. But as I did it, glancing one final time back into the street, I rebuked myself with the knowledge that to succumb to some maudlin mix of nostalgia and self-pity would do nothing for me except paralyse the very energies that I needed to keep moving, to have the will to get out of bed in the morning. And so I turned on the radio in the kitchen and listened to a voice telling me what I should do to avoid being scammed by some Nigerian con man with a computer. Then I switched on the kettle and sat at the kitchen table as the events of the day pressed themselves fresh into my memory. And at first like some bad taste in the mouth I tried to dispel the memory of Sean but the intensity of his words suddenly reasserted itself and I was conscious of the risk I had taken and a little shocked by what I had done.

In the shop I feel a curiosity about the lives that are represented by the objects that pass through my hands but it's a harmless speculation as I try to piece together the reality of a life once lived. But this thing with Georgie was different and broke the fundamental rule of never getting involved in things that have no predictable outcome and generally trying to avoid all risks and danger. I listened to the voice on the radio outlining how gullible people had lost their life savings in what sounded to me at least like the most preposterous and pathetically obvious scams, but then as I sat and sipped my tea I realised that all of them were rooted in the inescapable vulnerability of the human heart. And later on as I prepared the house for night it wasn't the pink swathes layering the sky or the lingering orange glow of a patio heater in a neighbour's garden that held my attention so much as checking all the windows were shut and my doors safely locked.

I had decided that it wasn't likely I would ever see Georgie again and that the taking of the money would prevent her returning to the shop. But that was one of many things I got wrong because two days later there she was and when no one else was looking she passed me a thank-you drawing Micah had done and to which she had added her own written thanks and an invitation to tea with the promise of a more ambitious menu. I thanked her and then tried to make an excuse, saying it wasn't necessary and keeping my voice low, increasingly conscious we had aroused Gwen's curious stare, and I suppose it was to avoid that continued scrutiny that made me suddenly accept. But when a day later I arrived at the flat and rang the bell I was greeted by Georgie and Micah ready to go out and I assumed she had forgotten.

'We're having a picnic,' she said as she handed me a red tartan blanket and a wicker basket to carry. 'It seemed a pity to waste this good weather.'

And I think I was happy enough not to reacquaint myself with the gloom of the flat in which no amount of fairy lights could dispel the sense of being underground.

'We're going to the park to feed the ducks, isn't that right, Micah?' she said breezily and there was a lilting lightness of anticipation in her voice and all her movements that felt like an invitation to share whatever promises the world could offer. And so we set off to the local park at a jaunty pace with Micah having to be constantly cautioned not to run too far ahead. Even though I felt a little self-conscious at carrying a wicker basket, the contents of which were covered by a chequered teacloth, it was pleasant to listen to her busy chatter. And whether it was her tribulations about a broken washing machine, the month of rain we'd just had or Micah's progress at school, she spoke to me as if we'd known each other for a long time and so there was never that hesitant, awkward first stage that most new relationships need to experience before they settle into their ease.

In the park we spread the blanket on the grass close to the lake that was more of a large pond and which joggers endlessly circled, but the ducks must have had forewarning that Micah was coming because all that could be seen on the water was the skim of dragonflies and trembling funnels of midges which occasionally drew a brief circle of ripples as presumably some fish surfaced in search of food. Georgie gave Micah two slices of stale bread and as compensation for the absence of the ducks he fed the pigeons and when the bread ran out amused himself by chasing them into scuttling flight.

Georgie removed the teacloth to reveal slices of ciabatta with a variety of toppings and a plastic container of home-made buns. As she handed me a napkin and a bottle of sparkling water she said, 'Sometimes I think I'd like to live somewhere the sun shines all the time and you can spend time outdoors and not be cooped up all winter worrying about your heating bills.'

'I'd miss the seasons,' I said, 'but it would make the winter more bearable if the sun remembered to shine in the summer.'

'I read somewhere we're all suffering from SAD – you know, not enough sunshine,' she said before warning Micah not to stray too close to the water.

'Where would you go?'

'I don't know, it's just a thought I get every so often. But a child anchors you to what you know, makes it harder to take risks.'

'After a while you'd take the sun for granted and you wouldn't get the pleasure that a day like this brings.'

'You're probably right,' she said and as she nodded the light suddenly flecked the colours in her hair into brighter life and burnished the metal stud and earrings. 'It's easy to take things for granted.'

I thought of the thirty years of marriage I had shared with Linda and wondered if I had been guilty of that but I couldn't do so without my head being filled with clichés of the you-don't-know-what-you-have-until-it's-gone variety and these combined to obscure any clarity of reflection, so in an attempt to dispel them said, 'It can't be easy being a single mum.'

'No, I don't suppose it is but after a while you don't think of it like that – it's just the way things are. You accept it, do your best and try not to waste time wondering how things might have worked out differently. I don't want anyone's sympathy.'

I looked away, staring across the water, unsure whether I'd been told off. The sky's reflection seemed to tease the rippling surface. There was silence for a moment before she asked, 'Was your life with Linda happy?'

I was momentarily distracted from the need for an answer by the breathless arrival of Micah in search of sustenance and as he flopped down on the blanket I wondered what it was I might say. She had prepared food for him and when he thought of wandering off with it she made him sit and eat under her supervision and not for the first time it struck me that she was a good mother who within the limitations of her resources did the best for her son. When he had finished and ambled off again to feed the pigeons with his leftovers I tried to answer her question because it seemed such an important one and one that couldn't be left hanging in the air.

So after she had gone to fetch Micah from going too close to the water's edge and I was alone on the blanket, its tartan pattern, its smell and the itch of the wool a reminder of distant seaside picnics, I said, 'Yes it was happy but because that's the way things are and mostly you don't realise it, don't ever tell yourself or her that it is, and then when you finally understand it, it's too late. And nothing can change that even though you tell her, trying to convince yourself that she's listening in the silence, when each time you speak to her she feels as if she's slipped even further away.'

As I watched Georgie lead a reluctant Micah back by the hand to the safety of the blanket I felt the fear of Linda's existence, the reality of her presence in my life for over thirty years, being finally lost and exerting no stronger grasp than the vague, half-formed recollections of childhood. And in that moment I wished I hadn't taken her things to the shop, let people disperse them to the wind. I should have held them close, tried to draw some sustaining sustenance from them – their touch, their smell, the memories that each might have evoked.

Not much later Georgie said that it was perhaps time to take Micah home and even though he protested we folded up the blanket and put the little left of the food back in the basket. I looked for a final time at the surface of the water and the trees that wept their branches into it and tried to focus on nothing but the present and the child who was complaining that he was tired and wanted to be carried and his mother who was insisting he walked in the belief that the more he tired himself out the more he was likely to sleep. But about five minutes from the house he refused to go any further and then with his mother's approval I carried him the remaining distance. He was already beginning to drift into sleep and so I had to take him into the flat and following Georgie took him to his bedroom then left her to undress him and slip him into bed.

In the kitchen I put the kettle on, an action that reminded me how increasingly at ease I felt, and as I waited for it to boil I looked at the washing machine that was not working and in a few minutes had diagnosed and solved the problem by removing one of Micah's socks that was blocking the drainage hose. Although I pride myself on my DIY skills it wasn't such a feat of mechanical expertise as I'd done it several times before so Georgie's thanks seemed unnecessarily effusive. I suppose it might have been the prospect of handwashing or a hefty engineer's bill that prompted her little hand-clapping jig which made me smile and I imagine it was in pursuit of that same feeling of being valued that saw me return at intervals in the subsequent months to rehang cupboard doors whose hinges had broken, bleed radiators and carry out various bits of painting.

Gradually we came to fill in the missing parts of our respective stories so I learned that her father and mother had split when she was twelve and during her teenage years she had lived with both, mostly depending, it seemed to me, on whoever tried to impose the least regulation. And despite what she had said earlier she admitted that she had never graduated, dropping out in the middle of her second year because she was bored. About Micah's father she never spoke and I never asked, sensing that he was a part of her past that she didn't want to revisit. And slowly over the months I felt I had got to know her more, to understand how often she could be buoyed up on hopes, sudden enthusiastic surges of future schemes, and how fragile these ultimately proved when obstacles that had not previously been envisaged gradually imposed themselves. I did some talking too but my story had fewer subplots, fewer divergences from a predictable medium way, so mostly I was happy to try and follow her convoluted lifelines that seemed to have constantly tangled in ways that were outside my experience.

Once she told me that she'd finally, absolutely finally, decided what it was she wanted to do and as she kicked off her pumps, her tanned insteps abruptly meeting the snow line of her toes, and slipped her feet under her on the settee I waited for her to reveal her latest plan for her future life.

'I want to be the person in a big store who does the window displays. I know I could do it and coming from an art background would give me a head start. Some of the ones you see have no imagination – I know I could do better. You would do a new one every season and at Christmas you'd push the boat out and have this display that would make people stop on the pavement and stare because they needed to take it all in. And you could have something that suddenly surprised them, made them jump.'

The flush of excitement quickened her voice and I nodded as encouragingly as I could and when she asked if I thought it'd be a good plan to put together a few sketches showcasing her ideas, I nodded again. And that is how I sometimes think of her as she conjured little future windows, moving and arranging the circumstances of her life to what she hoped was better effect. And because she was able to illuminate them with such a bright burst of enthusiasm it was difficult, at least at the moment of their conception, to shadow them with the doubts that would later emerge.

A week after she told me of her latest career plan she phoned me late at night about Micah whose high temperature had convinced her he had meningitis and I drove them both to A&E. They kept him overnight as a precaution but it turned out to be a virus whose worst effect was to leave him slightly dehydrated. She stayed with him through the night and at lunchtime the next day I drove them back home where she cried a little out of relief and took it in turns to hug us. When they both fell asleep I sat quietly in the living room watching the television with the sound muted and in those couple of hours felt like – I was almost going to say their good angel, but I know how that might sound so instead I'll just say their friend.

That was how we became part of each other's lives and like the shop you don't need to be an expert to grasp the need it fulfilled for me although below the surface there were occasions when I was conscious of other complications of feeling. And yes, while it's true there were times when I gave her money – once to cover an electric bill, once to replace the washing machine which broke down beyond my capacity to repair and at intervals smaller amounts to buy something Micah needed – I also want to believe that she got more from our connection than the opening of my wallet. They never came to my house because I never asked them and I wonder about that now. It wasn't anything to do with the neighbours because they know so little about my life that they would probably have assumed she was my niece or even my daughter. So why did I never ask her? I don't really know for sure but probably because it ran the risk of feeling as if they would have been intruding in a world that still belonged in significant part to Linda.

How long things might have continued on this course I don't know. Perhaps in time they would simply have petered out as we grew tired of each other, or she would have constructed some future window where I had no role to play. At that time I didn't think of the future much and tried simply to take things as they came because to analyse the flow of our relationship would probably have produced more questions than answers and there were things that I was happy to accept.

So what changed it? A question, really, a familiar question at that. I had come over on her invitation to look at a CV she had constructed on the library computer – because I had worked in the civil service she assumed I had insights into the mind of official-dom. When I got there with my laptop Micah was already in bed and if anything Georgie seemed quieter than normal and when she showed me it, she said, 'It doesn't amount to much, does it?'

I tried to reassure her by telling her that with a little polish and some layout tweaking we could make it look highly presentable and she perked up a bit and watched closely as I made a more effective copy of it on my laptop, asking her questions that enabled me to strengthen it, disguising absences and highlighting the positive.

'You need referees,' I told her as eventually we came to the end. 'Who would you like to use?'

'Mr Kerr, my old art teacher, would vouch for me. He used to call me his Tracey Emin and he encour-aged me to go to art college.' After a pause when she struggled to think of someone else she asked, 'Tom, would you be one for me?'

'Of course,' I said and typed in my name and address.

Then when it was finished she produced a bottle of wine and poured us each a celebratory glass.

'Depending on the type of job, you might need to take out some of the metal decorations,' I told her, but smiling.

'I can do that if I have to,' her fingers briefly brushing against her earlobe.

We drank the rest of the wine and then it was time for me to go. I promised when home I'd do a final check of her CV and then print some copies on good-quality paper. She was pleased but there was no flare of the optimism that usually lightened her face and animated her voice when she momentarily constructed some new future. I gathered up my things and said goodnight and then in the half-open doorway she pulled me back gently by the sleeve and offered me her cheek. I kissed it and then turned again to leave. That's when I heard her say quietly, heard her say it sincerely and without any trace of flirtatious play or the teasing lilt that she sometimes used in the shop, 'Is that the best you can do for me?' I looked at her and she stood looking back and then she kissed me and at first I simply let her.

In the bedroom I was suddenly unsure, but for every apprehension there was something stronger and her certainty served to undermine all my hesitancy. She stood at the side of the bed and slowly and deliberately began to remove the nose studs and the earrings. They knocked against each other as she set them on the bedside table, a tinkling descant to the drumming of my heart.

'You don't have to do that,' I said, my voice almost a whisper, as if to speak more loudly would risk it trembling into a nothingness. 'You don't have to do any of this.'

'I want to. I'm doing it because I want to. So do you think you can stop talking and just come and hold me, do your best for me the way you always do?'

So I did and when she stood naked I wrapped the skinny tremble of her body in the tightness of my embrace, felt her beaded spine pressing against the thin sheath of her skin. When I think about the rest now and I think about it often, it always begins with a pulse of shame, the shame of old flesh on young, the predictable old-enough-to-be-her-father refrain playing on a loop, and of course there's the voice that tries to insist it was nothing but the payment of a debt – a payment that a decent man would never have accepted. But after the voice has had its say and tried to stamp its shame on the memory there's something else that asserts the moment can't simply be defined by these things because what it felt like was no more, no less, than two hearts beating against each other, the way a moth beats its wings against the glass in the hope of finding its escape, and perhaps not much else matters when that's what happens.

Afterwards of course I was confused and embarrassed to the point of going back home almost immediately despite her invitation to stay. When I didn't appear back at the flat for a number of days she sent me a text that simply told me everything was all right and that they both wanted to see me. When eventually I summoned up the courage to return, all sorts of speeches readymade in my head, she greeted me as if nothing had happened and I was happy to be complicit with the unspoken agreement that we weren't going to talk about it. But I think now that's when I lost my courage and I've already told you that I wasn't a brave man to begin with. What it left me with was a sudden quickening and then a raw sense of something to which I couldn't give a name but which felt as if it might overwhelm me and threatened to spiral out of any sense of control. And it wasn't something that could be fed as data into a computer or plotted as a graph and I grew frightened of where it might take me, of becoming someone I wasn't supposed to be. But I couldn't simply walk away – I wasn't brave enough for that either.

It's probable – I realise that now – that I would gradually, if not suddenly, have drifted back into the safer and shallower waters of my life even if I hadn't been helped by what happened but I also realise now that although these things seemed real at the time they were merely the excuses I needed to avoid pushing my courage, or whatever the right word is, further than I was willing to go. So one morning as I was on my way to the shop I took a slight detour to the flat in order to drop in a leaflet from the local college that was offering various courses that I thought might interest her. It was one of those mornings when the light is misted, almost silvered, but you know the rising heat will slowly burn it away and in that promise there is an anticipation and a sense of pleasure only temporarily stalled. It was about a month after I had slept with Georgie, an event that often occupied my thoughts but which we had not repeated and which never established its reality in anything other than a shared if wordless memory. Doing this delivery seemed as good as any way to start the day and even though I intended to simply post the leaflet through the letter box it brought a connection, a sense of being anchored to something in the drift of those years after Linda's death.

I was nearly there, could actually see it from across the road, when someone came up the steps his arm pushing into the sleeve of a jacket. It was Sean, of course. I stopped behind a car and watched as he struggled for a second before his other arm found a sleeve and then made his shoulders ruck it into place. He was on the opposite pavement and took nothing in except his own hurry to be somewhere else. I watched him scurry away but even as he disappeared out of sight his physical reality was intense and formed afresh from the memory of his words, the hammer of his fist hanging in the air, and although I tried not to I couldn't stop myself thinking of that same hand pressed against her fragile spine where I had felt the vertebrae pushed against her skin like raised buttons on a flimsy coat. And, yes, it was in that instant when I heard the old-fool refrain breaking about my head and that first and worst flaring sense of foolishness. And, yes, despite the fact that I had no claim on her or any rights that precluded her from other parts of her life, it's true that I felt not just a sense of betrayal but one of loss, of being suddenly cast adrift again at that very moment when I had begun to feel steadied, even purposeful, in the pattern of my life.

I crumpled the leaflet but kept it in my hand until I passed a litter bin. I tried to make the walking filter out as much of the confusion as possible, temper some of the anger that had begun to flood through my thoughts and the bitter listing of my generosities, but as I increased my pace I could hear another, insistent voice telling me that it was not about what had been given so much as what had been lost. I thought of not going to the shop and simply returning home and closing the door but that frightened me more than any other course I could imagine so I went to work as usual and tried to focus as best as I could on the duties I was supposed to perform.

I didn't see Georgie for over a week and when she texted me I invented some family matters concerning my daughter with which I was supposedly busy. And then just as the summer turned its ear to the first whispers of autumn I went back.

'Hello, stranger,' she said as she opened the door while I stared at her face as if searching for some admission of what I couldn't help but construe as guilt. 'Get everything sorted?'

'Sorted?'

'Yes, whatever it was you were doing for your daughter.'

'Yes. Just some house stuff she needed help with.'

'You spend your life helping people.'

'I wouldn't say that,' I answered before I gave her a copy of the leaflet I had put in the bin. 'I don't know but there might be something that would interest you there.'

'You're always looking out for me,' she said, putting her hand on my shoulder and briefly kissing my cheek.

I almost asked her there and then about Sean but didn't and as she busied herself with clearing the kitchen table she offered me a coffee but I told her I couldn't stay, inventing a delivery for which I had to be home.

'A flying visit,' she said and momentarily stopped what she was doing. 'Is everything all right, Tom?'

But the desire to say something was repressed by the even greater fear of spilling into stupidities and assumptions that I had no right to make and so as an alternative to making a fool of myself I told her it was and left. I went back less often but I still went back and although there was never any physical trace of Sean, for which I searched endlessly, I felt his presence everywhere and I began to wonder what, if anything, she had told him about us. Did her ability to keep a secret extend as far as us? And she made new friends – a couple of young mothers, one of whom was also a single parent. I tried to be pleased for her and although I only met them once they seemed nice-enough people and I knew that any other reaction on my part was selfishness. They started a yoga class together and sometimes I looked after Micah during it. I had by then managed to wean him off television; if not completely, then long enough for me to read some of the children's books I got from my local library, telling the librarian it was for my grandchild when she made a joke about the change in my reading habits. And sometimes when he was bored of both books and television we'd build a den using an old tablecloth draped over the back of chairs as a roof. He liked that a lot and we'd furnish it with cushions and share some snack. It didn't seem impossible that some day we might go camping as I remembered the old tent that was stowed somewhere in my roof space.

But we never got to go camping and I often wonder about how he's getting on in school and how his reading's going. Wonder too about Georgie. Sometimes when I stand in the shop and the door opens I look up and anticipate her entry and at others I glance at the window, remember that day she walked past, her head unbowed by the rain, how she waved in and just for a fleeting moment it felt as if there was no glass between us. What did she see when she looked in? Was my life set out for her complete, arranged in its set patterns? Was it an old fool she saw when I raised my hand in reply?

One night after she had returned from the yoga class I saw the bracelet she was wearing. It had little beads of dark and light blue glass with a couple of small silver-type feathers strung at either end. I recognised it right away. I had bought it for Linda in a tiny shop down a narrow street behind the cathedral in Barcelona. I had bought it for her on that weekend trip we had taken to mark her birthday. It hadn't even cost much but she was fond of it and I remembered how pleased I had been that she liked it so much. It was part of her belongings I had stupidly taken to the shop and then had to stand as Gwen inspected everything before recording her valuations in the ledger.

'That's a nice bracelet,' I said to Georgie.

'Thanks. I like it.' And she held her wrist out towards me so that I could have a closer look.

'Did you get it in the shop?'

'Yes, that's right,' she said. 'About a week ago.'

'It's very pretty.'

Then she took it off and offered it to me to inspect and I wanted to tell her but I had to be sure so I handed it back and the next time I was in the shop I checked the ledger where every sale was recorded but found no trace of it. And of course I remembered Gwen's words about charity starting at home and decided that Georgie had stolen it. She had stolen something that belonged to Linda and in that realisation everything seemed to change until it felt that I had stolen something too. I tried to find reasons but none sounded stronger than an excuse and although the way I think about it all has changed over time, there's still some voice in my head that sounds accusatory and although I don't even think it's Linda's voice any more it still has the power to unsettle and knock me off course. And mostly it's a weakness, a cowardice, when we let others' voices drown out our own but perhaps better than anyone I should know there is no perfect flow, just a series of stops and starts, wrong turnings, roads not taken.

There wasn't a scene and I didn't say anything about the bracelet – I don't do that sort of stuff, don't know how to really. I just never went back and I think somehow she knew because she never returned to the shop or tried to contact me. There were times when I almost changed my mind. And then it was too late and a few months later, when I made an excuse to myself and passed her flat in the dusk, there was a To Let sign attached to the railings.

Some afternoons like this when the rain slants against the shop's window I think about her and remember how the first time her hair was beaded with droplets. How it was coloured like petrol splashed on water. And although it sounds crazy sometimes at home just before it's time to go to bed I want to build a den, drape a sheet over chairs for a roof, and sleep there rather than upstairs in a bed that's inescapably double. And sometimes like now when I'm working in the shop I stop and remember how she liked to construct those bright windows of the future and then I wonder if she were ever to shape the memory of our past what form would it take? Perhaps she'd see me hold these same things as I stand and look again at the objects in the box, lift them out one by one and wonder what value Gwen will place on them and which ones she will discard. I want to clear a shelf before Gwen has a chance to pass her judgement, and arrange these objects so they have their place – three carved wooden elephants trunk to tail; a child's tortoiseshell-backed hair-brush with withered and shrivelled bristles; an

269

old song about love; a faded wedding photograph in an ebony frame; a small bird with a chipped wing. It's the best I can do. The best I can do for them. I think Linda would understand this.

Crossing the River

In memoriam
Isabel Park
1925–2010

ITAKE THEM OVER. It's my job. As long as I can
remember and probably even before that, because
here time slowly unwinds, then just when you think
it's a straight line – the very way you want it to be –
it coils and spools in on itself and when you try to
pull an end to unravel it, everything tightens into
knots. Better not to try and better too just to concentrate on the rowing because that doesn't get any
easier. My palms are long sanded smooth by the
oars and fingers white-whorled with calluses – no
one could take my fingerprints any more. I have the
frequent, insistent complaint of my back and at
intervals there is a stab of pain that makes me
wince but I never share the reason with the passenger. They have passed through enough pain of
their own so why would they want to hear about
mine?

Sometimes I think about retirement and it's true I've enough buried coins to see me through, but I've had the licence a long time and it's not something that can be given up lightly, or even passed to an unenthusiastic son, who in any case has a different career in mind. And whatever anyone says about the wages there is a part of me at least that thinks of it as a calling. So I keep on rowing them and every time I try to give them the best crossing that I can and of course I know how to listen, and there's usually listening to be done, as the bewilderment of the journey finally shakes their voices free from the silent shroud of death.

There are younger ones working the river now, touting for business, offering cut-price rates, but none of them has the licence and some of them would slice your throat for it. But no one who has heard the stories of passengers being dumped halfway, and even worse if you believe the shoreline rumours, would risk stepping into their boats. I have the licence and that means the boat is sure and true, inspected once a year and hauled out of the water and subjected to the most rigorous of tests. The inspector won't renew the licence if there's any sign that it's not seaworthy and so for about three days I have to caulk and mend and scrape, give everything a brand-new lining of pitch and paint. Out of the water for three days always means there's a backlog. But there's no shortcuts to be taken and no one gets a skimped or shoddy deal because what I understand, and what the young ones with their customised and pimped carriers, all glittering with technology and toys, their sat navs and their entertainment centres, fail to grasp, is what the customer mostly wants is reassurance – a quiet listener if they wish to speak and silence if they don't. And if I'm asked for an opinion, or get to have a choice, then I think it's probably true that the steady rhythm of the rowing and the soft caress of the oars are best for calming and carrying their souls.

I never look at the schedule. I like to take it just as it comes, do what needs to be done just as it happens. So as I bring the boat alongside the jetty I have no need of name, or circumstance, and it's none of my business really and mostly it's just an unwanted distraction. In this, the first crossing of the day, my mind focuses on only the poorness of the light, the fretting choppiness of the water and the stirring, wakening swirl of the currents. He's waiting for me and as he sees my approach he looks deliberately at his watch to let me see his impatience but as I manoeuvre closer I weigh him with my eyes and gauge how low in the water the boat will sit. I offer my hand but he declines it as he steps aboard and takes his seat. His suit marks him out as a merchant and already he's brushing the weft of the cloth and running his hand through the thick rush of his hair, trying to refind the memory of who he is. I ask for the coin before the start because I know from experience that sometimes it is the wealthy who are most reluctant to pay the fare. He pats his sides and below his heart as if he's frisking himself and I see the moment of panic as he realises his pockets are empty and then finding the coin I watch him finger and turn it slowly in his hand. He's in no hurry to hand it over and he's a man who's always expected his money to work for him so I listen to him ask about an upgrade, as if there's some comfort, some hidden luxury, from which he's been excluded. I shake my head and hold out my hand for the coin but he's looking at it and weighing up the opportunities he thinks it brings. For a moment I feel a pulse of anger and want to tell him that where he's going he'll have no need of money but I know already that such words as these will only confuse and even stir him into movement that will put us both at risk, so I say nothing and merely pause and lean on the oars.

He tells me that in the other time and place he had his own boat and how much it cost and I nod as if I'm impressed. He tells me everything he owned and the list is long but after a while all I hear is the rising complaint of my back. Sometimes I think I need to caulk and oil it like the timbers of the boat. It's as if the coldness of the morning air has burrowed into my spine and now nestles at the very core. My hand is still stretched towards him and he narrows his eyes and looks at the rough patina of calluses, compares it no doubt to the softness of his own fingers with their rings and their manicured nails.

'Things fell apart,' he says and his voice is thinner than before, as if it too is shaped and shivered by the cold. 'Came tumbling down like a house of cards.'

I nod as if I understand and then slowly and with a sense of pained regret he slips the coin that is completely hidden in the folds of his palm into mine, slithering it between our touching skin, as if taking the final feel of the coin to store inside the vault of his memory.

He sits back on his seat and hunches his shoulders against the cold. He has not yet had time to unlearn himself, to know that now there is nothing he needs, so he asks me about names, about those who have gone before and people who were the players and shakers, about the contacts he might make, about deals that might be brokered, and I merely nod and keep the rhythm of my stroke. That's all that's true now, I want to tell him, but I know it's too soon for him to understand and so I let him talk and try to make his words distract from the voice in my spine that tells me my own best days are past and that one day I too shall make this journey for a final time.

'I had it all,' he says, gently massaging his throat as if the words have seared his flesh. 'I had it all and then it was gone. Do you understand?'

I bow my head several times and try in the gesture to show I understand and that I shall give him good service, all due respect in honour of who he was. It's an old trick but it's old because it mostly works and even now he seems to grow calmer, his hands stretching out to rest on his knees. The press of his trousers is still sharp, his leather shoes polished bright. They've let him keep his watch but I always think that a mistake. A watch in eternity – where's the point in that?

Despite his weight we're making good time and soon he's straining his eyes in the burgeoning light to see the approaching shoreline. I glance at him and see him measuring it up as the boat speeds on with a steady pull, the black waters bisected by the dip and rise of the sharpened bow. It's a good rhythm and perhaps the growing light will worm its way into my spine, quieten and swaddle the complaints with warmth. But I take nothing for granted because there are currents and random eddies to be navigated and I've crossed it often enough to know that nothing can ever be taken lightly.

'There's no shoreline development,' he says, his eyes narrowing into slits as he scans the distance. 'Wasted opportunity,' he says, 'whatever the market, people always like to look out over water. It's a sure-fire thing. Copper-bottomed. Can't go wrong.' And when he asks me what I think I nod again and puff a little stream of air through my lips to show that I need all my strength and concentration to bring him safely ashore.

We're almost there now and he's getting more excited. He's talking about deals, about opportunities, and he's offering me a chance of a guaranteed return on my investment which will see me in a comfortable retirement without the need to work another day. As I moor at the jetty he tells me he'll give me his card and I watch as he pats his jacket once more and then he burrows his hand into his inside breast pocket and when he pulls it out empty he stares at that emptiness before slumping back on his seat. Then he furrows a hand through his hair again, loosens his tie before opening his collar and that's when I glimpse the red scar of the rope and I turn my eyes away because it's not something I want him to know I've seen. So after we dock he slowly rises to his feet and this time he takes my helping hand as he steps ashore and I think he's rummaging in his back pocket for a tip, a tip that under the terms of the licence I wouldn't be able to accept, but he pats me twice on the shoulder as a thank you and then he's gone. And for a second I sit listening to the sound of his leather-soled shoes on the wooden planks of the jetty and then as they fade into silence I push off again and pull once more on the oars.

You get days like this when everything is tricky and the passengers present more problems than the currents. There are those whose lives have been taken from them and whose anger sometimes rocks the boat, who've had no time to prepare, and I have to watch them finger their wounds as they do a kind of autopsy on themselves, confused by the sudden flowering of their own blood-blossomed bodies, desperate even to deny their ownership as if there's been a mix-up and they've been issued with someone else's. Children, too, can bring their own problems, more than could ever be described – not least those who think they've stumbled through some cavernous wardrobe and are heading towards adventure where they will ride on the back of a lion. You have to tell them again and again to sit down, that they can't help with the rowing, that this river offers no chance of dolphin or whale sightings. And of course there are the frightened, those who want their mothers, and sometimes I have to talk them all the way across, tell them stories or, even though I've no longer the voice for it, sing some of the old songs I remember from the childhood I must once have had.

So now as she gets in the boat I feel only a sense of relief. These rarely give any trouble. They've been travelling such a long time that one more crossing means little to them. She scrunches up on the plain wooden bench that passes for a seat as if leaving room for others to join her and when I tell her there's no need, that she's the only passenger, she brings her hands together as if she's praying and smiles. She's dressed in black and her hair, too, is black as the water and tied in a ponytail that sometimes the wind stirs a little and curls into a question mark but from experience I know she will ask little of me, that despite everything that's happened to her she will do nothing but trust. It's always been all she's ever had to cling to even though she knows by now that there is no truth in trust. So I'll do my best for her, do my best to be true, take her only where she needs to go. And before I can even ask she's taking out the coin that she's hidden in her clothing and unfolding the silk handkerchief in which it's wrapped. I wonder how many other coins she's had to pay to those who promised to take her to where she wanted to go and how many of them lied.

Already she will have crossed water, perhaps many times, starting even in a boat not much bigger than this and then who knows in what lurching, rolling holds of ships, the captive air hot and fetid? Or in the backs of lorries for many days, pushed in tight with others who share no names but only the embarrassment of their bodies and who are forbidden to speak. I glance at her and know she's so used to silence that it's what's most comfortable for her and it's only the occasional flick of her eyes over her shoulder that says she's still worried about what may be following her. I want to tell her she's safe now, for a second ask her to tell me her story, but it's against the rules so it's only the oars I let whisper in their little flurries and frets of white.

She's not very old, young enough to be someone's daughter, old enough to be someone's wife,
and somewhere there will be people who wonder
where she is and when she's coming back. Her face
is open, curiously smooth and unbruised by death,
and her eyes are brown but strangely glittering and
shiny as if freshly washed by rain. Her hands hold
the edges of the seat as if she thinks we might hit a
sudden wave that will throw her into the depths. I
want to tell her that I know the currents, that I've
never yet lost a passenger, that she's safe with me,
but I know she'd only smile and that her eyes would
still be edged with fear. She looks out at the water
and as the boat lifts a little in the swell I see her
knuckles blanch as her hands tighten their grip.
And then I understand – it's been a while since I've
sat facing such a one so I've forgotten the signs. I
tell her it won't be much longer, that I'll soon have
her ashore, and she smiles quickly and bows her
head submissively. It makes me want to remind her
that I am her servant, not she mine, that I know
how frightened she is of the water, but because she
doesn't understand that we are destined to die only
once I pull a little stronger, ignoring the fresh complaint of my back.

'Will I be able to get in touch with my family, tell
them that I'm here?' she suddenly asks. Her voice is
fluttering, light-winged.

'In time they'll know where you are and in time all
of them will be able to come here too,' I answer,
avoiding the bright glitter of her eyes.

'Will you bring them across?' she asks.

'I'll bring them all.'

'But I have no more money to pay you.' And then she begins to cry and I know her tears are salted with the sea and even when I say that there is no need to worry she continues and then she looks at me and asks if there is some other way she can pay. But before I can answer she tells me how long it is since she saw her family, that they will be worried about her, that she has a younger sister and she's frightened that she too will be deceived by the promises, then sold. How she will do anything to prevent that happening.

I swear to her that I shall bring them all, that I shall row each one safely to where she is, and that I want nothing more from her than to do good service, to bring her to where will be her home, and I tell her it's a place where she will never have to pay someone, or be used by a man again. She lifts her face to me and I do not know whether she is able to believe my words or not. I want to tell her that all I traffic in is souls and for a moment I wish that I was her father and could look after her until she knows the words are true. It's breaking the codes of practice, of course, to think things like that but the mind is a strange thing and not always given to sticking to the letter of the law. I must be getting old because as the skin on my palms hardens I fear that something's softening inside and I know that's no use in a job like this – perhaps another sign after all that it's time to hang up the oars, sell the licence to someone younger.

We're almost there now and she falls calm and still. She knows that this will be her new home but probably sees it as temporary, a stopover until she finds where it is she really wants to go. They scatter across the world like so much ash blown on the wind and I do not know if they ever find the place they're looking for or if it exists only in their heads. I raise the oars and let our motion drift us closer to the jetty and now her face is marked by relief. She bows her head in gratitude and then I help her out of the boat and she feels so light that I think death has made her weightless, that all the encumbrances life burdened her with have finally fallen away. For a few moments she stands watching as I row again and then she turns and disappears into the veiled distance.

It's a busy day and there is no time for rest except the two official breaks that health and safety regulations insist on. Moored on the shore I take some bread and a little wine but measured out and not enough to push me over the limit. And then it's more crossings and here is a soldier, straight-backed, still in his uniform, his medal glinting in the light, and in the fix of his gaze I too try to straighten and find some show of discipline in my rowing. He has no fear that he will let himself parade for the likes of me and no words cross his lips and perhaps he looks at this as one more posting to some far-off land where there is a job to do.

There are others this day who call themselves soldiers but are now just the young boys they always were and they're shivering in their sportsgear, their hooded heads dropped towards their chests, their skittering eyes trying to understand their badge of honour, the neat little medal that gains them admittance to a world that lies beyond the only boundaries they once knew and thought they were defending. One calls me

'Old Man' and asks me what I'm looking at but in most of them their bravado has been burnt away by death and the shock of their own blood slowly haloing them on city pavements wet with rain, the terrible chasm of silence that opened up when the life-support machine was turned off, and as we approach the opposite shore they ply me with questions about turf ownership and neighbourhoods. But all I know is that when they die they die alone and it doesn't matter what the posted messages say – those text-spelt tributes in cyberspace about true soldiers. This now is their journey across the river and they're making it before their allotted span and when they shiver it's not just because of the coldness and so I take these, too, with respect and with all due care.

The day is almost over now and the fading light rather than the schedule tells me that I have one more journey to make before my back gets the rest it's started to demand. I approach the shore for this last passenger and narrowing my eyes I can see that she's small, white-haired, fragile in frame, trembling like the final leaf on a winter tree. When she sees me she holds up her hand as if she's hailing me. I raise my arm to let her know I've seen her, then grip the oars tightly and try to steady myself. It's the one I knew was coming and which I sought in vain to be excused. 'No exceptions,' was what they said when I begged to be released. 'You know the rules.'

I help her into the boat and put a blanket over her shoulders to try and stem the cold. Her eyes are fogged and webbed with death and she sits in the boat just as straight-backed as she sits in the chair in the small room they've allocated her – the place where I go to visit her while the plaques and the tangles spread and smother the light. But whatever the names the scientists give, I think of it as a thief, each day robbing something more of who she is, and by now there's only fleeting glimpses left, revealed in a little joke perhaps because that capacity, while worn thin, is still allowed to her, or a familiar phrase that suddenly sparks out of the cold ash of memory.

And after I've gone she will forget that I've been but they say I should be grateful that she still knows who I am. Now as I look into her eyes for that same recognition they are clouded and veiled by the bewilderment of death. I row more gently than I have ever rowed before, trying to steady the beat of my heart by synchronising it with my pull on the oars. There are so many things that I should say but don't know how, and if I were to say them perhaps their finality would upset her, so I hug them close and tell myself that perhaps in time I shall find words that will be worthy enough to carry her into an afterlife. So now I just row as lightly as I can.

'Don't you need a rest?' she asks after a while and she rubs her eyes as if she's been sleeping and is beginning to wake.

'No, I'm fine,' I say. 'It's my job to take you across. And it's not long now. Not long to go now.'

'You're doing a good job,' she says. But before I can answer she hesitates then asks, 'Is that you?'

'Yes, it's me.'

'I thought it was but I wasn't sure. I didn't know it was you taking me. Are you sure you know the way?'

'Yes, and I'll not lose you.'

'Will I be going home soon?' she asks and looks closely at my face as she always does when she asks this, as if she wants to gauge if I'm going to tell her the truth.

'You're going home soon.'

'That's good,' she says. 'I can't remember what the house looks like any more. I think in the street there's hardly any of the old neighbours left.'

'Just the Boyles and the Fallows – that's all who's left now,' I tell her.

'Just the Boyles and the Fallows, and George next door – that's right,' she says as if she's confirming something important to herself. 'I'm tired now. When you're going home will you turn off the lights and make sure all the plugs are out?'

'Yes, I'll check everything. Don't worry.'

There is a moment of silence before she asks again, 'Will I be going home soon?' asking again because already she's forgotten the answer to her question.

Yes, you're finally going home. You're going across the river and when you get there Bobby will be waiting and all your sisters who came before you. All of them waiting for you.

We're almost there. The last smear of light is draining from the sky and it's hard now to see where water and horizon meet. I feel the coldness flooding my bones as I glance behind me to take my final bearings and then when I turn again she's holding her outstretched hand with the shining coin.

'You forgot to take the money,' she says. 'You'll never be a businessman.'

'I can't take it,' I say.

284

'Don't be silly,' she tells me. 'What do I need it for?'

'I can't,' I say again, shaking my head.

'Then give it to the children.'

I have to look away, look into the distance where the water is inky black and spirals into the unknown mysteries of the currents. How can I take this coin when everything has already been paid so richly and in full?

'Take it,' she says and her voice is gentle but insistent so I hold out my hand on this last journey and receive the coin I never wanted to be given, then bow my head and carry her across the river, my oars slowly rising and falling in the final silent salutation of a son's love.

A Note on the Author

David Park has written nine previous books including *The Light of Amsterdam*, which was shortlisted for the 2014 International IMPAC Prize, and, most recently, *The Poets' Wives*, which was selected as Belfast's choice for One City One Book 2014. He has won the Authors' Club First Novel Award, the Ewart-Biggs Memorial Prize and the University of Ulster's McCrea Literary Award, three times. He has received a Major Individual Artist Award from the Arts Council of Northern Ireland and been shortlisted for the Irish Novel of the Year Award three times. In 2014 he was longlisted for the *Sunday Times* EFG Short Story Award. He lives in County Down, Northern Ireland.

A Note on the Type

The text of this book is set in Linotype Sabon, a typeface named after the type founder, Jacques Sabon. It was designed by Jan Tschichold and jointly developed by Linotype, Monotype and Stempel in response to a need for a typeface to be available in identical form for mechanical hot metal composition and hand composition using foundry type.

Tschichold based his design for Sabon roman on a font engraved by Garamond, and Sabon italic on a font by Granjon. It was first used in 1966 and has proved an enduring modern classic.

12/16

0 X 12/16 (1/19)